SHE WAS CHAINED TO THE BRASS BEDSTEAD!

Their lips met in a mingled shock of surprise. "Jesus, I'm sorry, Chance. I don't know why I did such a fool thing!"

Brian reached in his pocket, took out a key, and unlocked the handcuff. For a long, wordless moment they just looked at one another. Then he said, "Your hands are free. From here on you're on your own."

Then he took her in his arms and kissed her again. Until this moment she'd thought those men who'd murdered her Dad had killed all desire forever for her. But now no other man mattered.

"I'm going to have to stop right now, if I ever aim to," Brian whispered.

"You big goof, those buttons are scratching me. And if you mean to wear your spurs, I just might change my mind!"

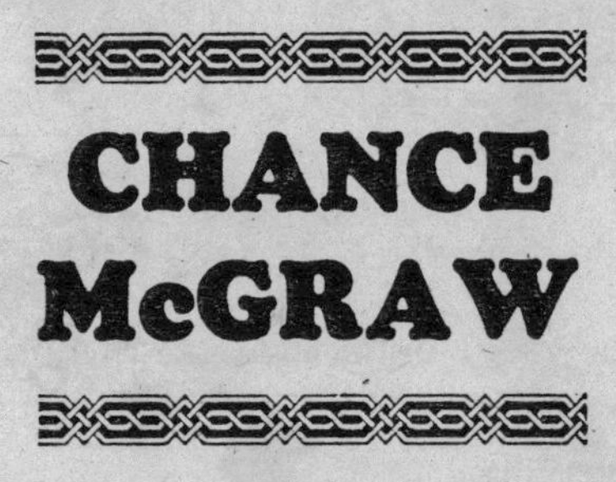

CHANCE McGRAW

by
Mary Louise
Manning

A DELL/BRYANS BOOK

Published by
Dell Publishing Co., Inc.
1 Dag Hammarskjold Plaza
New York, New York 10017

ISBN: 0-440-11523-X

Printed in the United States of America

First printing—November 1980

On the trail to Dodge, as the sun was setting, Chance McGraw watered the stock in the creek while her father built a night fire near their prairie schooner. They'd selected a campsite in a watered draw screened with cottonwood. For though the Kiowa were said to be quiet this summer, there were other wild creatures a fire visible for miles might attract and Dad was edgy about traveling alone with a pretty daughter, a Virginia walking horse, and one Henry rifle.

Chance was tall for a woman. So as she stood by the purling water she could see above the rim of the draw all around. The wide rolling prairie lay golden in the soft gloaming light, and the first stars were winking in the purple sky to the east as the sunset painted the clouds to the west the color of dying embers. Chance frowned slightly as she noticed dust above the eastern horizon. Surely the dust they'd stirred with their hooves and wheels over that way had settled by this time. But if other riders were following the trail they'd just left, Chance failed to see them.

From the fire Dad called, "That's enough for the critters, honey. Tether them to yon trees and rest your pretty bones a spell."

Chance nodded and led the horses away from the

stream, unconscious of the picture she presented as her father watched approvingly.

Chance was a tall, willowy brunette with cornflower blue eyes and a clear complexion tanned a shade darker than softer young ladies of her Victorian upbringing approved of. She was, at nineteen, aware that few men found her ugly. But she was unconscious of how truly beautiful she was, even in her dusty whipcord riding habit. As an army brat with a full colonel for a father Chance had always been treated with more respect than even the strict rules of military society called for.

She tethered the brutes and joined her father at the fire, carefully adjusting the folds of her Dolly Varden skirt as she sat on the blanket he'd spread on the dry grass for her. Dad hunkered on his heels like the old cavalryman he was, and Chance envied the easy way men moved in pants. She said, "I noticed some dust against the sky to the east, Dad," as he poked the fire under the coffeepot. Her father rose with easy grace and stared for a time before he sank back down and said, "It's settling. The evening breeze kicks up dust devils out here this time of the year."

Chance forgot the dust. Dad had fought out here before she was born and if he said it was all right, it was all right. Dad was the kind of man a woman would feel safe with even if he weren't her father. It seemed hard to believe he'd just retired from the army and was nearly sixty. Dad was one of those whipcord and whalebone men whose features set at thirty odd and never seemed to change. She couldn't remember when he hadn't looked a little gray, and when she'd been a little girl, she'd thought he was older than God. Now, grown herself, she saw he was surprisingly youthful. She wondered if he'd ever remarry now that he'd done his duty by the army and his orphaned daughter. He'd said they'd make a new life for themselves further west. But he seemed a bit vague about the details.

Chance saw that the coffee was perking and started to reach for the pot. But Dad said, "I'll pour, honey. You're likely to burn yourself."

Chance sighed and said, "Dad, I'm almost as old as my mother was when she had me. When are you going to stop treating me like I'm made of glass?"

Dad frowned, then nodded with a wry, surprisingly boyish smile and said, "Go ahead, but be careful."

He waited until she'd poured two tin cups of his strong cavalry brew before he sighed and added, "I reckon you have sort of sprung up on me while I was too busy to look. It's sort of hard to remember you're a grown woman."

He sipped his coffee as Chance held her tongue. She knew that he knew she remembered the strong words they'd had about her being a woman other men had noticed as such. But he'd been right about Lieutenant Duncan in the end, and Chance considered the matter settled.

But, as she sipped her own coffee, Dad said, "I reckon you thought I was sort of muleheaded. Ordering you to come west to Dodge with me and all, but . . ."

"Dad," she cut in with a weary smile, "you're not in the army giving orders anymore. I said I'd come with you because I wanted to."

"You're sure you're not pining for that shiftless young shavetail we had words about, honey?"

Chance sighed and said, "Dad, when you say a man has a drinking problem, you've said all there is to say. I'll admit I was swept off my feet for a time, if you'll admit I didn't need as much saving as you like to take credit for."

He chuckled and said, "You do get more like your mother every day. It's sure funny how you get your Irish temper from the Yankee side of your family tree. Us McGraws have always been the sweet, reasonable ones."

They both laughed, the tension broken, and Chance got to her feet, saying, "I'd better see about putting some supper on the fire."

Then she froze in place, staring into the sunset's glare as she softly murmured, "Dad, that wasn't a dust devil we saw to the east. Some riders have circled below the horizon. They're coming in from the west with the sun at their backs."

Dad got to his feet to stand at her side as seven dark outlines approached in the hellfire glow of sunset. Chance asked, "Kiowa?" and her father said, "White men. I can see that much. Just let me do the talking."

"Do you want me to see if I can reach the rifle in the wagon?"

"No. Too late for unfriendly moves. I'm hoping they're just cowhands who scout a camp before they ride in to hunker over coffee."

The seven strangers rode in spread out and walking their ponies.

Chance strained her eyes against the treacherous light. She couldn't make out their features, but there was something in the cautious way they were easing in that reminded her of coyotes skulking just outside of rifle range. They came to the rim of the draw and rode down the slope, spread out like skirmishers. A couple reined in and sat their mounts at a safe distance as the others stopped by the creek to water their ponies before approaching the fire. Finally one of them rode closer, and Dad called out, "Howdy, boys. We were just fixing to sup."

"The colonel and his lady was fixing to sup," the rider called out to his companions, and the draw was filled with taunting laughter that tingled the hairs on Chance's neck. Dad frowned and asked, "Do I know you, friend?"

The first rider was joined by a second who jeered, "Mebbe you do and mebbe you don't, Colonel. It was a long old war and you got to hang a *lot* of good old boys, didn't you?"

Dad said, "The war was a long time back, boys, and I doubt like hell I hanged any of *you* enough to matter."

A third rider sidled in from the side, covering Dad's gun hand as he chimed in, "Say, that's a pretty pinto pony you got over there in the trees, Colonel." And the first rider spat and added, "Your *gal* ain't bad either. You sure live good, Colonel."

"Who are you men and what's this all about?" Dad demanded in a voice that didn't give away the dry fear he must have felt. They were close enough now that Chance would be able to recognize them again and, despite her own growing panic, she concentrated on things to remember. The leader had a gold tooth. The burly lout on Dad's far side had his sleeves rolled up to expose a tattooed forearm.

Gold-tooth called out, "The colonel wants to know what this is all about, boys. Shall we tell him?"

A rough voice called back, "Hell, let's just shoot the son of a bitch."

Gold-tooth grinned and asked Dad, "You hear that, Colonel? The boys don't remember you as fondly as they might. I reckon a man who likes to play military policeman gets used to folks not liking him though."

Dad nodded and said, "All right, I was a provost marshal during the war. What were you boys, Union deserters or Reb guerrillas?"

Gold-tooth scowled and snapped, "Watch that *guerrilla* shit! We'uns was the Fifth Confederate Cavalry, you son of a blue-bellied bitch!"

And then with no further warning he drew and fired!

Chance screamed as her father staggered backward, staring up in wonder at the man who'd shot him as he tried in vain to make his gun hand obey. Then Gold-tooth's six-shooter roared again and Dad was down and Chance was running for the wagon. *The rifle.* She had to get to the rifle in the wagon. But as she ran she heard the pounding hooves behind her and a man laughed as his rope dropped over the frightened girl, pinning her elbows to her sides as it yanked her off her feet.

Chance fell, tried to rise, and then the rider who'd roped her was out of the saddle and pinning her to the grass with his greater weight. Chance got a hand free and tried to scratch, but he balled a fist and punched her full in the face to fill her head with pain, spinning stars, and evil laughter.

Another man dropped beside them to grab her thrashing, booted ankles, and he jeered, "I'll just tie her laigs with pigging string afore she kicks your balls off, pard."

But the man holding Chance snorted, "Shoot, you leave them laigs alone, boy! How in thunder can we *spread* a gal's laigs iffen they's tied together?" Then he started tearing her bodice off, popping the buttons as Chance gasped, "No! Not that!"

But it was going to be that, she knew in ever

growing horror as her head cleared just enough to see all seven of them, grinning down at her in the crimson light; and though the day was dying, she knew sickly that a night of hell was about to dawn.

As the sun was once more low after a long hot day, the tinker's cart paused on a rise. The sea of grass lay orange and purple and the draw ahead was a pool of hazy shadow. The tinker smoked his clay pipe thoughtfully as he rested their mule and gazed down the slope for a time. Then he turned to the tired old woman at his side and said, "Aroo, it's here we'll be after camping for the night, Annie macushla, for there's trees down there and the gleam of standing water."

The tinker's woman sniffed and said, "I'm for pushing on and about this place, Hughie O'Rourke. Can't you smell the woodsmoke on the evening air? There's someone *down* in yonder glen, I'll vow, and our kind is seldom welcome anywhere."

The tinker sighed and said, "Och, Annie, it's five thousand miles we are from the auld country with it's auld hates. These darling Yanks don't know a tinker from a burton, and if they did, it wouldn't matter. Has anyone accused you of witching a cow or causing a spud to rot since we crossed the main ocean more than a year ago?"

Annie shrugged and said, "The Americans seem dacent folk, for Protestants. But it's far to the west we've wandered, and thim down there may be *Indians*!"

The tinker laughed and said, "Jasus, now it's Indians! You heard me talking to thim settlers a day's journey back, Annie of the worries. We're too far south for Sioux and too far north for Comanche. The grand city of Dodge is only a day or so over the prairie to the southwest, and the settlers told us they'd seen divel a redskin this summer."

"What if they're bandits, then? What would you do if they was bandits, Hughie O'Rourke? You're almost sixty, and even when you was young you was short!"

The tinker shrugged and replied, "Och, you know I've ever been able to talk to the woild ones, Annie. In the first place we've nothing worth stealing. In the second place we've ever been outcasts ourselves. We can't avoid meeting folk on this great open plain and, damn it, there's wood and water down there."

He clucked the weary mule into motion as he added, "This night we'll put the kettle on a proper wood fire. For it's weary I am with the smell of dried buffalo chips in me tea! I can smell the smoke that worried you, now, and I'll vow you were worried for naught. Haven't you lived the roadside life long enough to tell a dead campfire from a live one? Aroo, whoever camped down among those cottonwoods left long before we got here, Annie macushla!"

The tinker let the mule have it's head as the thirsty animal broke into a downhill trot toward the winding streambed at the bottom of the draw. His woman put one hand up to hold her sunbonnet as she clung with the other to the seat between them. Annie knew better than to protest Hughie's driving. Like many small men the tinker liked to frighten bigger folk and Annie was big for a woman. In the years since she'd run off with the much younger, passing tinker, she'd learned his boyish pranks were tempered by a certain feline caution. Hughie was curious as a cat and sometimes forgot he was no longer a kitten. But like the auld gray cats of Kerry, he was mortal hard to be after hitting with a shoe.

The mule stumbled to a stop in the fetlock-deep water of the sluggish prairie creek and lowered it's head to drink as the tinker sprang lightly down and walked around the cart to help his weary woman to the sandy ground. Old Annie gasped and said, "Stop that, you fool!" as the elfin tinker slid his hand under her print cotton skirts while "helping" her.

Hughie chuckled as he placed her on her feet. He said, "Faith, you've put on a few stone since I stole you from your people, Annie macushla, but it's tight as a maid you still are where it counts."

"Och, you damned auld goat! It's auld enough to be a grandmother I am, and you're turning into a very dirty auld man!"

He laughed and said, "Ay, I told you I was dirty when you met me as a *young* man. I'll gather some wood and mayhaps make sure we're alone in this darling place. Then, after we put the kettle on, I mean to ravage you like the lusty wench you are!"

"Och, you damned auld fool!" she said, but Annie was smiling tenderly as she said it. She knew he meant what he said, and her heart was filled with the wonder of it as he patted her fondly and turned away.

Hughie got his Henry rifle from the dashboard boot and took an axe from the tool chest on the cart's off side. His woman stood there gazing after him as the tinker moved up the draw toward a clump of cottonwood. In the gloaming light he didn't look his age, for Hughie still moved with the feline grace of his tribe.

But if there was a certain swagger to his stride, the little tinker approached the dark tree line with a wary look in his eyes and a .44 round in the chamber of his rifle. Despite his assurances to the worried woman back at the cart Hughie knew just enough of this great tawny new land to know it held surprises, and his people had survived in the auld country by leaving little to chance and knowing what lay over the hill or around the bend of a lane. These endless days on the "sea of grass" had unsettled the tinker. America was a great brown land where even the birds sang different songs and strange new herbs grew by the side of the road. There was divel a hedge to hide behind, and you never knew how you stood with the people you met on the trail.

The setting sun was in his eyes. The cottonwoods were etched in black against the flaming sky. Hughie stopped and sniffed. The scent of smoke hung in the still air, mixed with the acrid reek of scorched paint and charred canvas. There was no sign of fire glow, but something had burned, and brightly, a while ago.

The tinker hunkered down for a better look at the inkblot outlines, and then he spied the square mass of a prairie schooner parked under the trees. The hardwood hoops above the wagon bed were bare against the sunset. The canvas top had been burned away. There was no trace of the wagon team. Hughie rose to his feet and called out, "Is anyone there?"

There was no answer. Or was there? Hughie frowned as the breeze seemed to carry a faraway moaning sound to his keen ears. He called again, and this time there was definitely no answer.

The tinker moved in, gun muzzle sweeping in line with his wary eyes. He was close enough to the prairie schooner now to see why it was so black. The wheels and wagon-bed were charred and the burned-out wagon stood in a bed of fluffy gray ash. He nodded and said, "Ay, someone didn't know how quickly cottonwood burns to ash with divel enough heat to matter."

He stood undecided. Whoever had burned the wagon out had held red thoughts for them who'd come this far in it. It might have been a private quarrel. It might have been renegades or Indians. Mayhaps the smartest move for a wandering tinker and his woman would be far and sudden. "Och, they've gone. Whoever they was," he told himself aloud, adding, "This is the least likely place they'd be after returning. Run like a rabbit, Hughie me lad, and who knows but what you'd run *into* thim?"

The fire had left most of the wagon intact. There might be something worth the salvaging, and Hughie's kind lived by the leavings of others.

The tinker circled in, unaware that a wary coyote did the same before approaching carrion. Whatever was in the wagon would wait until he made sure it was unguarded.

He stopped again and sucked in his breath as he spotted a prone figure in the charred grass between the burned-out prairie schooner and the stream. It was a man, or at least it had been. The clothes had been burned off, and the bloated body looked like it was made of toasted marshmallow. Hughie crossed himself with his free hand and murmured, "Sure, I hope they had the dacency to shoot you before the flames got to you, whoever you was!"

The tinker walked over gingerly and rolled the

blackened corpse on it's side with his boot. As he'd hoped, the parts against the ground hadn't been as badly burned, but if anything, the body was now more ghastly to gaze upon and he was grateful for the dim light. The face was that of a middle-aged man. Some of his linen shirt still clung to his damp chest, but the heat had dried the blood stains to the texture of spilled chocolate. It seemed impossible for a face to look so peaceful after such an ugly death. He hadn't been dead long. The swollen features were the result of heat, not decay.

Hughie swept his eyes over the flattened grass where the body had protected the stems from the flames. He'd hoped for a watch or a few loose coins. But they'd obviously robbed him too.

Hughie moved on. Then he froze as once again he heard a low moan.

"I see you!" he lied, training his gun in the direction of the sound as he squinted into the shadows. There was another soft moan, and this time the tinker's eyes locked on a dim, pale form at the base of a tree.

Hughie said, "I see you and I have a gun. Are you hurt?"

There was no answer. The tinker smiled thinly at the stupidity of his own question and moved closer.

Then he stopped and murmured, "Jasus, Mary, and Joseph!"

It was a woman. Stark naked and sprawled spread-eagle on her back in the dry leaves under the tree. As the tinker came closer, she rolled her head and weakly sobbed, "No. Please, not again!"

He knelt beside her on one knee and soothed, "Easy, lass. You've fallen among dacent folk this night. Me name is Hughie O'Rourke and it's from

Kerry I've come. Who might you be, and who was after treating you so savage?"

The woman didn't answer. He saw she was young and well-formed if a man liked his women willowy. Her eyes were closed and what he could see of her face was pretty. But it was half hidden by blood and swollen about the lips and one eye. He put his free hand out to move a tendril of matted black hair aside and whistled softly, "Jasus, it's backwards through the keyhole you've been dragged, and shot in the head to boot!"

"Please stop," she murmured.

He ran his eyes over her bruised body, noting the bite marks on one firm breast and the bruises between her thighs. As she tried weakly to push his gentle hand from her hair, he saw the rope burns on her wrist. He said, "They've gone, and back to the divel who spawned them I'll be hoping. I'll take you to me woman and . . ."

The girl suddenly bared her teeth and dug her nails into Hughie's wrist as she hissed like a frightened cat. The tinker snatched his hand away and marveled, "Jasus! Shot in the brain and fighting like a vixen in a trap she is!"

He rose as she passed out again. He said, "Rest easy then, and I'll fetch auld Annie. Sure I can see you've taken a sudden dislike to men, and that's a fact!"

He jogged back to his own smaller cart, where he found his woman squatting over a fire, brewing tea. Annie called out, "Who was you talking to over there, Hughie?"

The tinker said, "Two murthered travelers. One of thim's a gorl, and still breathing. I don't know why."

"Murthered, you say? How can you say they was both murthered if one of thim's still alive?"

"Och, I said she was still breathing. I never said she was alive. It's a gorl in her twenties they was after beating, raping, and shooting in the head. She should have died by now, but she's stubborn for a lass. We'll try and make her comfortable until she breathes her last. But I doubt she'll last through the night."

So this was death. Chance McGraw hadn't expected to die so young. But now that she had, it didn't feel so bad. She was numbly surprised that she could still think here in . . . wherever she was. She tried to open her eyes, but the effort was too much and there'd be time enough to get used to death. She'd waited long enough for it back there under the cottonwoods. Toward the last she'd prayed to die. But they kept pawing her and hurting her for what seemed like an eternity in hell, and near the end she'd started to wonder if she wasn't already dead and *down* in hell. Surely those grinning faces hadn't been the faces of human men. What was it Dad had called them—guerrillas? That was a funny name for fiends from hell. Maybe he'd meant they were guerrillas killed in the War Between the States a few years back. Her childhood had been haunted by the savage tales of border fights between guerrilla bands, and if half the tales had been true, men who'd died fighting for both sides belonged in hell forever. But the gang who'd ridden in back there on earth hadn't been in hell. They'd been in Kansas. There was something very odd going on in the universe tonight.

Chance McGraw floated among the stars and willed herself to return to oblivion. It had been better right after she'd died and didn't have to remember. She had no reason to remember now. It didn't seem fair to have to remember such horrors after you were dead.

An angel said, "I think she's coming out of it," and Chance opened her eyes. The angel who'd spoken was a motherly looking fat woman with a firelit face outlined by a starry sky. Chance felt warm and cozy albeit still naked under the wool blanket by the tinker's fire. She moved her hands and saw they'd untied them, or . . . wait, she'd struggled free of the rawhide thongs herself while she'd been waiting to die that afternoon. She licked her swollen lips and said, "I came to and the sun was beating down on me like an open furnace door. I rolled to the creek, and after I'd soaked a while, the rawhide was easy to stretch. So I broke free."

A small, elfin man smoking a clay pipe across the fire from them nodded and said, "Ay, I saw where you'd crawled up into the trees from the water, lass. That was good thinking. The sun would have cooked you like a lobster had you stayed out in it with divel a stitch to cover your white skin. I've been telling Annie that you must be Irish. For it's Irish you look and the luck of the Irish that saved you. Did you know they shot you in the head before they rode off?"

The girl raised a hand and felt the bandages around her head as Annie soothed, "He's a tinker and he likes to tell tall tales, darling. The bullet was only after grazing you, bloody as your scalp was left. Sure I've put a few stitches and a poultice to set you to rights, and the scar won't even show after the wee bit of hair I had to shave is after growing back."

Hughie chuckled and said, "She's a witch, you see. That's what they call auld wimmen who practice medicine without a grand degree. It's my belief they left you for dead after knocking you galley-west with a poorly aimed pistol ball. In God's truth *I* thought your wound was morthal when first I saw you there. And you was moving, too."

Chance tried to sit up, saw she was still too weak, and took a deep breath before she asked softly, "Did you see what they did to my father?"

There was a moment of silence before Hughie said, "I buried him near the wagon, lass. You'll want an accounting after you've recovered your strength. If it'll save us having you search through our pockets and cart, I'll vow I found nothing of value on or about the two of you. I'll look again in broad daylight. But it's my belief they robbed you down to your boot heels and that's a fact."

The girl nodded and said, "I believe you. My name is Chance McGraw. My father was Colonel Tyrone McGraw of the Eighteenth Kansas. We were on our way to Dodge."

O'Rourke laughed and said, "I knew you was Irish, and it's to Dodge City auld Annie and me are bound! I'd be Hughie O'Rourke, and Annie you know. Since you're Irish, you'll want to know up front it's *tinkers* we are. But we're *dacent* tinkers and, what the hell, we're in a new country."

This time the girl managed to prop herself up on one elbow for a look at her surroundings, holding the blanket over her breasts as she frowned and said, "I'm not sure I follow you, sir. My folks have been in this country a long time and I've never heard of a tinker, save as a man who *fixes* things."

"Jasus, your people wasn't Orangemen, was they? Most of the Irish who came over before the potato famine was Orangemen, I've heard."

Chance shook her head, winced at the sudden dizziness, and lay back down, saying, "I'm still woozy. I'm not really very interested in Irish history right now. My grandfather came to Texas from some place in Ireland. Both my grandmother and late mother were native-born American."

Hughie looked relieved and said, "Ah, it's all right then. I heard about Mexico granting land to Catholic English, Irish, and Americans back in the twenties. Had your grandfather been an Orangeman, he'd not have emigrated to Texas."

He knocked the dottle from his pipe against a heel and added, "Sure, thim Mexicans thought they was the sly ones, granting lands to Catholic families in hopes of a buffer between thim and the Yanks. They should have known blood was thicker than mescal. Austin and Houston was auld Irish names, begorrah, but what Irishman born of mortal woman would want to be a Mexican whin he could be a Yank?"

Annie said, "Hughie, the lass was just after telling you she ain't *interested*! Would you be a darling man and be after fetching me a bucket of water and some more wood?"

The tinker glanced at the cottonwood sticks piled beside the fire and raised an eyebrow. Then he nodded thoughtfully and got to his feet. As he walked away, Annie leaned closer and confided, "It's not a thing you'd want to talk about in front of men, but Hughie was right. When I was washing and putting you to rights, I could tell they'd had their way with you."

"There were seven of them," the girl replied bleakly and added, "I don't want to talk about it."

Annie shook her head and said, "We have to talk about it now, for though Hughie means well, he'll be jabbering at us half the night and we'll get few further chances. He told you I had certain skills. I did what I could, but the timing is important. How far away from your monthly curse was you when they had their way with you, lass?"

The girl's voice was ominously calm as she replied, "They didn't have their way with me. I was gang raped and shot down like a dog. As to the less important details I had my last period about a week ago. Why?"

Annie smiled and said, "I don't think you'll pay for their pleasure with any bastards related to thim."

Chance sat up again, and this time she willed the dizzy stars from her injured head as she said, "You're wrong. *They'll* pay! Every mother's son of the seven!"

"Och, you know who they were, lass?"

"No. But I'll never forget their faces as long as I live. And they won't live long once I catch up with them!"

"Ay, if you can identify thim to the law . . ."

"What law? I'm not about to turn them in to any lawman, Annie. In the first place it would be my word against theirs, seven to one. In the second place juries out here are funny when it comes to old scores left over from the war."

Annie nodded and said, "Och, we heard of your grand Civil War before we crossed the main ocean. Was it the Blue or the Gray your dear father was fighting for, Chance?"

"Blue," said Chance, "But it may be more complicated than that. You see, my father never rode against the regular troops of the Confederacy. The Eighteenth Kansas was a police unit. They patrolled the prairie against renegades and guerrillas from *both* sides."

The old Irishwoman obviously didn't understand her, so Chance elaborated, "Kansas was a border state. Even before the war broke out, they called it Bleeding Kansas. Mad idealists like John Brown raided slaveholders. Southern sympathizers like the James Boys and Quantrill shot abolitionists before and during the war. Many a man pretending to be fighting for either cause was simply a bandit or worse.

"My father's politics were moderate. We had friends and neighbors on both sides. But as a soldier he fought firm and fair. Dad's orders were to round up any irregular not in uniform and bring him into Leavenworth for a hanging and . . ."

"Aroo! Thim killers could have been on either side during the war. Or maybe neither side at all at all!"

Chance shook her head and said, "Dad recognized at least one or two of them. It all happened so fast, I'm a little fuzzy about the details. But I remember them riding in as we were making camp and, yes, the name of an irregular band."

"Do you remember either the man or his regiment, then?"

"No. It all happened so fast and everyone was shooting at once. I saw Dad fall and I tried to run and . . . Never mind."

Both women stared into the fire for a time before Chance sighed and said, "They were from the fifth something. Fifth Cav, I think one of them said. He was correcting my father, who'd called them something else I can't bring to the tip of my tongue."

The tinker came back, carrying some firewood. He tossed it down with the other pile and said, "I've been thinking about making this gorl dacent, Annie."

Annie said, "She's already dacent, you auld fool. Sins done against one's own free will don't count. As you'd know if you'd been raised by a Christian woman who'd known your father's name!"

Hughie laughed and said, "Flattery will get you nowheres. I wasn't thinking of what's over and done with. It's the preventing of *future* misadventures I've been straining me wee brain over."

Both women looked blank. Hughie said, "Jasus, hasn't it occurred to either of you that thim divels is still out there in the night somewhere?"

Annie wailed in terror and he quickly added, "Whist! They'll not be coming back to this particular place, for it's a terrible deed they left behind thim here. But this gorl can't tell us who they was or where they was headed. It's my feeling that should we meet up with thim again, they should never learn the one they left for dead is still alive on this earth."

Chance brightened and said, "You're right! Whatever their reasons were for killing my father, they think they left no witness. They'd have no reason to attack the two of you between here and Dodge."

"Ay, but the thrubble with this prairie is that there's so little to look at out here between the settlements. If they spy us between here and safety, they'll move in on us, if only to sniff us over like the dogs they are."

"They'd recognize me," said Chance, adding bitterly, "God knows, they know me well enough to remember now."

Hughie nodded and said, "Ay, and even if we disguised your face, we know they're not gintlemen when it comes to a pretty colleen. In the morrow we're going to have to thurn you into a tinker lad."

Chance frowned and said, "I still don't know what a tinker is, male or female!"

Hughie smiled and said, "You might say we're Irish *gypsies*. Though some say the burtons and not the tinkers is the true Romany men back home. You see, in thoims of thrubble many a lad born of Christian croft folk has run off to join the hedgerow clans and . . ."

Annie cut in to explain, "I ran off to be a tinker when I was younger than you, Chance McGraw. So some of us is gypsy and some of us ain't. Tinker, burton, or rom, it's all the same when you pass through a town with a narrow-minded priest or a rough tavern gang."

Chance nodded and said, "I think we call you *hoboes* over here. But I've never seen a hobo with a wife or a gypsy cart before."

Hughie said, "Well, it's not a very civilized country yet. As to how we get along, us tinkers are dacent folk who work at honest crafts like mending things or playing a fairy tune at a country wedding. The burtons tend to be horse thraders, or they'll cure a sick cow or a child cheaper than the regular grand doctors. The Romany tell fortunes and poach, and we all pay for it in the end."

"That's why we came over here," added Annie, explaining, "Since the famine the roads are crowded with wanderers and the auld guild crafts have broken down. I've had to doctor and Hughie, here, has been known to poach or worse."

Chance knew they'd tell her more than she really

wanted or needed to know if she let them. So she said, "I sure would like some of that tea now. I'm wide awake at last, and I can see things are more complicated than I first thought. You two might be better off leaving me to fend for myself if you could spare a dress, some shoes, and a gun."

The two tinkers exchanged glances and Hughie said, "Och, any of Annie's auld gowns would hang on you like a tent. You're taller than me, but built no wider, and I've some boots and a hat that will fit you, too. We'll dress you as a *boyo,* and if anyone asks, we'll say you're our half-witted son. That way you won't have to answer questions in your Kansas brogue."

As Annie handed her a tin cup of tea, Chance said, "I like the part about dressing as a man. If I put my hair up inside a man's hat and make sure the shirt is loose, I might pass for a teen-age boy at that." She took a sip before she added, "You'd better travel on without me, though. You've already done so much for me, and those seven men are killers."

Annie said, "Don't be mad, macushla. It's miles we are from any town, and we've neither a mount nor a rifle to be sparing. It's to Dodge City you'll be going with us and I'll hear no more about it."

Hughie smiled fondly at his fat old woman across the fire and said, "We never had any childer, you see. God knows we've tried, but mayhaps it's just as well. All in all it's better to adopt grown kids than it is to bring them into this world behind a hedge."

Chance swallowed more tea, as well as the lump in her throat, as she looked at the aging couple in the firelight and said, "I don't understand why you're being so kind. We're total strangers and you know you're putting your lives in danger by helping me like this."

Hughie shrugged and said, "Whist, you said your gradfather was Irish, didn't you?"

Chance smiled through her tears as she gently chided, "You don't fool me, Hughie O'Rourke. You'd do the same for anyone you found in a fix like this, wouldn't you?"

"Well, as long as they wasn't Orangemen."

Annie laughed and said, "He hates to admit he's not really a Druid, but I fear you're right, Chance McGraw. I remember one time when we came on this *Protestant* with a broken axle on his jaunting cart and . . . well, I'll not be the one to tell his awful secrets."

Chance said, "Listen, if you do get me safely to the Western Union wire at Dodge, I'll wire our bank for a money order and . . ."

"Whist!" the tinker cut in with a genuine frown as he added, "I know you've had a rough time, lass. But that's no reason to be after *insulting* us!"

"You get some sleep now, daughter," said Annie firmly. "We'll talk of your great fortune after we get you safe among your own people. You did say you had relations in Dodge City, didn't you?"

Chance McGraw said, "No. Dad was my only living relative. My mother died years ago. Dad was all I had. We were on our way to his new business venture in Dodge and . . . I wish you could have known him, Annie. He was a wonderful man as well as a wonderful father, and now I have nobody."

Hughie O'Rourke threw another stick on the fire as he scowled darkly at the flames and muttered, "Jasus, it's a saucy child you've adopted, Annie macushla! First she offers silver as if the saving of a human life is something to be bought and sold. Now she has the cheek to call us *nobody!*"

"She's hurt and tired, Hughie. She meant no harm, I'm sure. When she said she had nobody, she wasn't speaking about *us!*"

By the second day on the trail Chance McGraw's swollen face had gone down, although she still had a black eye and the stitching under the band of her borrowed hat itched. The tinkers had had no underwear to lend her and the woolen pants she wore itched too. The loose linen shirt she wore over her small, firm breasts was the only comfortable thing she had on. She didn't have to walk, seated between them on the cart seat. It was just as well. She was taller than Hughie, but his boots were a size too big for her even with paper wadding in the toes.

By now they knew each other better. In truth there was little to add to the tinker's tale. Hughie had been everywhere and done everything since he'd been born by the side of the road to an unremembered woman who might have been a gypsy and the tinker who'd owned this cart before him. Hughie's father had been a morose drinking man who'd beat him until he was twelve and then, as Hughie put it, "had the dacency to be shot poaching rabbits by the gamekeeper of a grand estate." Since that time he'd lived from hand-to-mouth in a series of minor adventures that all sounded much the same. He'd stolen everything from apples off a roadside tree to Annie from a roadside farm. He'd fought more men than he could remember, but didn't think he'd killed anyone in his time and was cheerful about the few wounds Annie had nursed him through. It was the growing frequency of the attacks by village louts that had sent them across the main ocean where people were less religious in his view.

As a pagan Hughie had been getting caught between the ruffians who were beginning to take such matters seriously in Ireland. He said he'd never had trouble convincing Fenians he was "a dacent Papist like thimselves" until lately. Now, with Orange and Green at one another's throats, a man was expected to say his catechism cold sober in a tavern yard without a moment or a pint to remember who was the Father and who was the Son. Hughie was still confused as to whether Saint Bridget had been the sister of Mary as he'd said or the Druid goddess those boyos who'd tried to hit him with a rock had insisted. Annie, of course, could say her beads with the best or the worse of them, but she'd been frightened by the black looks the village women gave a woman with a dark tinker at her side.

It had taken all their savings and a bit of gentle robbery to get them and their cart this far. Chance assumed the mule was stolen. But she didn't ask. She didn't want to talk about herself, but they insisted.

Forced to face things in the cold, clear light of day, Chance mused, "I don't think they were trailing us. They were dressed like cowhands and probably work near Dodge. We just stumbled over each other miles from anybody, and they grabbed at the opportunity to settle some old score."

She pounded her thigh and swore, "Damn! If only I'd been his *son* instead of his *daughter!*"

Hughie said, "Whist, it still would have been two against seven."

"I know. But we'd have had a *chance* at least. If only I'd had a *gun!*"

"You'd have been dead instead of cursing yourself about what can't be helped, macushla. What would a wee gorl like yourself have done with a gun if you'd had one, eh?"

"I'd have *fought* them, by God! I may be a girl, but I'm not a shrinking violet. Dad taught me how to shoot a gun when I was little. I used to hit bottles set up on the fence three out of four times."

The tinker said, "Ay, but bottles don't shoot back, and three out of four ain't good enough when you're facing seven. All in all I think it's as well you had no weapons in your hands then. I know they savaged you and left you for dead. But they'd have killed you out of hand had you been a man or even a woman armed."

Chance grimaced and said, "That's probably true, but do you know what bothered me the most while they were taking turns with me?"

Annie gasped, "Whist, *gintleman* present, gorl!"

Chance shuddered and said, "The thing that haunts me is the *helpless* horror I felt through every minute of it! You see, I fought them tooth and nail. I knew they'd killed Dad. I knew what they were doing to my body and I wanted to just die and I hoped that if I fought them hard enough they'd kill me."

She stared out across the sun-bleached prairie as she shuddered again and murmured, "They didn't *have* to kill me. I was helpless as a child. They knew it. When I raked one man's face with my nails, he laughed and said he liked a gal with spunk. Then he . . ."

She buried her face in her hands, and Annie put a motherly fat arm around her, crooning, "Hush now, macushla. Auld Annie understands."

But Chance knew she didn't understand. No one would understand how . . . how *unfair* it had been. They hadn't torn her clothes off and ravaged her as an act of perverse desire. They'd done it to humiliate her and to show their power over her and the man they'd murdered. The real humiliation hadn't been the things they'd done to her. It had been the jeering *contempt* in their jovial insults and casual brutality. Chance sniffed and said, "They didn't even take me serious enough to make sure I was really dead. They just used me as their plaything until one of them said it was time they rode off. Then the man who was using me got off, hitched his belt with one hand, and shot me with the other!"

Hughie's teeth were gripping his pipe hard as he asked in a very quiet tone, "Was that when they set fire to your wagon and all, lass?"

Chance shrugged and said, "I don't know. I was unconscious for hours. It was dawn when I woke up again, surprised to be alive." She looked away and added, "Surprised but not delighted. You know the rest. I kept passing out and waking up again. And every time I woke up I cursed myself for still being alive."

"Ah, well, you *are* alive, and if we can keep you that way, you well may pay them back."

"I'll never pay them back. I may kill all seven. But I'll never pay them back."

Before the tinker had time to think of a sensible

answer to the girl's bitter promise, he reined in on a rise and said, "Whist! Look down there, the both of you!"

Chance stared down the slope and spotted two ponies and as many men by a water hole in the otherwise featureless draw. The ponies were both bays and hobbled to graze near the water hole. The two men hunkered over a tiny fire near the water had spotted them too. One rose to his feet, a Winchester cradled across one arm. His bigger companion went on stirring the tin pot on the coals. The short one waved.

Hughie said, "They look like cowboys. Do you recognize the ponies or anything about their outfits, Chance?"

The girl frowned and said, "No. Not that I could be sure at this distance."

Annie said, "We'd best ride around them, Hughie."

But the tinker said, "The fat's in the fire either way. No matter who they might be, they'd think it odd of us to shirk their company. It's two to one, and our mule would never outdistance thim two ponies if they decided to question our manners."

Chance said, "It's not two to one. It's two to two if you'll hand me a gun!"

Hughie shook his head and said, "We've one gun and it's in me lap it must stay, lass."

"But if I recognize one of them and he recognizes me at the same time . . ."

"Ay, I said the fat was in the fire. Remember you're my half-wit son, Sean, and we'll hope they won't remember you if you remember them."

"Damn it, you think I'm not fit to handle that gun because I'm a woman, don't you?"

He chucked the mule forward before he answered, "Now it's yourself who's saying foolish words about who's fit and who ain't, gorl! For one thing I was potting rabbits with a gun before you were born, male or otherwise. For another thing you're too wrought up to be trusted with a gun, and I'd say the same if you was Woild Bill Hickok in the flesh. We're not going down there for a gunfight, damn it. We're going down like innocent travelers in the hopes of avoiding a fight at all at all!"

They were now close enough to make out the features of the standing stranger. He was a heavyset man of medium height. His face was almost as brown as his week's growth of beard and the eyebrows meeting over amber eyes. He wore his gun high and cross-draw and was dressed in various shades of brown, too. Hughie murmured, "Jasus, he looks like a bear. Is he someone you know, Chance McGraw?"

She answered, "No," even as she repressed a shudder at the thought of the ursine stranger's greasy, buckskin-clad arms around her. She knew it would take some time before she would no longer think of each new man she met as a prospective rapist. Since the man they were approaching had never done a thing to harm her, Chance overcompensated with a bright smile as he called out, "How do. My handle is Anthony Despres and I hail from the Red River of the North. My friends call me Tony."

Despres indicated his silent partner still hunkered over the cow chip fire and added, "That's Brian Pio yonder. He's all right, when you get to know him."

O'Rourke reined in and answered, "Me name is O'Rourke and I was born in County Kerry near a place called Castle Maine. This is me auld woman, Annie, and the lad's our son, Sean. He's a bit faible in the head. So you mustn't think he's pouting if he's not up to conversation."

The man by the fire rose. Then rose some more. He was nearly seven feet tall in his Texas boots and, though lean and lanky, must have weighed over two hundred pounds. Brian Pio put two fingers to the brim of his black Stetson and said, "We're bound for Dodge. Have you folks seen a band of riders in the past few days? We think there are six or seven of them in the bunch."

Hughie shook his head wordlessly. Then, to gain time while he sized up the situation, he said, "Brian is a foin Irish name, but I've met divel a Pio on the roads of Erin and that's the truth."

Despres laughed and said, "Hell, he's a dago. Can't you tell?"

Chance studied the tall dark man as his oddly blue eyes were fixed on the tinker across the seat from her. Brian Pio needed a shave, too, but he was a handsome man. His jeans and hickory shirt were dusty as those of his more flamboyant companion, and like Despres he wore his Colt .44 in a cross-draw rig. The holster was untooled and waxed. The walnut grips of the Colt had been crisscrossed with the grooves a quick draw artist was said to favor. The gun rode on his right side. So she knew he was left-handed.

Hughie was saying, "Eye-talian, are you? Well, as long as you're not an Orangeman I say live and let live. If you've room at your fire, we've tea and a bit of sugar to share with you."

Pio nodded and said, "You're welcome to join us, but don't you mean to water that mule? It's nearly three and hot as the hinges."

Hughie nodded and handed the reins to Chance as he sprang down and turned to help Annie, saying, "Be a good lad and water the stock, will you, Sean?"

Chance nodded wordlessly, and as the tinker and

his woman stood by the strangers, she drove the mule over to the water hole. Hughie said something about the tea and followed casually. As the weary mule lowered it's head to drink, he joined her and said softly, "Don't let him bloat himself. I take it you don't know either of thim, but what do you make of thim, lass?"

She murmured, "They're gunslicks. They said they're looking for seven men. I don't know how to take that."

"Ay, they could be meaning to join the gang. On the other hand they could be lawmen *looking* for thim."

"Two men, looking for a fight with seven?"

"Ay, they're either brave or bandits. Be careful about standing tall in me auld shirt. We wouldn't want them to spot your wee titties before we got to know thim better!"

He got the canisters and Annie's tea kettle and headed back to the fire, trying to stave off possible trouble by saying, "Sure, it's poor as church mice the three of us are, but at least we've tea and sugar. Ain't it grand that the cowshit burns so nice on this dry plain? Sure, we haven't enough between us to be after buying firewood."

Chance finished watering the mule, her mouth dry and her heart beating hard as she strained to hear what they were saying. All four knelt around the fire and spoke more softly. She saw the mule was drinking too much and got down to lead him away from the water. The mule was still thirsty and fought her stubbornly. Chance dug in her heels and hauled on the reins. She was still weak from her ordeal and the thirsty animal was too willful for her to manage. She cursed it and said, "That's enough, you fool critter!"

Then a long, lean arm reached past her and took

the reins near her hands as the tall Brian Pio said, "Let me give you a hand with that brute, son."

The mule shook it's muzzle and fought the bit as its head rose unwillingly from the stagnant pool. Pio laughed and said, "It's no use, pard. I've dealt with drinking men like you before!"

Chance saw she was only in the way and let go to step aside as the stronger man took charge. She said, "Thanks," and then she caught herself. She was supposed to be a feebleminded boy. Had he noticed her womanly voice or the lack of a brogue in the same?

Pio said, "You go on over to join your folks, son. I'll lead this brute up the draw and set the brakes."

She nodded numbly and headed for the fire. She tried to walk like a man. Damn it, what did a man walk like?

Aware he might be watching her from the rear, Chance gave herself a slight limp and tried to keep her slender waist from swaying naturally as she moved slowly to join the others. She saw Annie was sitting on one hip in the grass. Hughie and Tony Despres were squatting on their heels. Chance sank into the same position, balanced on the heels of her borrowed boots. The crotch of Hughie's wool pants pressed hard against her groin, and she wondered if the hefty man across from her could see anything down there as he smiled at her and said, "I see you picked up a gimp leg with that black eye, kid. What did you tangle with, a railroad train?"

Chance looked down and didn't answer. The tinker laughed casually and said, "Sure, he tried to ride the mule and it bucked him galley-west the other night. The lad means well, but he hasn't much common sense, you see."

Despres nodded and said, "Playing cowboy, eh?

Well, don't let it fret you, son. I've been throwed a few times my ownself."

To change the subject Hughie said, "Despres is a French name, ain't it?"

Despres said, "French canuck. I told you I was from the Red River. My daddy was a trapper for the Hudson Bay Company, but I'm a Yankee. Rode with the First Iowa Cav during the war. Old Brian over there fit for the South. But what the hell."

Chance cursed inwardly but held her tongue. She was bursting with so many questions, and the tinker who'd saddled her with this ridiculous disguise didn't seem to know enough to ask the questions she wanted him to. Who were these men and why were they looking for the seven?

Hughie glanced over to where the taller of the pair was braking and chocking the wheels of his cart. He nodded and said, "Ay, the war's been over for a time and what's done is done. What are you lads up to these days of the grand new peace? I'd say you was cowboys from the looks of you."

Despres chuckled and said, "It ain't all that peaceful west of the Big Muddy. But we get along. You might say we was hunters."

"Hunters, is it? Sure, they told us the south buffalo herd had been about shot off. Ain't it up in the Dakotas you hideskinners should be hunting?"

Despres wasn't smiling as he replied, "Some folks hunt buffalo, and some folks hunt other critters."

Hughie had sense enough to drop it. He said, "Well, your business is your own. It's a tinker, or a traveling repairman, you might call me. We heard there's farming around Dodge City, and where there's farms, there's things to be mended. You boyos don't have anything broken that could be fixed with a spot of solder and bailing wire, do you?"

Despres said, "Not hardly. We keep our gear and possibles in good repair, but I thank you for the neighborly offer."

Brian Pio rejoined them, and as he hunkered down, the tinker nodded at Annie's kettle and said, "Tea will be ready in a minute. What's that stuff you're boiling in the other pot?"

Pio didn't answer. Despres said, "It's mostly water with some parched corn and jerky. I'll allow it smells awful, but it does stick to your ribs and you can see we've enough to go around."

The tinker laughed and said, "Sure, it's a grand party we'll be after having before we move on. Would either of you know how far we are from Dodge City now?"

Despres said, "About a day's ride aboard a sudden bronc. You'll take a mite longer ahint that mule."

Hughie glanced up at the sun and said, "In that case our best bet would be to call this day a day and camp here by the water for the night if it's all right with you gints."

Despres looked silently at his taller partner. Pio's thoughtful blue eyes were on Chance as he nodded silently. Despres said, "Hell, we don't own this draw. We'll probably be pushing on come sundown, so it'll be all yours."

"You ride at night?" asked the tinker.

Neither man answered. There was an awkward silence. Then Hughie smiled and said, "Sure, I've ever been too curious for me own health. I mind me sainted father used to hunt at night now that I think about it."

Annie murmured that the tea was ready, and

Hughie got up to fetch some tin utensils from the cart. Chance could have killed him for not sending her as she found herself alone with the shy Annie and the two mysterious "hunters."

Despres said, "The boy, here, got throwed by their mule. Ain't that some shiner he's got?"

Pio smiled thinly at Chance but didn't answer. Her heart was pounding again as she felt undressed before them. She felt a turgid nipple against the linen of Hughie's shirt. Could they see it? She didn't dare look down. Nervously she leaned forward to hug her own knees with her elbows, eyes lowered to the smoldering cow chip fire.

Annie sensed the tension in the air and, licking her lips, said, "I knew some folks named Pio once. It was in County Mayo they had a garth."

Despres laughed and said, "Shux, Ma'am, everyone knows it's a dago name. What would dagos be doing in Ireland?"

"Spanish Armada," said Pio softly. Then he added, "There's an Irish clan called Costello, too. The De Wolfs used to be De Lobo before *their* galleon ran aground on an Irish strand."

Annie looked relieved and said, "Och, then you are an Irishman after all, Mister Pio?"

Pio shrugged and said, "Not lately. My Dad left for Texas during the Famine of Forty-eight. I was born on the Brazos and grew up just in time to ride with the Texas Volunteers."

Despres chuckled and said, "We was on opposite sides, but we never met up until after the war. That's likely why we're still both breathing. We never have settled on who'd beat who to the draw. It wouldn't be neighborly."

Pio sighed and said, "You talk too much, Frenchy,"

and Despres nodded cheerfully and answered, "Somebody has to talk when they rides with such a moody cuss." He winked at Annie and added, "I keeps him out of trouble by jawing polite with folks. He makes some folks uncomfortable the way he just sits and stares like a durned old hoot owl."

Chance suppressed an urge to smile and nod. The tall, sardonic Brian probably knew he made less laconic people nervous with that silent smile and unwinking, unreadable expression. He'd probably been an officer, like Dad. As an army brat she knew the reserve of men used to command. There were so many questions she wanted to ask. But she knew he might not answer even if she were free to ask, and, damn it, what did it matter? They'd said they were riding on. They'd probably never meet again, and it was just as well. She'd had her fill of men of late. He was nice-looking, but he was rather frightening and for all she knew an outlaw.

Hughie came back with plates, cups, and spoons to go around. Despres invited Annie to serve, and the next few minutes were spent in eating the trail stew and washing the vile taste away with Annie's surprisingly tasty tea. Like most country folk neither the strangers nor her tinker friends saw fit to converse as they ate. Chance was used to more gracious table manners, but as a half-witted boy she could hardly make small talk as she dined.

When they'd finished, Annie got up to wash the utensils with wet sand at the water's edge. Chance wondered if she should offer to help. She was uncomfortable by the fire, but unwilling to miss anything.

Despres took out a cigar for an after-smoke. Pio reached in his shirt pocket and took out three thin black cheroots. He offered one to Hughie and another to Chance, who numbly shook her head. Hughie covered by saying, "The lad don't smoke. But I'll be proud to. Sure, ain't this a grand cigar, though?"

Despres said, "Brian lives high for a dago. You ought to see him gussied up in town with a clean shirt and smelling like a whorehouse."

Chance tried not to blush as she reminded herself he thought there were no ladies present. Pio plucked a grass stem and put its end in the fire to light his smoke without comment.

The others did the same, and the tinker, more relaxed now, said, "I've been thinking of these seven men you was asking about. We stopped for directions a few days ago and I do seem to remember the settlers saying something about some riders passing through."

This time Pio answered as he asked quietly, "Can you remember anything else about them?"

"Well, you understand I never saw them meself. But the settlers said they was a mean-looking bunch and, let me see, I think they said one of thim said something about thim being the *fifth* something."

Despres asked, "Fifth Confederate Cav?" and Hughie answered, "That might have been it. I wasn't there when they was after boasting."

Despres nodded and said, "It was them, sure as hell. Didn't old Quantrill call his irregulars the Fifth Cav, Brian?"

Pio grimaced and said, "Not where Robert E. Lee could hear him. The sons of bitches were never recognized as soldiers by the Confederate Army and you know it!"

"Well, whatever they was, they called themselves the Fifth Confederate Cav. Old Quantrill was gussied up in a gray uniform with a gold *V* on the collar when we shot the son of a bitch and scattered his outfit to the four winds. We know that Dawson joined up with some of his old war buddies after he jumped bail in Missouri. We know there's seven of 'em now. I *told* you they was headed for Dodge!"

Pio blew a thoughtful smoke ring before he said, "This don't make sense. Why in thunder would anyone who'd ridden with Quantrill be *telling* folks about it this far north?"

"Hell, I don't know about his friends, but we know *Dawson* ain't got a lick of sense, Brian. Maybe they thought them settlers was old Rebs. Maybe they was trying to scare them. Dawson is a borned bully who likes to scare folks. Who in hell would jump bail and then hit a gal in a whorehouse wearing a red checkered shirt if he had sense enough to pour piss out of his own boots? We'd have never trailed him this far had he had sense enough to change his duds and mind his manners!"

Chance felt her breath catch as the meaning of his words sank in. This man they were talking about, Dawson, had been the one who'd lassoed her! None of the others had worn a red checkered shirt! Who *were* Brian and Tony? What did all this *mean*?

As if he'd read her mind, the tinker said, "Aroo, I see now what it is you're after hunting! The two of you'd be *lawmen*, wouldn't you?"

Pio didn't answer. Despres shrugged and said, "Sort of. You might say we're acting as a *posse comitatus* under the ruling of the Supreme Court decision of Taylor versus Tainter, 1873."

"You're *bounty hunters*!" Chance blurted, forgetting herself for the moment.

Brian Pio nodded and said, "And you're a girl.

Don't you think it's time we put our cards on the table, folks?"

Hughie started to protest. Then he grinned sheepishly as Tony Despres laughed and said, "I was wondering how long it would take you to figure that out, Brian."

Pio shrugged and said, "Nothing much to figure. They have her dressed like that to keep men like the ones we're trailing from messing with her. I reckon two men out of a dozen might take her for a boy who moves like a sissy and looks too pretty, even with that black eye."

Despres saw Chance was frightened and soothed, "Don't you fret on it, honey. We ain't ornery like that to gals. But it's lucky you met up with *us* instead of *them*! I don't think you'd fool a man who's been out on this prairie alone very long."

Chance's voice was bleak as she met his eyes levelly and said, "I know. I've already met them. They killed my father and shot me. Hughie and Annie just happened along in time to keep me from dying after they'd finished with me."

Despres whistled silently. Then he asked, "Jesus, I hope shooting you was all they had in mind."

Pio cut in with, "Don't ask stupid questions about men we already know about."

"Yeah, I can see they knocked her around some, but you're right. It ain't the sort of question you asks a white woman."

"They shot me in the head and left me to die by our burning wagon," said Chance, forcing herself to meet Pio's eyes. The tall bounty hunter's eyes were gentle as he nodded and said, "That ain't what I aim to trouble you about, Ma'am. I noticed how you flinched when mention was made of a red shirt. The man we're after was last seen in the same."

"He was the one who roped me after his leader shot my father. What about the other six? Are you after them, too?"

Pio shook his head and said, "Not if they stay out of our way. We're packing a warrant on Black Jack Dawson, wanted for jumping bail in Clay County, Missouri."

"What did he do, and why was he out on bail in the first place?"

"Don't know. It don't matter. We ain't working for the County of Clay. We're trailing him for the bail bonding company he skipped out on afore his trial came up. It ain't nice to jump bail. The bondsman stands to lose his bail to the court if he can't produce the rascal for the judge and jury at the appointed time."

Despres explained, "Dawson's bail has already been forfeited to the court. The folks who contracted with us have losted five hundred dollars. So they're set to pay a thousand for the rascal, dead or otherwise."

Hughie O'Rourke looked puzzled as he asked, "What good will that do the bail bondsmen he ran out on if the money's already gone for good?"

Despres said, "You might call it an educational experience. The U.S. Constitution says ever'body's entitled to bail, pending a trial. Dawson don't seem to understand his bail was a *loan,* not a license to run off and join his old guerrilla sidekicks in Kansas. You might say he welshed on his just debts. No bail bondsman can stay in business long if he lets folks treat him like an idjet."

The tinker nodded in dawning understanding and said, "Och, it's an example to others who might get the same idea, eh? You mean to teach this Dawson that it's far safer to stand trial and take your chances with the jury than to run off like a woild goose and cost dacent tradesmen hard-earned money!"

Annie had put the utensils away and rejoined them at the fire. Chance ignored her to ask Pio soberly, "You say you're only after the one called Dawson. What would it take to make you kill the other six?"

Pio shook his head and said, "It don't work like that, Ma'am. I know what they say about the Wild West in Ned Buntline's magazine, but we really do have laws out here."

"Damn it, they killed my father!"

"I'll take your word for it, Ma'am. But it ain't legal to gun a man just on a lady's say-so. We'd be proud to shoot the rascals for you if you had a warrant on them and they was dumb enough to resist a citizen's arrest. But you're putting the cart before the horse, no offense. You've got to swear out charges afore a grand jury and get them to issue you a probable cause. Then you've got to get somebody dumb enough to serve them with the same and hope he wins."

"Listen, I don't have a penny on me right now. But my father has property and a bank account. I could make it worth your while if you were to let me point them out to you and . . ."

"Forget it," said Pio flatly. Despres was gentler as he explained, "We ain't hired killers, Ma'am. Brian and me never shoots folks unless it's legal."

"You're *afraid* of them!" she spat, unthinking in her bitterness.

Pio didn't answer. But Despres said, "We wouldn't be looking for 'em if we was fearful, Ma'am. You may git lucky and Dawson's friends may back his play if and when we catch up with them. If they have sense enough to stand aside, our hands is tied. This ain't generally knowed back East, but they *hang* you for just gunning folks for the hell of it, even out here."

Pio said, "Dawson may come quiet. He may even have a thousand bucks on him and want to settle up peaceable. If we have to take him the hard way, we'll have to satisfy the coroner's jury we acted lawful."

"My God, you mean there's a chance you won't even get to kill *him?*"

Pio smiled morosely and said, "We ain't in the business of killing folks, Ma'am. Our job is to recover the bail he skipped out on or to make him sorry as hell he done it."

He rose from the fire and added, "It's time we rode on, Tony."

But as Despres got to his feet, Chance joined them, saying, "Wait a minute. You have to take me with you!"

Pio said, "Not hardly. The man we're after is armed and riding with rough company."

"I know that only too well. But I can point them out to you!"

"We know what Dawson looks like, Ma'am. It won't matter who he's with, unless they want to mix in our business with him. You're safer here with these folks. When you get to Dodge, you'd best swear out a warrant on the gang and maybe the State of Kansas will see fit to do something about it."

As he started to turn away, she clung to his sleeve and sobbed, "No, don't leave it just like that! I don't even know their names! It's only my word against all of theirs! I'll never be able to prove they were the ones!"

Brian Pio gently disengaged her hand as he sighed

and said, "I know. You've got a hard row to hoe, and I wish there was something I could do about it. Get the ponies, Tony."

As Depres moved off to gather their mounts, Chance pleaded, "Just let me have the satisfaction of seeing you take Jack Dawson."

He shook his head and said, "It ain't a satisfaction, Ma'am. If he tries to stand agin' us, it figures to just be ugly. I know how you feel right now. But I can see you was brung up gentle. Your best bet is to try and forget what happened and leave them rascals to heaven. Men like that don't live long, Ma'am. You go back to your family and friends, and in a year or more they'll all be likely dead in any case."

"Damn it, they *killed* my family. Dad was all I had. I can point them out, and if need be, I can handle a gun, too!"

To his credit he didn't laugh at her. But he shook his head and said, "We've got all the gun hands we need, Ma'am. By the way what's your name, in case we ever meet up in happier times?"

"I'm Chance McGraw and I'm going to kill those murderers whether you help me or not!"

He saw Despres was bringing the horses over. He smiled and put two fingers to his hat brim as he said, "I'm proud to meet you, Miss Chance. I'm sorry we couldn't get to know each other better."

Then he turned, took the reins from his sidekick, and swung up into his saddle with surprising grace for such a big man. Despres nodded to her as he mounted his own pony. Then the two bounty hunters were riding out of her life, and Chance could only stand there, crying silently.

Hughie O'Rourke joined her, saying, "Och, it's

good riddance, lass. Men like thim are little better than the ones they're after hunting."

"I've got to get to Dodge," she said flatly, adding, "I'm going to find that Dawson and the others before they do."

"Och, child, you're daft! Haven't you had enough of thim sevin divels?"

"No," she snapped. "The last time we met I didn't have a gun! I mean to wire home for money. Then I mean to arm myself like a man and hunt the seven of them down!"

"Sure, and we'll talk about it on the way to Dodge City. But what's that Pio rascal coming back for?"

Chance followed his glance with her own tear-filled eyes and saw that Brian was riding back their way as Despres sat his pony up the slope to the southwest.

Pio reined in, sighed, and held his free hand down to her as he said, "Come on, you can ride pillion behind me."

She took his hand, and as he lifted her lightly from the ground with surprising strength even for his size, she gasped, "Thank heavens! I see you've changed your mind!"

He settled her astride atop his saddle roll, and as she put her arms around his waist, he said, "Not hardly. I think old Tony's right. I suspicion you aim to keep after the seven on your own, and life gets complicated enough."

He nodded to Hughie and said, "We'll meet up again in Dodge. Lord willing and the creeks don't rise." Then he swung his mount around, and they started jogging up the slope with his saddle carbine digging into Chance's right knee. As he rejoined his shorter partner, Despres grinned and said, "I admire a man who thinks on his feet. If she's with us when we meet up with Dawson, we won't have to worry where she's *at!*"

"You talk too much," said Brian, adding, "Let's move it out. They'll be in Dodge by the time we get there, and I've been studying on how we might get some papers worth having on some of the others."

They rode through the sunset and as far into the night as the moon would let them before it set in the west. Brian Pio reined in and said, "We'd best stop here until sunup. We're close enough now to run into one of them damned new glidden wire fences in the dark."

Despres dismounted as Brian lowered Chance to the prairie grass. The bear-like Tony dropped to one knee and said, "Yep, somebody's grazed cows through here. I know better than to ask, but you won't want a fire out here on this flat, right?"

Pio didn't answer as he dismounted to join them. He started to unlash his bedroll as he told Chance, "You'd best get some shut-eye. We'll be doing some hard riding as soon as it's light. I'd like to ride into Dodge afore they unroll the sidewalks if it's possible."

"You . . . want me in your bedroll?"

"It's the only one I've got for you. I aim to stand watch while you two catnap. I'll crawl into Tony's when the time comes."

Despres said, "I ain't that kind of a boy, you dago

bastard." Then he laughed and said, "I'll be standing watch by then, Miss Chance. We ain't really *that* friendly."

Chance didn't answer either. She was beginning to see why Brian opined he talked too much. Tony Despres had a way of explaining everything to her as if she were a child from back East.

She waited until Pio had spread the roll on the short grass and told Tony to hobble the ponies before she said, "I'm not very tired and it's sort of hard to hold a conversation with a man's back when he insists on trotting his mount."

He said, "I'm sorry about that. I know it's uncomfortable to ride at a trot with no stirrups, but you said you wanted to come along. You get in that roll, tired or no. If you can't sleep, try to rest your bones at least."

She got down on her hands and knees to do as he asked. By the time she was snuggled in the blankets under the canvas, Despres had rejoined them. He hunkered down and said, "We can't brew nothing. If you're hungry, I got some chocolate here for you to chaw, Ma'am."

"I'm not hungry. What about you two?"

"Shux, we're used to traveling light, Ma'am. I could tell you tales of riding up and down the Shenandoah so hungry, you'd think I was bragging. I figure I'm living high on the hog if I eat ever' other day now."

Pio said, "Leave her be. She don't want to jaw with us. She's so tired, she thinks she does. I figure to boot you awake in a couple of hours, Tony. So you'd best get your beauty rest while there's time for the same."

Despres got up and walked off, saying, "You call

me if he trifles with you, Miss Chance. You know what they say about dagos."

Chance grimaced but didn't answer. Pio said, "He didn't mean to bring things up you're trying to forget, Miss Chance. Sometimes I suspicion he had a tooth pulled with laughing gas and he's just never got over talking silly."

She said, "I know, but I like him. You don't have to treat me like I'm made of glass, Brian. I'm an army brat. I'm tougher than I look."

"I know. That's why I come back for you. You've got to get over that idea of yours about the seven, Chance. I told you I'd drop by the town marshal's when we get to Dodge. If any of the others has wanted papers out on 'em, me and Tony will split such rewards as we get with you. But you still ain't promised me you won't buy a gun and start acting foolish."

"You men are all alike. I told you I know how to shoot a gun. I know you think I'm a weak silly woman, but how much strength does it take to pull a trigger?"

He shook his head and said, "That ain't the part that's hard. I ain't putting you down because you're a gal. I noticed this evening you can ride some. But what you've been toying with is dangerous for a man as well. Men like Dawson don't just stand there waiting for you to pull a trigger. He's a gunslick, and a good one. The men he's riding with rode through a war and come out the other side alive."

"I know. My father said most of the men killed in battle die in the first two weeks on the line. Any man who lasts longer has learned how to stay alive. That's why old soldiers never die."

He shifted his weight uncomfortably and said, "I

didn't mean to bring this up, Miss Chance. But since you mentioned your late father, he *was* an old soldier. He was likely pretty handy with a sidearm, too, wasn't he?"

"That's not fair. It was seven to one, and they had the drop on him before he could go for his gun!"

"I know. Meaning no disrespect to your dad, he never had a hope in hell. Men like the seven don't *give* fair odds."

"Do *you*, Brian?"

She propped herself up on one elbow to ask, "All right, how would you or Wild Bill go about taking the seven?"

He said, "His name's James Butler Hickok, and he don't like that fool name the reporters hung on him much. As to how Jim, me, or any other professional would go about it, it would take a week or more to show you the basic moves. You'll be better off catching forty winks. I know you feel like talking. That's from being tired and all you've been through. I must be a mite tired my ownself or I wouldn't be jawing at you like this neither. So I'll say buenos noches for now."

But as he tried to leave, she said, "Wait, I have a proposition for you."

"A what, Chance?"

"A business deal. Cash on the barrelhead. I know you won't gun those men for me illegally. But there is a legal deal we can make for ready cash. What would you say to a hundred dollars a day?"

He frowned down at her and asked cautiously, "Just what do you have in mind for that kind of money, Chance?"

"I want to go to *school.* If you and Tony aren't

afraid of seven gunslicks, and I know you're not, you must be good."

"We're tolerable fighting men if push comes to shove. But it ain't a trade they *teach* at any school, Ma'am."

"I know. That's why I mean to start my own. With a class of one and you two as my teachers."

He shook his head and said, "No, that stuff about two badmen meeting face-to-face for a friendly shoot-out in the town square is plumb silly. You know what I'd do if some damned fool was to send word he'd be waiting for me at high noon in front of the saloon for a quick draw contest? I'd git there at eleven and be up in a steeple with a rifle. That's if I had papers on the idjet."

"What if he wasn't wanted by the law? What if he was just tough?"

"I reckon I'd ride out of town and leave him to meet whomsoever on his lonesome. Men like that ain't tough, they're loco. I got no call shooting crazy folks just for the hell of it."

"Have you ever actually backed out of a gunfight, Brian?"

"Sure, more'n once. Do I look like a teen-ager who's been at hard cider ahint the barn?"

"Tony seems to think you're pretty tough."

"There you go. My friends *know* how much sand I got in my craw. So it don't matter what my *enemies* think of me. I've never seen much sense in fretting about what folks think if they don't like me in the first place."

"I promise never to call you a sissy. But what does all this have to do with me and the men I'm after?"

"Ever'thing. You're still thinking like that teen-aged kid I was just speaking of. You think you can just strap on a brace of six-guns and go stampeding after seven growed men like Wild Bill Hickok. Only I know old Jim Hickok—to give him his right name—and *he* wouldn't do it neither!"

She heard him snort in annoyance and quickly added, "Wait, I know I have a lot to learn. You just taught me something I never might have thought of about engraved invitations from the town bully. I know you have a lot more you've picked up the hard way between here and your Texas boyhood."

"Honey, it'd take you years and at least one good war before you could hope to stand agin' me or Tony, even if you was built less winsome."

"I don't need to be as good as you. I just need to be better than the breed you hunt. Will you give me two weeks at a hundred dollars a day?"

"That's fourteen hundred dollars, counting Sundays."

"I know. I've got it. Consider how long you've been trailing Black Jack Dawson for a thousand, less your expenses. Surely you can spare me two weeks for almost half again as much."

He shook his head and said, "I'd be robbing an orphan and that ain't my style. Besides, we ain't *got* two weeks to spare. Dawson's just a day or so ahead of us."

"He might stay in Dodge if they feel safe there. If he's ridden on, we'll have to hunt him down in any case. I used to hunt deer with my father. Sometimes when we were following a spooked deer, Dad would sit down to have a smoke. Hunted critters stop running when they feel nobody's trailing them close and . . ."

"I got my first deer when I was nine. You might have noticed we're trailing Dawson *easy*. He don't know we're after him. That ain't the point. What you want from me is loco. I wouldn't try to turn a kid like you into a gunslick for twice the money."

She sat up and sighed, "I don't have twice the money to spare. I haven't anything left to offer but . . . well, my body."

Brian Pio stared silently down at her for a breathless moment in time. Then he said, "You mean that, don't you?"

She nodded and said, "If it's the only way."

"What about Tony?"

She shrugged numbly and said, "If I have to, I have to. I *need* the two of you and those . . . animals destroyed my pride in any case."

Brian Pio leaned to place a firm hand on either of Chance's shoulders as he pressed her down on her back. She smiled wanly and said, "Try to be gentle. I'm still a little sore, but . . ."

"Shut up!" he hissed, shaking her to silence her. As she stared up at his dark head haloed by the Milky Way above them, he said, "Now listen to me and listen tight, Chance McGraw! Them seven never destroyed a thing important unless you *let* what happened scar your soul. You're still a lady 'til I say different, and I don't remember saying nothing of the kind!

"You got to get it out of your head that you've been shamed. You've been maltreated and humbled, like a kid throwed from a sassy bronc. You can lay there in the dust, feeling sorry for yourself, or you can get up, dust yourself off, and climb back in the saddle!"

She laughed despite herself and said, "You sound just like my father did the first time I fell off a horse."

"There you go. That horse you met up with in your girlhood likely made you eat some humble pie. Are you still cut up inside about being bucked off in front of your folks?"

She wiped her face and answered, "No, as a matter of fact I'm sort of proud about the way I finally broke that horse. Her name was Ribbon and she was mean as anything, but I taught her to behave and . . ."

"And the next time you went to a party you was wearing a new dress, and nobody could see the dust you'd washed off after Ribbon throwed you, right?"

"That's true! How did you know about the new dress Dad bought me for the regimental dance?"

"I know gals and I've been to regimental dances. I know about the hurts folks wear under their new duds as they smile and do the two-step, too."

"Brian, it's not the same. I wouldn't be able to meet your eyes as we spoke like this if the sun was shining."

"Then you ain't worth much. You think you was the only gal at them dances who'd ever lost some dignity? How many bright-eyed wives do you reckon had birthed a baby, screaming in pain and soaked with their own blood and sweat? How many belles of the ball was there who'd slept with more'n seven men, or done worse?"

"Eight," she corrected with a sigh, explaining, "I've been had by eight men, counting one lover. I kept telling myself it wasn't as if I was a virgin, but it didn't seem to help much."

He shrugged and said, "Let's not take complaining into *bragging*, damn it! Eight ain't all that many."

Again she found herself laughing, and before she'd

thought, she'd asked archly, "Are you suggesting I get back in *that* saddle, too?"

He shook his head and said, "Nope. You said you was bruised and I'm trying to convince you you're still a lady. If you make a fool suggestion like that a day or so from now, though, you'd best be prepared to meet your maker. For you're pretty as hell and I'm only human!"

"Do you expect to be around a few days from now, Brian?"

He let go of her and straightened up, saying, "Hard to say. You asked for two weeks. We'll work out your tuition later. Right now I'm giving you an entrance examination."

"A what?"

"Got to see if you're worth teaching or just frothing at the mouth. I got me a trick question for you, Miss Chance. You'd best study some afore you answer."

"What is it, Brian?"

He paused before he asked soberly, "Are you after the seven because of what they done to you or what they done to your father?"

She sat up again and said, "Both, of course!"

He shook his head and said, "One more try is all you get. You're not worth teaching if you can't learn to *think* afore you sound off!"

She nodded and said, "All right, if it's a choice of one or the other, I mean to pay them back for killing Dad."

Brian Pio put out a hand and said, "Shake. I'm giving you a gold star on that one."

She took his hand in both of hers and gasped, "You mean you'll teach me, Brian?"

He shrugged and said, "I mean I'll try. I doubt like hell you've got the makings of a gunslick. But you may as well commit suicide with a little style."

"God damn it, girl," said Brian, "That's a loaded six-gun on your hip, not a powder puff. Do it *right* this time!"

Chance faced him on the open prairie as Tony Despres watched, amused, holding the ponies.

Chance had borrowed Tony's gunbelt and strapped it on over the tinker's pants amid some sardonic remarks as Despres punched a new hole for the buckle. Like her, he was right-handed, so the holster snuggled against her left hipbone, and she'd noticed the care he'd taken in fitting the gun to the curve of her body. Brian faced her from ten paces away, his own left-handed rig ready, although both guns in truth were empty.

Brian yelled, "Well, what are you waiting for?" and she asked, "Isn't there supposed to be some sort of signal?"

Brian took his hat off, threw it on the ground, and kicked it. Then he said, "God damn it, nobody *signals* when they aim to draw on you!"

Tony called, "I told you she's been reading Ned Buntline, Brian."

A sly thought crossed Chance's mind, and as Brian bent, grumbling, to retrieve his hat, Chance went for the gun at her side. She drew smoothly and well, for Dad had let her practice with his own and she was not the total greenhorn they took her for. She had the hammer back and almost in line with Brian's tall form when his own gun clicked three times and he said, "You're dead. I *figured* you'd try when I bent over."

Chance clicked her own gun futilely as she wondered how he'd moved so fast. Tony called out, "He's good at riling folks into foolish moves, honey. At the risk of giving away a trade secret, he's been cussing at you to get you flustered. Sometimes you can get an edge on a gent by saying something mean about his mother just as he's set to slap leather."

Brian grinned sheepishly and said, "Let's try her again. Remember now, I'm giving you a point you'd never get in a real showdown. You *know* I won't draw *first*. So don't get sassy if you beat me. *Real* enemies has a way of drawing anytime they *feel* like it!"

Chance put the muzzle of the six-gun in the holster and then, without seating it firmly, whipped it out and thumbed the hammer as she cheated.

Again Brian's empty gun clicked three times before she made it, and he said, "Better. But I can see you're having trouble with that single action. They say there's a double action S&W on the market now. But it's a bitty .36 as'd be an insult to draw agin' a grown man. We're going to have to work on that lazy thumb of yours."

"Darn it," she frowned ruefully, "don't you ever fire *four* times, or *twice*? Every time you beat me, you click that thing three times and it's getting tedious as anything!"

Brian walked over to her, smiling, and said, "Three rounds is about right. A man can still kill you with one bullet in his heart. Three rounds in the trunk generally make him lose interest in further plans he might have had, even if he's only gutshot."

"The two left in your gun is what you might call insurance," added Tony.

Chance frowned and asked, "Two? Don't you mean *three*? These guns hold six bullets, don't they?"

Brian said, "Five, if you value your own toes. You keep your hammer on an empty round until you're serious about wanting the fool thing to fire."

Tony said, "Tell her about that Pinkerton man we worked with who shot hisself in the leg that time, Brian."

Brian said, "It was a natural mistake. He knew enough to keep an empty round in one chamber. But we were moving in and he cocked the gun while it was still in the holster, hoping to be set for a quick draw if the men we were after were home."

Tony chortled and chimed in, "This door busted open and this colored gal came out with a bucket of slops to throw. Old Pink slapped leather and the gun went off in the holster. Damn near took his kneecap off."

Brian said, "That's another point to remember. The address they'd given us was wrong. The colored girl was an innocent housewife throwing out her slops. The Pink slapped leather like a greenhorn, and had he not managed to shoot himself, he'd have had the killing of an unarmed woman to answer for."

Tony said, "You got to be careful about alleyways, too. Sometimes there's a kid sleeping on the other side of a thin wall ahint the man you're out to knock down."

Chance shuddered at the grim picture his words

painted in her mind. She asked, "How do you avoid a mistake like that in an alley?"

Brian said, "Easy. You don't *go* down a blind alley after anyone. You wait for him to come out. If you go in, he's got you outlined and any accidents to innocent bystanders are on your shoulders."

He added, "They've always got a terrible edge against us when we're working *legal*, Chance. You see, we have to *answer* for everything we do. They don't. You'd be in a mess if you gunned the wrong man on sight. An owlhoot don't have to make sure. He can smoke up anybody who don't look right to him."

Tony said, "Tell her about that jasper you shot in Leadville that time. The one who looked sort of like somebody else we had papers on."

Brian grimaced and said, "I was new at the game then. He went for his guns when I ordered him to freeze."

Tony said, "We was sweating bullets just the same. When we drug the rascal out in the light, we seen his eyes was brown. The man on our warrant had blue ones."

Chance gasped, "My God, you mean you shot the wrong man? How did you get out of it, Brian?"

"I was lucky. You see, I really did give him the choice of coming quiet, and he really tried to kill me for my polite words. So it wasn't such a great surprise when the sheriff told us he was wanted on *other* warrants."

Tony said, "The durned sheriff kept the whole reward, the rascal. He said he only owed us his heartfelt thanks for gunning a wanted outlaw in his county, since we didn't have the proper papers to go with said cadaver!"

Chance said, "I had no idea it could get so technical," and Brian replied, "I know. That's why you hired us to teach you. I keep telling you that you can't just go around shooting folks whenever you feel like it."

"Oh, come now, everyone knows about the gunfights in Abilene and Dodge. Are you saying they never happened?"

Brian said, "Sure they happen. Folks get drunk and shoot one another almost as often as Ned Buntline writes about it. Then the survivor generally runs like hell. There ain't all that much law out here, the way it's sort of empty. But such laws as they enforce are the same ones they have everywhere else. They can hang you legal for stealing a horse in Colorado. Most juries take shooting a man even more serious."

"Then it's hit-and-run for the most part?"

"That's what I just said. Sometimes the local law ain't paid enough to stand up to a gang of drunken trailhands. So they might sort of swagger out by the time a grand jury hands down its findings. But there's usually a murder warrant out by the time the killer sobers up. That's where gents like me and Tony here come in."

"I see. What's this posse comitatus business Tony keeps talking about?"

"English common law. The laws of public hue and cry. Posse comitatus is a highfaluting way of saying the power of the county. All law-abiding citizens has the duty to assist the sheriff or other peace officer in arresting a fleeing outlaw. It ain't enforced, but an able-bodied man can be arrested as an accomplice if he stands aside and lets a wanted man get away."

"Then if I meet one of those men and have to shoot him . . ."

"Wrong. I keep telling you that'd be plain murder,

revenge or no. You want to argue about law some more, or shall I show you what you're doing wrong with your thumb?"

Tony Despres came closer, leading the ponies, and chimed in, "She's going to have to web-draw, Brian. Her hands is too small for them thumb-busting Colts."

Brian shook his head and said, "I don't care for that flashy, border stuff. A web-draw can hang your gun up in the first place, and you only get off one shot with it in the second."

Tony insisted, "One shot's better than none. Hang my nails if you ain't blind. Look at her *hands*, damn it!"

Chance raised the six-gun in her hand and studied her own hand on the walnut grip. She cocked the gun with a little effort and asked, "What's wrong with my hands, Tony?"

"They ain't *big* enough. Meaning no disrespect to your gender, Sam Colt never designed that gun with a woman's thumb in mind."

Brian said, "Old Sam Colt died before these Peacemakers came out a couple of years ago. But you got a point, Tony."

He smiled ruefully at Chance and added, "This here is what they call a web-draw."

Then his big left hand skimmed across his waist, there was the sharp crack of tortured leather, and the gun was pointed at her as it clicked once. It all happened too fast for the eye to follow, and the only difference she noticed was the single click.

She was getting tired of them joshing her about her lack of gun lore, so she nodded as if she knew what was going on and said, "I see why you only get one shot with that . . . web-draw. I've been meaning to ask, though. Dosen't it hurt these guns to be clicking them empty like this? My Dad always said you could break the hammer firing dry."

Brian shook his head and said, "He was from the old army and likely set in his ways. The army uses dry firing lately. It beats hell out of pointing *loaded* guns at folks you ain't really mad at."

"You mean it's just a superstition?"

"No. I mean we're talking about different kinds of guns. Up until just after the War Between the States the only six-guns was cap-and-ball. A flat hammer hitting agin' a little nipple on the cylinder. If you didn't have the copper cap on the nipple, it could chew up the hammer face and collapse the nipple if you kept snapping an empty gun. These center-fire jobs drive their pins into the cartridge base or into plain air if the gun ain't loaded."

Tony added, "Colt's hammers is forged steel. The pin's a solid part of the hammer and you'd have a time busting it off with a rock. In fairness to your Dad, though, some cheap belly guns is made with cast-iron hammers as brittle as glass, and I have heard tell of fancy furrin guns with the pin screwed into the hammer as a separate part. You could likely mess one of them fool guns up with or without dry fire. But old Sam made his guns right, dead or whatsoever. You go on and snap my pisoliver all you like. But let's learn you to do it *sudden!*"

She nodded and replaced the borrowed weapon in it's holster as Brian said, "I'm going to do it real slow this time. Watch close."

She tried to follow his actions as he moved more slowly for a man born with lightning in his fists. Again the gun appeared as if by magic in his left hand, and she protested, "Not so fast. I missed something."

Brian snorted in annoyance and replaced his gun in its holster. He said, "All right. How's this?"

He was grinning at his own pantomime as he moved his hand like it was going through glue. She saw his thumb and fingers were spread wide, like a leaping wolf spider, as he dropped them on the gun on his right hip. The web between his thumb and fingers came down on the hammer, cocking the gun in its holster. Then thumb and fingers closed around the weapon and he drew it slowly but smoothly and gripped loosely. As he brought it across his torso to train her way, she saw he shifted his grip to get his thumb-web off the hammer while sliding his trigger finger deeper into the guard. He didn't dry fire this time. He held the gun on her, cocked and ready, and said, "You can see how it's cocked. But from here on you've got to do it right."

He pulled the trigger and the gun clicked three times. Chance shook her head and said, "Do that last part again slowly."

Brian sighed and put his thumb on the hammer. He cocked and fired slowly three more times, and Chance saw there was no trick to it. Just a strong thumb and plenty of practice. She shook her head and opined, "Tony's right. These guns are too big, or my hands are too small. I heard some soldiers talking one day about something they called *fanning* a gun. One of them said that was how Wild Bill shot so fast."

Both men laughed. She sighed and asked, "What's so funny? Can't you really fan a gun?"

Brian said, "It's possible. It ain't sensible."

Holding the gun in his left hand, Brian brought

his right down on the hammer in a slow, chopping motion she could follow as he explained, "As you see, you can cock her this way, if you don't miss and tear hell out of your knuckles. You also throw the aim to one side if you ain't careful. When you're all done waving your arms around, all you wind up with is a gun you could have cocked with one hand in the first place."

Tony said, "I read about that fanning business in a dime novel one time. They said some jasper filed the sears off his action so the hammer was loose from the trigger. In the story he just beat hell out of his gun like he was spanking it for being stubborn, and bullets flew ever' which-way. You reckon it would work with the sears filed off, Brian?"

Brian looked disgusted and said, "Mebbe. You don't win a gunfight by throwing lead ever' which way. You win by putting *one* bullet where it *matters*! How the hell would you fire a gun from the saddle if the trigger didn't work no more?"

"Hell, I said it was a dime novel. Try doing her some more the hard way, honey."

Chance replaced the borrowed weapon and tried to web-draw. She thought she knew how Brian had done it. But when she slapped down at the gun on her hip she missed and tore a little divot out of her palm. She hissed in pain and put the heel of her palm to her mouth to suck it.

Brian didn't laugh. He glanced up at the sun and said, "I reckon that's enough for now. We'd better move on if we aim to reach Dodge in the gloaming."

Chance knew they'd delayed their journey by a day for her already and she felt foolish and helpless. She wasn't sure if Brian was trying to teach her his skills or if he was trying to show her the futility of her plans. She said, "It won't matter if we ride in an hour later as long as it's dusk or darker, will it?"

Brian said, "Never be first, never be last, and never volunteer. Next to three strangers coming in broad daylight there's nothing that draws more attention than three strangers riding in late at night. Best time to arrive is suppertime. Folks don't notice much when they're staring at beans."

"Just let me try a few more times?"

"All right. Don't just stand there. Do it."

Chance took a deep breath as she planned her draw, then went for her gun. This time she hooked her thumb in Tony's belt.

She blushed beet red as she waited for them to laugh. Tony grinned fondly, but Brian was expressionless as he said, "You're overanxious and your hand is tired. We'll ride on a spell and mebbe try her some more the next time we rest the ponies."

Wordlessly she unbuckled the belt as Brian began to reload his own weapon. She handed the rig to Tony, who said, "Don't feel bad, honey. Your *head* will go on practicing as we ride. Sometimes when you can't get the hang of a thing, your mind keeps chawing at it without you knowing it. Have you tried to remember something, put it out of your mind, and had it flash sudden into your head when you wasn't thinking about it?"

She said, "Of course. I didn't know manual skills worked that way, too."

Tony strapped on his gun and began to reload himself as he insisted, "Ever'thing we do is started inside our skulls. Put it aside for now and let her simmer on the back of your stove."

Brian took the reins of his own pony and mounted up before he reached down to help Chance aboard.

As she settled behind him, Tony mounted and said to Brian, "I figure we'll make Dodge in the sneaky shadow time if we take two more breaks along the way. Do you reckon she'd do better with a side-draw rig?"

Brian didn't answer as he spurred them forward. Clinging to his waist, Chance asked the back of his neck, "What's he talking about?"

Brian said, "I'm still studying on it. Him and me favor cross-draw because it's a handy compromise for gents who never know when they might want to fill their fists with hardware. As you can likely see, I could draw as fast mounted with this rig as I could afoot."

She glanced down at the holster between his hip and her thigh and agreed, "Of course. That's why Wild Bill favors a cross-draw, right?"

"Forget Jim Hickock. He ain't all that big a shux in spite of the way he brags. What Tony means by a side-draw is just what it sounds like. You wear the gun low on your right hip, grips facing aft. It's closer to your hand when you need it, and the draw's more natural. You'd have less trouble webbing, too. Some border buscaderos are said to tie the holster flat with a thong around their thigh. I don't know if that's a good notion or not. I told you I have to study on it."

Chance mentally pictured the feel of such a rig and found her right hand itching to slap down at her hip. She said, "It does feel more natural. But if you tied the holster to your thigh, wouldn't the gun ride almost horizontal when you were mounted?"

He chuckled and said, "There you go. If she didn't fall out at a lope, you'd have to swing under your bronc to find the fool grips."

She laughed and they jogged along in pleasant

silence. The prairie was rolling more now, and whoever had named it the "sea of grass" had chosen aptly. The rises all around were gently rounded like the ground swells of a vast stagnant sea, frozen in midwave and sewn with grass. The grass was summer-dried and the color of a lion's mane in the sunlight. When they passed a bovine skull bleaching in a clump of grama, it seemed more to be floating half-awash than embedded in the soft prairie loam. Chance asked, "Isn't that a buffalo skull?" and Brian said, "Yep. Old bull the bone pickers missed. Used to be a mess of bones out here, but somebody found out they make good bone meal fertilizer. Some old boys with strong backs and a big wagon have made almost as much off the bones as the hide hunters did with the shoot-off."

He fell silent for a time before he added, "I tried a season of buffalo hunting right after the war. Didn't like it much. Takes more skill to shoot a *duck*! Ducks have enough sense to fly away when they hear gunfire. Dumb old buffalo just stand there looking mournful. I've never understood why Bill Cody brags so much about all the buffalo he shot for the Union Pacific that time. The poor brutes are almost impossible to miss."

Chance smiled and said, "You're a funny man, Brian Pio. You hunt *men* for a living and here you are waxing sentimental about buffalo!"

He shrugged and said, "The buffalo I shot that season never hurt nobody. We don't hunt just *any* men, Chance. We hunt the *ornery* ones. You might say me and old Tony are like the bone pickers. We neaten up the country by removing unsightly debris."

"But you say some of them have only jumped bail or skipped out with the contents of a till. I understand killing killers. What about the men you've killed who were only common criminals?"

"Criminals ain't common, Chance. Nine out of ten or more people are honest. It don't matter if a man's birthed white or Injun. Most Mexicans I've met wouldn't steal if they was hungry, and a lot of 'em are. I'm a southeron, but fair is fair and most colored folk is decent too. You have to look hard for the rotten apples in any barrel. When you *find* 'em, you have to take 'em out and get *rid* of 'em. That's why our job don't fret us. I've never shot a man who wasn't out to kill me save for the war."

He fell silent for a moment before he added, "Sometimes *that* bothers me a mite. I was a fool kid, not dry ahint the ears, and the bands was playing and the gals was smiling and waving the Stars and Bars when they marched us off to kill other kids who didn't know what *they* was doing neither."

"My father always said the war was a tragedy that never should have happened, too."

"Your dad sounds like a sensible cuss, even if he did ride for the Blue. It's a funny thing, but the only regrets I have wore blue. The first man I killed was coming at me with a bayonet and I was scared as hell. Then, when my bullet put him on his knees, he dropped his musket and sort of stared at me in wonder, holding his hands to his belly. I stared back, and then I said I was sorry. He never answered. He just kept staring at me reproachful as he keeled over, slow. And then more Yanks was coming and I forgot about him 'til later that night when it was all over. I kept wondering if he was still laying out there in the field or if they'd carried him away. I wondered if there'd been papers or a watch or something he'd want sent home to his kin. I always thought he'd meant to *say* something as he knelt there staring at me like that. I don't reckon he believed me when I said I was sorry, but I was."

Chance's voice was gentle as she asked, "How old were you then, Brian?"

He said, "Sixteen. The war was over afore I got old enough to vote. But I sure had learned a *trade*."

Before Chance could answer, Tony shouted, "Smoke ahead, folks. You reckon it's a grass fire, Brian?"

Brian reined in and studied the smudge against the sky before he shook his head and said, "That's woodsmoke. Coming from one place just over that distant rise."

Tony said, "We're too far out to see smoke from the railroad or Dodge. Do we circle her or shall I scout ahead?"

"Neither. We'll fan out and approach from two directions. Fire your saddle gun if you see something important afore we do."

Despres nodded and spurred his pony to a lope, drawing his saddle gun as he rode off at an angle to their right. Brian walked their mount forward, trending more to the left as they approached the rising smoke on the horizon. Chance started to comment on their different paces, but she held her tongue as she realized Tony had more ground to cover. She knew men who worked as a team needed fewer explanations than someone merely tagging along. She asked Brian, "Do you want me to hold your Winchester? I'm pretty good with a rifle."

He drew the rifle with his free hand and held the stock back to her without turning as he said, "Hold it, but keep cool and point it at the ground. There's no round in the chamber, so remember to lever her if you need to fire. We'll dismount on this side of the last rise and move in afoot. I'll want you to hold the reins and hang back as I pop my head over for a look-see. Make sure you don't line up with me so's one field of fire covers us both, hear?"

She took the Winchester and held it out to the side as she hooked her remaining fingers in his gunbelt. He said, "Don't do that. Grab a fistful of shirt if you're afraid of falling off. My gun rig ain't no handle. It's a tool of my trade."

She shifted her grip, abashed and anxious, but pleased that she seemed to be part of the team. She had a better view of the rising smoke now as they angled to the left. She said, "It's too much smoke for a campfire. What do you suppose could be burning over there?"

He said, "Don't know. That's why we're riding in careful."

Chance stood by the pony's head, holding the reins, as she watched Brian Pio moving up the slope toward the mushrooming plume of dirty gray. The pony was nervous about the woodsmoke in the air and pawed at the turf. Chance murmured, "Easy, boy. It's not a prairie fire. You don't have to run away from it."

She saw Brian drop to his knees and right hand, holding his drawn pistol as he crawled smoothly for the crest. She remembered soldiers training at Fort

Leavenworth when she was younger, and though he wore dusty denim now, it was easy to picture Brian in the butternut gray of the lost cause. He moved like a stalking cat and it was obvious how he'd lived through the tragic days of his youth. She knew the invisible Tony Despres was working in from another angle and probably with similar skill. When she'd first met them, she'd assumed the two bounty hunters approached their prey side by side. Now she saw why there were two of them. She could see the advantage of having someone covering the back door when you knocked on the front with legal papers.

Brian flattened out on the crest and seemed to be watching something. He didn't signal her. She shifted the rifle's weight in her free hand and wondered if she should load the chamber. She decided not to. She was more afraid of being teased as a greenhorn than she was about what he might be staring at up there. She knew he wouldn't let anything come over the crest to hurt her. Anyone who tried to get past Brian Pio would be in big trouble.

Chance was stabbed by an angry little pang as she thought back to those jeering strangers riding in on her and Dad that night. Poor Dad had tried. But if *Brian* had been there . . .

The tall man on the crest of the rise got to his feet and waved her forward with his gun hand. As she walked the pony up the slope, Chance saw him putting the gun in its holster.

As she joined him, he said, "Stay up here. It figures to be ugly."

Chance looked down into the next draw and gasped. The smoke was rising from the gutted ruins of a sod house. A dead milk cow lay in the wagon yard. Just beyond a human body lay spread-eagled, dead in the dust. The body was that of a woman. She was naked save for her high-button shoes. You couldn't tell from up here what she'd looked like in life.

"The seven!" Chance gasped. But Brian said, "Mebbe. Might have been Kiowa. We'll know better after we scout for sign. You stay here with the critter while I poke about a spell down there."

But as he started down the slope she followed, saying, "I'm coming, too."

He didn't answer.

Chance saw Tony coming down the slope from the far side of the burned-out homestead, leading his pony. As the three of them got closer, a stray tendril of breeze carried a ghastly sweet scent to her nostrils and the pony she was leading tried to break free. Chance dropped the rifle in the grass and grabbed the reins with both hands to keep its head down as it whinnied in terror. Brian turned, grabbed the reins from her, and said, "Easy, boy. Pick up the rifle and put her in the boot. *You* may have a strong stomach, but horses is more sensitive about the smell of death."

Shamefaced, Chance retrieved the fallen Winchester and put it away as he held the spooked mount steady. Then he led it to a nearby fence post and tethered the reins to it, observing, "They hadn't gotten around to stringing their wire yet, so this post is likely fresh-drove. It ought to hold. Old Thunder here is rein-trained, but he'd drag 'em sure with that smell in the air. You sure you want to see what whomsoever done?"

Chance licked her lips and nodded. He shrugged and said, "Well, I told you to stay back here with Thunder. We ain't got no smelling salts."

She followed, frowning, as he walked toward the

ruins. She didn't know if he'd passed that last remark to annoy her or to put some spine in her. But she knew she wouldn't faint no matter what.

It was just as well she'd steeled herself firmly. As they circled the dead cow, Tony was standing over the woman sprawled in the dust, and Chance bit her lower lip to keep from screaming.

The woman hadn't been very pretty, even alive. She'd been about forty with a flabby belly and sagging breasts. She'd been shot in the forehead and was staring cross-eyed at the clean blue sky above. There were human tooth marks around both nipples, and Chance knew that had been the one with the anchor tattoed on his forearm. The one the others teased about his size. She felt her groin freeze as the memory of his stubby penis defiled her once again with its premature ejaculations.

The biter's latest victim lay with her legs apart and bluebottle flies crawled over her gray pubic hairs. Tony looked around, spotted a burlap seed bag near the yawning doorway of the burned-out house, and went to fetch it. Brian shoved the woman's legs together with his boot tip.

Chance said quietly, "One of them bites."

"I noticed. Didn't reckon it was Kiowa this close to town. She's still got her hair, too. Kiowa cotton to long scalp locks."

Tony came back and said, "There's another couple in the house. Man and a kid. Can't tell if the kid was a boy or a girl. They're sort of toasted."

He dropped the sack across the woman's lap. Had it been up to Chance, she'd have covered the face. She said, "The child they killed must have been a boy. We'd have found her out here with her mother if she'd been wearing a skirt when they found her."

Tony nodded and said, "Yep. It sure looks like them boys is in a rut. This lady wasn't as lucky when they blowed her a good night kiss, though. I reckon practice makes perfect. You reckon we've time to bury 'em, Brian? Might be some tools about somewheres."

Chance expected him to nod, but Brian said, "Leave 'em be. We'll tell the sheriff what we found when we get to Dodge."

Tony protested, "This lady figures to be mighty messy by the time anyone rides out here again, Brian."

Brian said, "I know. I *want* them to see. They're nesters, and graves don't stir men much. I want the posse mad as hell when they start searching."

"Hell, ain't we already searching for the rascals, Brian?"

"We only have papers on Dawson. Chance here can identify the others. It's still only her word agin' theirs, but if the folks in Dodge are riled enough, they might not want to be too technical about the rules of evidence. The town is spanking new. It ain't incorporated yet, and save for the county sheriff the only law is likely to be a vigilance committee, if you follow my drift."

Tony nodded, bent over, and removed the improvised burlap shroud. As he cast it aside, he said, "Lynching's too good for the rascals, but it do save time and paperwork, don't it?"

Brian said, "Let's ride. There's nothing we can do for these folks now."

Chance waited until they were all riding out the far side before she asked Brian, "Does this mean we'll be changing our plans about getting there at dusk?"

He asked, "Why should it? I don't make plans to change 'em."

"I thought you'd be anxious to report what we just found back there."

"You thought wrong. Nobody will ride out here this far afore sunup tomorrow in any case. There's no sense in giving them owlhoots an edge by riding in like Paul Revere. We'll mosey in quiet and get you bedded down outten the way afore I drop by the sheriff's."

"Won't you need me there as a witness?"

"Not hardly. Tony and me seen what they done back there."

"But I can identify the men on sight!"

"I know. But I might be able to spare you the discomfort of relating your misadventures to strangers if it works out right. Once I tell the sheriff what happened and he starts gathering a posse, ever'one in town will hear about it. If Dawson and the other six are hiding out in town, they'll hear it, too."

"Then they might make a break for it?"

"Wouldn't you? Like I said, we'll cache you someplace safe afore we spread the word. Then Tony and me will be waiting in the railroad yards to see what happens."

"How do you know they'll try to hop a train? What if they just ride out of town on their horses?"

Brian didn't answer. But Tony had been listening. He said, "They never would be headed for Dodge if they wasn't out to hop a freight, honey. Them seven rascals has been riding careless, leaving a bloody trail and letting ever'body know they're looking for seven mounted men."

She frowned and started to ask him what he was talking about. Then she nodded and said, "Of course.

They've been on the dodge since the war and must know all the tricks by now. I read how the James-Younger gang leads the posse a merry chase cross-country and then abandons the horses to split up and take public transportation far and fast. Where do you think they're headed, California?"

Brian shook his head and said, "Most likely back toward Missouri."

"But that's where they just *came* from!"

"I know. *Coyotes* double back, too. The hounds never seem to catch on. Dawson and his pals lit out of Missouri riding hard and acting careless. By now they must have a dozen lawmen looking for 'em. All remembering 'em *mounted* and headed *west*."

She nodded and said, "Missouri and Kansas is their home territory. They have hideouts and friends to the east. And you're right. *I* never would have searched for them back along their trail. It's sort of like playing chess, isn't it?"

Brian said, "You do have to think ahead. It's a big country. You can't just tear-ass around asking which way did they go. You got to narrow it down to what's possible."

She said, "I feel like such a fool. No wonder you laughed at me when I asked you to teach me the tricks of your trade."

Tony said, "Don't feel bad. Lots of men wearing a badge don't know what you've larnt already. They hunt outlaws the way a kid hunts deer. They just run about in circles shooting and yelling until they get tired and give up. That's likely why there's so many outlaws."

Dodge City was only four or five years old as they rode in that summer evening. It looked it. The town had taken its name from the nearby Fort Dodge, which guarded the crossing of the Arkansas River on the old Santa Fe Trail. The trail was dead now. Replaced by the Atchison, Topeka & Sante Fe. The railroad gave Dodge its reason for existence.

It was a cow town pure and simple. It had nothing much to offer but a place to load bawling cattle aboard the trains to be shipped to the slaughterhouses further east. The railroad yards and cattle pens around them covered more of the town's gridiron than all the buildings put together.

The housing was mostly jerry-built of canvas and raw lumber, not yet weathered enough to matter by the sun. Some few of the saloons and stores along the main drag sported false fronts. Most were little more than shacks. Chance commented on how quiet things seemed, and Brian said, "The workday's over and the nightlife ain't started yet. I timed it with that in mind. You won't see much action tonight in any case. It's a weeknight, so the hands working the spreads out of town won't be riding in unless they work close. The big cattle drives from Texas ain't due for nigh a month. Between roundups it ain't that big a shux in Dodge."

Tony said, "I was out here when the first steers

come north from the Panhandle. Got to go to the funeral of the first man kilt in Dodge. He was a colored cowboy named Tex. Never larnt his last name or why they kilt him. It's quieted some since then. The railroad said they'd bypass the town if folks didn't act more polite of a Saturday night."

Chance spotted a sign over a door and said, "There's the Western Union office! I'll run in and wire home for money."

But Brian said, "Not yet. You won't need money tonight and it'll still be there come sunup. I aim to bed you and these ponies down and get over to the sheriff's afore the boys come out to set on the steps for an after-supper smoke."

Tony asked, "Where are we staying this time, Madam Moustache's?"

Brian said, "Not hardly. The Drover's Rest Hotel is clean and down at the quiet end of Saloon Row."

Chance blinked and asked, "Is, uh, Madame Moustache what I think she is, Brian?"

He shrugged and said, "I wouldn't know. I never asked her. I only know her to play cards with, and she sure has a good poker face."

"What about this place of hers?"

"She calls it a hotel. It might be one. Last time we stopped by, all we got for our money was our rooms. There was a mite more action in the barroom downstairs than you'd find in the Palmer House up in Chicago. Her bartenders wore high heels and low-cut bodices. But I can't say if they served more than likker. I never asked."

Tony said, "I did. But since ladies is present, I'll say no more about it. What the hell, it ain't that far from the Drover's Rest." He threw back his head and began to sing, "First down to Rosie's, and then to the cardhouse. Shot in the breast and I'm dying today!"

Brian snapped, "Shut up, you danged fool! We're almost home free and you start wailing like a coyote! Sometimes I wonder how General Billy Sherman got a wink of sleep, if you really did march through Georgia with him like you say."

Tony Despres fell silent and they reined in near a barn-like two-story building with DROVER'S REST painted across its raw lumber false front. Brian glanced at the cherry red sky and observed, "The light's likely to be even dimmer inside, Chance. You just keep quiet and let me do the talking whilst I hire us some rooms. Pull that hat down a mite and they may take you for a boy."

As he lifted her down, she asked, "What difference does it make now that we're safe in town?"

He swung himself out of the saddle and began to tether his mount before he said, "You're in town. That don't mean your *safe*. The rascals who killed your dad and them other folks don't know you're alive to point 'em out in a crowd. Let's keep her that way until we find out if they're here in Dodge, and have the drop on all seven."

Tony tethered his own pony as he added, "You being a manchild saves questions in any case, honey. This here's a hotel for cowboys and you ain't wearing no wedding band."

Chance nodded wordlessly as she followed them up the plank steps toward the open doorway. She caught herself running a thumbnail over the base of the finger she'd worn Duncan's engagement ring on. She'd left it on the dresser with her note to Duncan when she'd left. She wondered if he'd pawned it for drinking money.

It was very dark in the lobby. A bored-looking

room clerk sat at the desk playing solitaire by the light of a penny candle. Brian greeted him by name and asked for adjoining rooms near the bath. As he put some coins on the counter, the clerk handed over two keys without looking her way. Chance felt relieved. He wouldn't remember her.

As she followed Brian up the narrow stairwell, Chance wondered why she felt so oddly guilty. It was true she was sneaking into a hotel with two men, but he'd mentioned two rooms and it wasn't as if she'd signed in as anyone's wife under a false name. Brian unlocked a corner room with one of the keys. As Chance followed him in, she could barely make out the sagging brass bedstead and a table lamp in the gloaming light coming through the window. She asked if either of them had a match and Brian said, "Wait a minute."

He went to the window, stared thoughtfully out, and drew the roller shade before he thumbed a match head and lit the lamp. Tony had brought their saddlebags and Winchesters. He asked, "Where do you want this stuff, Brian?"

"Leave my rifle here with Chance. We'll be bunking down next door."

He stepped over to a side door, tried the key, and said, "Yep. This is an ajoining door betwixt the rooms of this suite. I thought I remembered the layout."

Then he tried the other key and swore softly. Tony nodded and said, "Cheap locks, right?"

Brian sighed and said, "I'll bet one key fits every lock on this damned floor. Hand me my possibles, Tony."

His sidekick gave him his saddlebags. Brian put them on a nearby dresser and opened one. He took out a small toolkit and a barrel bolt. As Chance stepped nearer to see what on earth he was up to, Brian explained, "We spend a lot of time in these cheap hotels. You'll sleep easier with real locks on your doors."

As he began to work silently with awl and screwdriver, Tony moved past him to deposit their belongings on the bed in the next room. Chance asked how they were going to lock the suite from the outside and Brian said, "We don't have to. You'll be here when we get back. We'll give a tap and you can let us in."

"Then why are you installing a lock between our rooms?"

He shot her a thoughtful look before he said, "I figured you'd want one. I got four of these barrel bolts and it only takes a jiffy."

"Brian, I've spent a couple of nights on the trail with you two. Don't you think I trust you by now?"

He smiled and said, "Right," as he stopped drilling the screw hole in the jam. He stepped around her and went over to the outer door to fit the lock as Tony said, "I'll get the other one next door."

As he left them alone for a moment, Chance asked, "Are you always this careful? Those men don't even know we're in town. How could they possibly know where we might be staying?"

He said, "Three minutes of prevention beats a night of worrying. By the time word gets around that somebody's been asking about that red checkered shirt and an anchor tattoo . . ."

"Of course. I just learned another trick of the trade, didn't I?"

He smiled grimly and said, "*One*. You still got a lot to learn, girl."

She watched his hands as he skillfully and quickly installed the lock. She asked, "Have you forgotten you promised to give me two full weeks of schooling, Brian?"

He said, "I didn't promise. I said I'd teach you what I could in such time as I could spare. We might catch up with Dawson tonight. We might take a month. Don't push it, Chance."

She started to protest. Then she asked, "What happens if you and Tony catch him tonight?"

He shrugged and said, "Depends on what he has to say about running out on the folks we work for. If he has the money, which don't seem likely, that'll be that. If he don't want to come quiet, he'll be going back to Missouri in a box. We'll have him embalmed here, of course."

"But you don't intend to kill him if he doesn't resist?"

"Nope. That wouldn't be professional. I know he deserves to die gutshot, Chance, but we ain't in this business for pleasure and we don't break the law."

"The man's a murderer! Can't you turn him over to the local sheriff at least?"

"Not hardly. I aim to report what we found out on the prairie to the law as soon as we leave the hotel. If they catch the rascals afore we do, we'll be good sports about it. If we catch Dawson first, he's *ours*!"

He finished driving the last screw, threw the bolt, and turned to face her. He saw the bewildered hurt in her eyes and said, "Look at it this way, honey. He's got a better than fifty-fifty chance of beating any charges you can press on him here in Ford County. He's been convicted in absentia back in Missouri."

"But you don't know if it's a hanging offense."

"Sure I do. It ain't. He'd have never been held on

five hundred dollar bail if the charge was serious. But he'll go to jail for a spell for sure, which is more than I can promise you here."

"Damn it, Brian, I told you *I'd* give you a reward for gunning the monsters for me here and now! Don't you think I'm good for the money?"

He started for the other room as he said, "I don't doubt you'd pay us. But you don't listen good. We're bounty hunters, not hired killers. How long do you reckon I'd have my license if I started killing folks for friends on the side?"

She followed and they found Tony putting the finishing touches on the other barrel bolt. He said, "Ain't nobody coming in without an invite now."

Chance ignored him to ask Brian, "License? I didn't know you had a *license!*"

Brian had picked up his saddlebags on the way and was putting his tools away as he nodded and said, "You have to have a license as a bonded private detective if you don't want to get arrested by ever' small town lawman you trip over. Did you think you could just run about smoking folks up without papers to show the coroner's jury?"

He took his wallet out and opened it to take out a card, saying, "This is issued by Clay County, Missouri. I got one from the State of Illinois and another from Colorado. Texas is sort of muleheaded about free-lance lawmen, but the Rangers don't arrest you if you can show 'em you was working for a bonded agency."

She nodded and asked, "How do you get one of those things?"

Tony said, "You don't. You're a gal. We got us a lawyer to set us up an incorporated detective agency. We had to post a bond and such and satisfy the state attorney general that we know what we're doing and know our law. I hear tell the Pinkertons has some lady agents. But they'd never license a gal on her own."

Brian said, "We'll talk about it later. After we have us a look-see for the rascals. You lock up after us and don't let nobody in while we're gone, Chance."

"I want to go with you! You don't know any of them on sight save for Dawson!"

But he shook his head and said, "Dawson's the one we're after. We'll talk about the others after we have him, one way or the other."

And then he opened the door and stepped out into the dark corridor. Tony patted her on the arm and said, "Don't try to follow us, honey. I know how you feel, but Brian's sort of set in his ways."

She stamped her foot in helpless anger as the burly Despres followed his partner out, shutting the door after them.

She went in the other room and sat on the bed. But she was too nervous to sit still. She got up and paced for a a few minutes. Then she blew out the light and went to the window. She raised the shade and peered out. It was dark now. But the street was illuminated by lamplight and getting more crowded. She stood there, watching men and an occasional woman passing below her. Somewhere a piano was playing the "Gerry Owen," and a bell rang off in the distance. She counted and snapped, "Damn! It's only eight o'clock!"

She turned to see the Winchester gleaming in the wan light atop her shabby bedspread. She hesitated. Then she picked it up.

She unlocked her door, had second thoughts, and went to get the other rifle and their saddlebags before she left the rooms. She carried them downstairs and told the clerk, "I'm going out for a while. Would you mind these things for my, uh, sidekicks?"

The clerk took the spare rifle and saddlebags with a knowing grin and said, "Sure, son. You headed down to Big Nose Kate's or Madame Moustache?"

Chance made her voice growly as she answered, "Mebbe both," and the clerk chuckled as she turned to swagger out, her borrowed Winchester cradled on her left elbow.

She tried to clomp her heels on the boardwalk outside as she walked tall, pretending she was a soldier on parade. The trick of walking like a man, she decided, was to keep your spine stiff at the waist and take bigger steps. In truth she was walking with the self-conscious dignity of a young drunken hand. The men she passed on the streets of Dodge spotted the walk about the same time as they spotted the Winchester. So they tended to pass around her quietly.

She was almost to the Western Union office when a short, elfin figure moved partly out of her way, froze in its tracks, and said, "Top of the evening to you, Chance McGraw! I see you made it to the grand city in one piece. But you're drunk or I'm blind!"

"Hughie O'Rourke!" she gasped with delight, and would have hugged him had not she realized what it would look like with both of them in pants.

The tinker said, "Herself is with our cart down by the stockyards. I offered silver to the lad in charge, but he's a Mayo man and said we was welcome to camp under a water tower by a foin pile of railroad coal. Come away with me now and we'll share some of Annie's tea while you tell me all that's happened since last we met."

She said, "I haven't time to join you at the cart

right now. I have to send some wires back to Leavenworth if the Western Union is still open."

"It is, for I just passed it. But who would you be after sending a telegram to? Have you forgotten them men left you for dead?"

She frowned and said, "That's right. If I wire Dad's lawyer it will be in the papers that he was murdered and that I'm still alive!"

He led her over to the edge of the walk and they sat down in front of a closed and shuttered shop as she brought him up to date. He laughed when she said she needed money to obtain her own private law license. But when she insisted she meant it, he said, "Well, you'll need meself as well as a lawyer then. What you say about gunfight lessons from them two rascals is all right, but you need advice from a boyo who's used to dodging artful."

She started to protest she was hunting, not dodging, and Hughie cut in with, "Jasus, don't you see it's all the same craft, gorl?"

He stabbed her knee with a finger for emphasis as he explained, "Back in the auld country I used to laugh meself sick as the grand gentry hunted the fox. All jumped up in red coats they wuz, blowin' horns and crashing into fences like they wuz drunk while the fox played tag with 'em."

"I know about riding to hounds, Hughie."

"Ay, and so does every fox. I told you me father was a poacher, and I've never been one to sleep on an empty belly when the hedges wuz there to provide meat in me pot and to hell with your English laws."

"You've told me all this before, Hughie."

"If I did, you didn't listen. A good hunter hides as well as the hare. When I set a snare along the hedge, I don't post a sign pointing to it. I don't leave anything the gamekeeper might notice neither. Sure, it's fairy snares me people have the skills for, and we don't run about in great circles, calling out, 'I say, Fox, where are you?' "

Chance laughed, but said, "I thought you were talking about rabbit."

He shrugged and said, "Rabbit, fox, a vicious farm dog who could use a lesson, I've hunted them all, and *caught* them, too! It's vicious dogs I'm good at, for they haven't the cunning of a rabbit or hedgehog as they go snapping through life at dacent people's heels."

Chance nodded and said, "You're right. It's best they think they left no living witness to Dad's murder. I'll just wire my bank as if nothing happened. I'll say I need money to buy a horse and . . ."

"Whist, wait and make sure you're not putting your foot in a cow pat, gorl! You say them killers knew your father. Don't that mean they know you?"

Chance shook her head and said, "I never saw any of them before and it was an accidental meeting. They killed Dad and attacked me without much conversation. They might not have known I was his daughter. They might have thought I was his young wife."

Hughie nodded and said, "In that case you may be safe in wiring if you don't say anything they'd be after printing in the papers. But how can a gorl like yourself make a bank send her money? Ain't it in your late father's name?"

"It's a joint account. Dad always said it saved time and probate court problems if everyone in the family had access to the funds. I never realized how much he wanted to protect me when first he mentioned it."

"Ay, I can see he *trusted* you, too! I'm sorry I never

met the gint, darling. He sounds like a foin dacent man and a wise one, too. For if he was thinking ahead to this night, he must have sensed his days wuz numbered."

She shuddered and said, "He never spoke much about the war. But I know he was a provost marshal during the early Reconstruction. He must have made a lot of enemies. And these days the old Rebs have the right to bear arms again."

She added something about sending a night letter and got to her feet as Hughie tagged along. As they walked the rest of the way to the telegraph office, he pondered and suggested, "This provost thing is like a military policeman, ain't it?"

"Sort of. Why?"

"Your father recognized at least one of thim as an enemy, but it was over for him before there was a long discussion of the booger's past misdeeds. Have you thought that the man might not have *been* a Rebel?"

"That's absurd! Brian says Black Jack Dawson rode with Rebel raiders."

"Ay, but Dawson might not have been the one he knew as an enemy. The gang is made up of outlaws, not auld soldiers! You say they wiped out another family. They can't know *everyone* they've been after attacking. It's *mad dogs* we're tracking. The one who knew your father may well have been a Union deserter or, indade, a common criminal who rode with neither side!"

She paused and said, "You're hired, Hughie. I don't think even Brian thought of that. I can see my quest needs tinker cunning as much as it needs gun lore!"

He laughed and said, "Ay, them big Yanks may

know how to win a fight a lad like me would stay out of. But the ins and outs of the highways and byways is important, too, and I've been dwelling in the shadows since before thim bandits was born to disturb the peace of this world."

Chance led the way into the Western Union and found a pad of telegram blanks and a stub pencil on the battered counter. Hughie made small talk with the bored-looking clerk as Chance wrote a night letter, keeping her face shaded by the brim of her man's hat. When she'd finished, she made her voice gruff as she said, "I'd like to send this collect, please."

The clerk glanced at the message and nodded. He said, "I don't have money like that in my safe, but I send a lot of these for you young hands. What did you do, run up the national debt at Madam Moustache's?"

"I'm buying some stock. How much can you handle by wire?"

"A hundred bucks is my table stakes unless I know you better. Let me reword it for you and your bank back home can send you a draft on the bank across the street. I told you I do this all the time."

Chance thanked him, and the clerk scratched out a few words and wrote some in. Then he said, "That'll do her. But you can't send a night letter collect. No offense, but Western Union has no way of knowing your bank will accept the charges until nine in the morning."

Chance looked stricken and O'Rourke asked, "How much is it as a straight wire?"

"Five cents a word. It's kind of a long message and . . ."

"Och, say no more about it. I thought we wuz talking about a great sum."

He put a ten-dollar gold piece on the counter as Chance said, "I can't take your money, Hughie."

The tinker said, "Sure, *you* ain't taking it. *He* is. Send the wire, me bucko."

The clerk glanced at Chance and, seeing no further objection, took the coin and handed the tinker back his change as O'Rourke took Chance by the arm and steered her outside. As soon as they were alone on the walk, he said, "Jasus, you're not a good actress and that's a fact. A lad could be named Chance, but if he didn't see you're a woman he's bloind!"

She shrugged and said, "What difference does it make as long as he sends the wire?"

O'Rourke rolled his eyes heavenward and sighed, "Jasus, Mary, and Joseph! What difference does it make, she says! How many wimmen do you think there might be roving about in pants?"

"If one of the gang's in town and hears some gossip, they still have no way of connecting it to the girl they left for dead."

"Mayhaps, but why have them thinking at all at all? Hunted men are best left not to worry, gorl. It's at every shadow a hunted man is peering with unhealthy interest, and we've got to get you off this street. Sure, it's attention you're attracting with that rifle and pants too short for you. Let's go down to the cart now."

But Chance said, "In the morning. Now that I've had a chance to talk to someone and send for money, I'm thinking more clearly. I can see I've been a little foolish, but cooped up so helpless in those rooms at the hotel . . ."

"Ay, you'll sleep better now, knowing you have money on the way and friends in town. Ain't it odd how we make mad plans when we're broke that seem so pointless after we've the sound of silver in our pockets? You'd better take the change that lad gave me, too."

"I don't know, Hughie. What if something happens and I can't pay you back in the morning?"

"Och, I'll have to steal some more somewhere. Stop acting like a blushing maid and take the silver, gorl! I want you to have the feel of it in your fingers this night, for the price of a few pints is better than a rosary for the calming of your nerves."

Chance laughed and took the money. As she put it in her pants pocket, she said, "You're right. I don't want a pint of ale, but it's nice to know it's my choice and not . . . well, *helplessness.*"

The tinker walked her back to the hotel. He left her there after getting her promise to visit him and Annie at their camp as soon as she heard from her bank in the morning.

She went inside and asked the clerk for her key and the things she'd left with him for safekeeping. Feeling expansive, she left a dime tip on the counter. The clerk grinned as he handed over the rifle and saddlebags. He said, "You look satisfied with yourself, sonny. I can see you didn't go down to Madame Moustache's for a card game. Was she any good?"

Chance said, "Tolerable," and walked rather grandly up the stairs as the clerk made a lewd remark about young men and jackrabbits.

Chance was red-faced but grinning as she went inside and locked the doors. Raised by loving parents in a Victorian home, she was unfamiliar with the banter of men when they assumed no ladies were present. It was most educational, but she knew she'd feel better in the morning once she was properly dressed again.

The strain of posing as a youth was wearing. She knew she'd never be able to pass as a man in broad daylight. How on earth was she to explain her appearance to the bankers when she went to get her money?

Chance put the gear aside and turned up the lamp. She removed the hat and let her hair fall around her shoulders as she regarded herself in the cracked mirror over the dresser in her room. Holding herself erect so her breasts showed under the shabby shirt, she smiled at her image and explained, "I've been helping my father drive stock, and you know you can't do that sidesaddle."

Her black eye was fading and the other swelling had gone down. She was tall for a woman but quite attractive, even wearing such an outlandish costume. Her blue eyes looked turquoise in the lamplight, and her normally ivory complexion had tanned in the prairie sun. She looked like a wild tomboy, she decided. But at least she wasn't an *ugly* tomboy. Had Brian noticed she was pretty? It was hard to tell what Brian was thinking.

Chance undressed before the mirror, feeling a bit improper but enjoying the sensual pleasure of the air on her nude flesh. She needed a bath and they'd said there was a bathroom just down the hall. She hesitated. Then decided to forego the pleasure. She didn't feel like coping with the complication of the locks, and should she need to relieve herself, there was a chamber pot under the bed.

Putting her man's attire on a chair, Chance pulled down the covers and got into bed. The linens were rough and patched, but clean on her naked skin. The night was cool, and it felt good to pull the covers up in a real bed for a change. She knew she wouldn't sleep. She had too much on her mind, weary as she was. She wondered when Brian and Tony would get back and what they'd have to tell her when they did. She suddenly remembered she'd have to let them in and murmured, "Damn."

She threw the covers off and swung her bare feet to the worn carpet. She pulled the chair over to the bed and blew out the lamp before she got back under the covers. The room was dark, but she could see the yawning doorway to the next room and wondered why it looked so spooky. She started to get up to close it. But she was more tired than she'd thought and told herself not to be a ninny. She stared at the dark ceiling and decided to just rest her bones until they got back. It didn't matter if she fell asleep or not.

And so, not trying to fall asleep, she was asleep within minutes. And then the jeering faces closed in around her in the flickering light of Dad's burning wagon and grubby hands were tearing her clothes away as she sobbed and begged for pity. But there was no pity in their coarse laughter, and while two of them held her wrists to the dust, she felt her knees being forced apart and she cried out, "No, not that! Dear God, not that!"

And then as the one with the tobacco-stained beard was mounting her, another started pounding on the door and Chance awoke with a strangled scream.

As she shook her head to clear it and realized she was in a man's arms, Chance screamed again. Brian Pio shook her gently and soothed, "It's all right, Chance. It's me. You were having a nightmare."

Chance shuddered but stopped struggling as he held her in the dark and reality returned. To her relief the linen sheet was above her naked breasts and between her and Brian's hickory shirt. She whispered,

"I'm not wearing anything, Brian," and he said, "I noticed. I throwed the sheet over you before I woke you up. You were having a hell of a fight with the covers when I let myself in." He chuckled and added, "You were winning, too."

She grimaced in the dark and said, "I was back there at the wagon. How did you *get* in? Where's Tony?"

Brian released his firm grip on her shoulders, but she remained in place, aware that her nudity was less obvious when she reclined on one elbow against him. He said, "Them locks were meant to keep out the uneducated. I figured you'd be sleeping and didn't mean to waken you, until I heard you yelling for help. Old Tony's staked out down on Tin Pot Alley behind the opera house. I have to go back and relieve him in a while."

Chance gasped and asked, "Have you found out where those men are hiding?" and Brian answered, "One of 'em maybe. A lady of joy that Tony got to talking with says a man answering to Jack Dawson's description rented a friend of hers for the night. He's up in her room at the moment. The light's out and it promises to be a long, uninteresting wait."

Chance frowned and asked, "Why do you have to wait outside for Dawson? I thought once you knew where he was . . ."

"You ain't thinking, honey. I keep telling you there's *rules* to the game. We don't know for certain it's Dawson, and even if it is, we have to consider the lady's feelings. The local law could take a mighty dim view of our activities if a gal who's bought and paid for protection got caught in the cross fire of a dark bed chamber. Folks get shot a lot in dark rooms. It's safer for all of us if we just wait out back, polite.

Whoever it was who went in, he'll be coming out in the cold gray."

"And then you'll kill him, right?"

"Wrong. We aim to take him alive if it's possible. There's a fifty-fifty chance it ain't Dawson we have staked out. In that case he'll never know how interested we were in his love life."

Chance said, "Let me up. I want to go down there and wait with you."

But Brian shook his head and said, "Simmer down. You ain't going nowhere. Taking a man in an alley can get complicated enough without outsiders in the way."

Chance stiffened in his arms and her voice was bitter as she said, "Oh? I didn't know I was an outsider, Brian!"

He said, "Don't cloud up and rain on me, honey. I know you have personal reasons for seeing Jack Dawson full of lead."

"You've just been humoring me! All those lessons with the gun were a joke to you and Tony!"

He shook his head again and said, "Not really. You've gotten pretty good with a gun in the last few days, considering."

"Considering I'm just a silly female?"

"Nope. Considering me and Tony are better and don't need help. We haven't even told the town law about that stakeout in Tin Pot Alley. Taking a man alive is sort of delicate, even for a pro."

Chance pushed at him and said, "Let me go. I'm getting up, and I don't have any clothes on."

Brian chuckled and said, "I don't reckon I will. What we've got here is a Mexican standoff. If I don't step into the next room, you *can't* get up, and since I don't want you to get up . . ."

"That's not fair!" she cut in, smiling despite herself. Brian was using no force to hold her, and as she pushed him again, he leaned back, still sitting on the bed with her. But it was still an impasse and she knew he knew it. She said, "Damn it. I've a good mind to shock you."

He shrugged and said, "I don't shock easy. But maybe I'd better sit on your duds."

He shifted his weight, and Chance knew he meant to impound the clothing she'd draped over the chair. She sat bolt upright and grabbed his sleeves. The sheet fell around her waist, but it was quite dark and she knew if she let go, he'd have her trapped in bed. Smiling despite her annoyance, she said, "This is getting silly, Brian."

He nodded and said, "You're right. I've never seen such a willful little gal."

"Pooh, I'm taller than a lot of men I know. I'll bet I'm a better fighter, too!"

"Maybe, but somehow I ain't scared. You're not going down to Tin Pot Alley, wearing duds or no. One way or the other you're going to stay right here until we find out who that man we've staked out might be."

"What are you going to do?" she asked defiantly. "Tie me hand and foot?"

Brian grinned and said, "I might have to handcuff you to the bed post at that."

"You wouldn't dare!"

He hesitated before he answered, "I dare all sorts of things, but I'll admit it ain't polite to chain a lady to her bed. Why don't you sort of cover yourself up and promise to behave? Behaving is a chore for both of us to study on right now."

Chance took a deep breath, as if she were a child

about to dive naked into a cold, unfamiliar swimming hole; then she swung her legs from under the sheet and announced, abruptly, "I'm getting up. If you were any kind of a gentleman you wouldn't be watching while a lady dresses."

But she suddenly found herself flat on her back as Brian sighed and said, "Hell, who said I was a gent? I can see there's no other way to make you behave, so . . ." And then as she struggled to rise, he held her down with one hand while he reached for the handcuffs on his belt with the other!

"You brute!" she protested, frightened as well as excited by Brian's surprising strength as she struggled in vain to rise. Chance was much stronger than most women and she knew it. Yet she felt helpless as a kitten as the big bounty hunter gently but firmly disciplined her. The sheet was wadded and cast aside between them as they wrestled on the mattress, but Chance was hardly aware of her nudity until she felt her right wrist gripped in the steel vice of Brian's big fist. He raised it above her head, holding her down with his chest. The cloth was rough against her heaving breasts and her heart pounded like a trip-hammer as she whimpered, "No!" And then the cold handcuff snapped around her wrist and she realized with mingled panic and resignation that he'd made good his threat. She was chained to the brass bedstead!

The struggle had excited Brian, too. He started to ease his weight off her. Then as their eyes met in the dim light, he suddenly lowered his face to hers. Their lips met in mingled, shocked desire, and she felt herself responding. Then he sat bolt upright and muttered, "Jesus, I'm sorry, Chance. I don't know why I did such a fool thing!"

She sighed and said, "I liked it better than being handcuffed."

Brian didn't answer for a moment. Then he reached in his pocket, took out a key ring, and unlocked her wrist. For a long, wordless moment they just looked at one another. Then he said, "Your hands are free. From here on you're on your own."

Then he took her in his arms and kissed her again, and as she wrapped her arms around his rough-clad shoulders, she knew it was going to be all right. Until this moment she'd thought those men who'd murdered Dad had killed all desire forever for her. But in Brian's rough albeit tender embrace no other man existed. He lowered her to the bed and started petting her with his free hand until, as his palm cupped over her mons, he sighed and said, "I'm going to have to stop right now if I ever aim to."

She murmured, "It's all right, darling. I don't want you to stop."

"Are you sure, Chance? I never meant to start up with you like this. Leastwise not so *soon*."

"You big goof," she sighed, "those buttons are scratching me. And if you mean to wear your *spurs* in bed, I just might change my mind!"

Someone was pounding on the door again and Chance wondered why Brian didn't answer. She smiled sleepily and reached across the bed. Then as she felt the empty pillow at her side, she was wide awake. She heard the tapping again as she got her bearings in the dim light. The sun was shining outside, but Brian had pulled the shades and . . . where *was* Brian?

Chance swung her bare feet to the carpet and slipped into her shirt and male pants as she called out, "I'm coming. Who is it?"

Tony's familiar voice replied, "It's me, and keep it down to a roar," through the panel of the locked door. She went over and let Tony in, saying, "I thought for a minute you were Brian. He must have gone out while I was . . . never mind."

Tony came inside and locked the door after him before he said, "I sort of wish I was Brian, but never mind is a good notion. He joined me just as things got interesting down in Tin Pot Alley. I've never met a gent who times things as neat as old Brian. I don't reckon we had ten minutes to wait."

"What happened? Where *is* Brian?"

Tony said, "On his way to Missouri. He said I was to sell the ponies and settle up here in Dodge afore I followed. Jack Dawson come gentle as a lamb after Brian pistol-whipped him some to teach him the error of his ways."

"You *caught* one of them!"

"That's what I just said. Brian cuffed him and the last time I seen 'em they was boarding the flyer east. Like I said, he left me to tidy up and follow after."

Chance sank defeated on the bed as Tony lit the lamp. He saw the tears rolling down her cheeks, and his bearish face softened as he swung a leg over the chair and sat astride it, facing her. He nodded and said, "I wanted to kill him, too. But Brian is a stickler for the durned old law. He did chip the rascal's teeth a mite, and I ain't sure he'll ever see out of one eye again, but once he'd told us all he knowed, Brian said it wouldn't be professional to deliver him dead."

Chance sobbed, "That's not fair! He's the one who killed my father! Brian promised to teach me and help me get the others, and now he's run out on me and Jack Dawson will never pay for his crime!"

Tony said, "You don't listen, girl. Just simmer down and stop raining on me whilst I tell you the whole tale. After catching Dawson, we went to the local law, like we said we aimed to."

Tony took a wad of papers from his vest pocket and started to unfold them as he said, "In the first place there's this wire from Missouri. Dawson kilt a man and stole his hoss right after he jumped bail on the lesser charge of cattle theft. So after Brian delivers him to the bonding company, he'll be charged with murder. It ain't the murder of your dad, but what the hell, they can only hang you once."

"What about the others? Brian was going to teach me how to be a bounty hunter and . . ."

"Honey, he was just funning you and you know it. We carried you along to keep you out of trouble and in case we needed a witness to a crime on Kansas soil. Sometimes these county sheriffs can get muley about us taking a man outten their jurisdiction. But the law here in Ford County is neighborly. They have enough homegrowed outlaws here in Dodge to keep 'em busy. So Brian's on his way home with the man we come after and that's that."

"You don't *care* about my father and those other people!"

"That ain't fair, honey. We told the sheriff about the settlers we found dead out on the prairie, and he said he'd do something about it. We gave him as good a description as we could, and after we caught Dawson, we whupped some names outten him. After Brian boarded the train with our prisoner, I moseyed back to the sheriff with the names he gave us, and we've just been going over the wanted fliers half the morning. I *told* Brian he might be acting hasty, but you know how he is. Anyway, we're in luck. All but two of the rascals is wanted on ever' charge but smallpox. You was right about 'em being Rebel raiders for the most part. One's wanted for treason and desertion from the Union Army during the war. The sheriff says the county DA has enough to swear out material witness warrants on them. Their names is Slade and Dodd. The leader of the gang rode with Quantrill's guerrillas in the war. That one's Slade," Tony added, "and he has a gold tooth, like you said. Another one's called Sailor Flynn."

Chance gasped, "That must be the man with the anchor on his forearm!" But Tony shook his head and said, "Nope. The tattooed wonder is Stubby Hawkins. He's a deserter. Brian hit Dawson a couple of extra licks to make sure on that point. The other two are Nails Kinkaid and Lefty Shaw. Both unreconstructed Rebels, wanted for murder and worse."

Chance grimaced as he handed her the wanted fliers. She spread them out on the bed at her side and said, "So now I have names to go with my nightmares. But Brian's deserted me and . . ."

Tony swore under his breath and said, "I just sent a night letter to old Brian telling him about these other rewards. He might decide to come back. He might not figure it's worth our time. With Dawson took and the county looking for the others, they'll likely split up and head out in ever' direction. I'll wait for Brian to write back afore I make any further plans."

He chuckled and added, "The telegraph clerk said he saw Calamity Jane Canary last night. Ain't that a bitch?"

"Calamity who?"

"Jane Canary. Crazy old gal who traipses about in men's duds. He said she sent a wire, using another name, but he knowed it was her. He said there ain't another gal as crazy as Calamity Jane out here. She was with some little runt she'd picked up. But he said he was just paid to send the wires, not to ask fool questions."

Chance began to laugh, a bit hysterically, and Tony frowned and said, "Hell, it ain't all *that* funny! I feel sort of sorry for old Calamity. They say she used to be a pretty gal afore she got dosed up and went crazy. She used to work for Madame Moustache here in Dodge. Then her luck ran out and it got to be a calamity to trifle with her and she's taken to drinkin' and cussin' like a cowboy."

Chance said, "That was *me* he was talking about, Tony! I went down to the telegraph office to wire for money and I met Hughie O'Rourke along the way."

Despres stared soberly at her from under his bushy brows as he said, "You was told to stay here, girl."

"Pooh, I don't have to do anything you two tell me, damn it! You've been false with me since first we met!"

He shrugged and said, "Brian was funning you. I didn't like it much. I told him it wasn't fair to get your hopes up with them fool lessons. But he said you didn't have no knitting and it wouldn't hurt to let you try."

"What about *you* teaching me some more, Tony? You won't hear from Brian for a day or so, will you?"

Tony said, "It's no use, honey. The men you keep

talking about are too good for most *men*, and you're just a *gal*."

"I'll pay you, Tony. I know you're not as good as Brian but . . ."

And then a gun muzzle was staring her in the eye, cocked and loaded, as Tony said morosely, "I ain't as pretty, but if anything, I'm *better*."

She gasped as he lowered the hammer and put the gun away. Then she grinned and asked, "How on earth did you *do* that!"

He said, "I practiced. I mean, I practiced a long time. Longer than I've got time to spend giving lessons."

Then he saw the hurt in her eyes and said, "Hell, I'll play with you until I get word from Brian. But it's only something to fill the waiting. You wouldn't be able to larn in a year, even if you was a boy."

Chance insisted, "I'll buy a gun and you can show me how you draw so fast. Do you have any other tricks, Tony?"

His hand moved in another blur and something thudded gently into her middle, just under her breasts. Tony said, "You're dead again."

Chance glanced down to see an eight-inch bowie in the bearish Tony's hand. Butt-first against her ribs and the blade facing safely away. She laughed incredulously and said, "I didn't know you had that knife *on* you!"

He made it vanish as he grinned back and said, "You ain't *supposed* to see the knife as *gets* you. I've never been cut by a blade I saw ahead of time."

"Heavens, have you been stabbed often, Tony?"

"Nope. Just once, when I was young and foolish. The man who cut me never announced his intentions neither. When I *see* a blade, I just laugh and tell 'em to put it away afore someone gits hurt. You ever been hit good with a drover's whip?"

"Good heavens, no!"

"I'll show you about them, too, come morning and we can find some place to practice quiet. Whips is a lot like knives. Men who mean to kill with either don't wave 'em about waiting for you to draw on 'em."

He got up from his chair and said, "Stand up, Chance."

She rose wordlessly and he said, "Look at my feet and tell me what you see."

She glanced down with a frown. Tony was standing at apparent ease and she saw nothing remarkable about the position of his feet. He said, "You see a man with his feet planted like this and you know he's about to draw." He moved one foot and added, "This is the way most folks stand when they're just talking to hear themselves. Nobody draws when they're standing like this. Now watch."

He moved his right foot and again the gun appeared as if by magic in his hand. Chance nodded and said, "I see how you balanced against the sudden movement of your arm now."

He shrugged and said, "Side-draw man stands like *this.* Make a mistake reading a *southpaw's* stance and you're *dead*! The one called Shaw is a southpaw. You see how silly you're being, girl?"

She shook her head and said, "I'm going to get a gun, and then you're going to teach me some more. Will you help me select my rig, Tony?"

He sighed and said, "Damn, you sure are stubborn for such a pretty little thing."

There was an awkward pause before he sighed

again and said, "You likely knowed I thought you was pretty, didn't you."

Chance licked her lips, not knowing how to answer. She *needed* Tony and she liked him, but could she keep him at her side that way? It wouldn't be as bad as being raped, and Brian had used her that way, but . . .

He nodded and said, "Yeah, I know I'm sort of an ugly cuss. I know no gal as pretty as you would see fit to marry up with me, but . . ."

Chance felt a wave of relief as she gasped and said, "Oh, you mustn't say things like that, Tony."

His jaw dropped as he stared at her in the lamplight and demanded, "You mean, if you wasn't stuck on Brian, I'd have a *chance*?"

Her fond smile was genuine, despite the gentle lie, as she put a hand on his sleeve and kissed him on the cheek, saying, "I think we've said enough for now, Tony. It's too early for me to even think of such things, but you're very sweet, and I'm very honored."

He grinned from ear to ear and muttered, "Hot damn. I just growed eighteen inches!"

He almost swaggered as he stepped into the next room and closed the door after him. Chance stared at the closed door, wondering why she felt so shabby. She hadn't really led him on, and it was the least she could do for his friendship. She knew that if there'd been no other way, she might have gone farther. Or would she have?

"It's not fair," she sighed as she blew out the lamp and began to undress again. In a man's world even well-brought-up young women knew how to get their way with fluttering lash and timid smile. But wasn't there some way to compete with men on equal terms?

There had to be. For she meant to avenge her father's death and she meant to do it right. Flirting with some man to make him fight for her was almost as degrading as selling her body outright. If anything it was more dishonest. As she finished dressing, she murmured, "That's not the way, Chance McGraw. Dad has to be avenged as he would have been by a son. The son he never had. Not by a daughter who'd shame his memory as a whore!"

The money came at noon. Before that, of course, Chance had bathed and breakfasted with the tinkers. Tony came along as an ursine escort, and if the few townees they passed thought she looked funny, one look at the husky Despres discouraged verbal comment.

The timid-looking banker treated her with respect, too. Chance was bigger than he was, and a lady who can sign for a thousand at a time is worthy of respect in pants or not.

She put most in a local checking account and found a notions store near the bank. The two old maids who ran the shop seemed nervous, too. It was hard to tell if they approved her new clothes or simply wanted to humor her. But when she'd changed to a feminine but sensible riding outfit of tan whipcord with a veiled black derby, Tony shook his head and said, "You look pretty enough to eat, honey. But you'll have to ride sidesaddle just the same in them skirts."

Chance grinned back and said, "I can afford a proper saddle now. I'm going to need your advice about my gun rig, though."

The old woman making out her change looked startled but didn't say anything. Tony frowned and asked, "Do you aim to strap a gun on over that skirt and bodice, Chance?"

She said, "Certainly. Wouldn't I look silly trying to draw if it was *under* the skirt?"

He grinned and said, "It'd sure be worth paying a quarter to *watch*! There's a gunsmith I know down by the livery. I'll carry that stuff you're fixing to give back to the gypsies."

As they were leaving, one of the fluttery old women gasped, "Excuse me. I know it's none of my business, but . . ."

"This here's Calamity Jane and I'm Wild Bill Hickok," said Tony with a lewd wink as he added, "I'm making an honest woman of her."

They were both laughing as they got outside. Tony said, "Wait'll Ned Buntline hears *that* one for his magazine."

"You're awful. Is it true Wild Bill is Calamity Jane's lover?"

"Not hardly. He's a happily married man, and I told you why they called her 'calamity.' Gunsmith's yonder under that swinging sign."

As they approached, she asked, "Why do I need a smith? I meant to buy a *new* gun, Tony."

"Hell, you don't get a good gun outten the factory box. Old Pop and me has had dealings afore. He'll give you a gun with balance, seeing you're with me."

He led her into the oil-scented gloom where an apparent gnome in a green eyeshade glanced up from his combined counter and workbench to ask, "What have you done with it now, Despres? You been using the gun I fixed for you to pound nails again?"

Tony said, "It ain't good enough, Pop. This here's Miss Chance McGraw and she needs her a man-sized gun she can handle with them dainty little hands of her'n."

Chance braced herself for a snide remark about women, but Pop said, "Hold out your hand, Ma'am."

Chance did so, and the gunsmith took her fingers and turned them over as if reading her palm. Tony said, "He don't cotton to small talk. But he does know which end the bullets come out."

Pop snorted in annoyance and pressed a sheet of carbon paper to the girl's palm, rubbing it with his thumb as he muttered, "You got good wrists for a gal. I got a Harrington Richardson .32 you could likely handle well enough."

Tony said, "Hell, she ain't hunting *prairie dogs*, Pop! She needs a .44! If you give us a good buy on a Winchester, the same rounds will fit both guns."

The gunsmith shrugged and let go of her hand as he reached under the bench by feel and placed a Colt Peacemaker on top. He didn't ask her if she liked it. He picked up a screwdriver and started to remove the factory grips as he asked, "Cross-draw or side-draw?"

Chance looked at Tony, who thought a moment before he answered, "I reckon she ought to wear it low on her right hip and draw natural. She rides sidesaddle when she ain't afoot. I'll be damned if I know *how* you draw, mounted sidesaddle!"

The gunsmith nodded and said, "It ain't possible. When she's mounted, she'll move the gun around to her lap and hope for the best."

He turned and opened a cigar box filled with blank wooden grips. He fumbled out a pair and wrapped the carbon paper around them. Chance saw it left a barely visible set of smudges on the raw wood. Tony said, "We'll go next door and have us some pie and coffee while you whittle them grips, Pop."

But the little gunsmith said, "No you won't. I can't fix these durned grips to a hand I can't *see*!" He pointed with his chin at a nearby barrel and said, "You can set there 'til I need you, Ma'am. Only take a minute or so to rough her out for the final fitting."

Chance nodded and sat on the edge of the barrel as the old man picked up a rasp and began to file madly at the unfinished walnut. Tony picked up the unstocked gun and hefted it, saying, "It's a might barrel-heavy, ain't it?"

Pop said, "Don't try to teach your granny to suck eggs, boy. You know I put lead ballast in a serious gun."

Chance wondered how he knew what she wanted the gun for, since he hadn't asked. Then she realized she was in the company of a professional and that they'd asked for a bigger gun than most women might want. Pop was a professional, too.

He stopped what he was doing and turned again to take a folded gunbelt and holster down from a shelf behind him. He handed it across to her and said, "Put this on while I fit the grips for a bit of study."

Chance wrapped the gunbelt around and once again she was surprised by the old man's keen eye. From a dozen belts up there he'd selected one that fit almost perfectly around her hips. The holster lay flat just below her right hipbone, its hard, waxed leather snuggled to her thigh as if it wanted to stay there.

Pop handed her the assembled empty pistol and said, "Let's see how good you are."

Chance holstered the gun, then drew, pointing it at

the counter between them. Pop asked, are you pointing it like that because you're polite or because it cants to the left?"

Chance nodded, reholstered, and drew again to throw down on the old man. Tony sighed and said, "Jesus, that's too *slow*."

Pop said, "Hand her back a minute, Ma'am. I need to take some off where the heel of your palm's shoving it a mite high and to your right."

She handed it back, saying, "It feels much easier to hold than any other gun I've ever held in my hands, Mister, uh, Pop."

He said, "Names ain't important if you're paying cash. *Better* ain't as good as *perfect*. I like my customers to leave here gunned up proper."

He filed some more wood away, smoothed it with sandpaper, and the next time she drew it, the gun seemed to have a life of its own as it pointed almost in obedience to her thought. She laughed and said, "No wonder Brian made me look so foolish, Tony! I had no idea the fit of the grips could make such a difference!"

Grudgingly the gunsmith said, "You're pointing good. But he's right about you needing practice. The ballast is the real secret. Them dudes in Hartford make a fair gun, but the Colt's a mite heavy at the business end. I've moved the center of gravity aft."

Chance held the gun out and relaxed her grip a bit before she nodded and said, "I see what you mean. It just sort of, well, *floats* in my hand. I'd have thought the extra weight would make it clumsy."

The gunsmith looked slightly pleased with himself as he shook his head and said, "The center of gravity is just a hair ahead of your hand's relaxed strength. When you grip tight, it's locked in line with your arm bones and you just have to point her like a finger. The ballast soaks up some of the recoil, too. You don't look like a sissy, but a .44 do kick. Hand her back and I'll put some finish on the wood."

She did, and as the old man started to rub the raw wood down with a rag he'd taken from a coffee can, she asked, "What is that, varnish?"

Pop looked pained and said, "Hell no it ain't varnish! This here is a *gun*, not a *piano*! It's an insult to any hand tool to varnish her. This here's linseed and wax with a little thinner to help it soak in. It'll season better as you sweat some of your own juices into her. Old wood is like old wine. It improves with age."

Tony asked, "Don't you reckon she needs some crosscut grooves, Pop?" and the gunsmith replied, "If I thought so, I'd have cut some. I put them grooves in *your* grips 'cause you've got horney callus, slippery as soap when you're sweating. This gal's hands have seen some work, but they're softer and . . . Hell, Despres, I *told* you I fit these damn grips to go with the shooter's hands, didn't I?"

He held the gun up to the light and wiped the grips dry before he handed it to Chance, saying, "I got some rounds for it here. The box has been opened, but the bullets is new from the factory. They had some awful sticky stuff on the brass to keep 'em from tarnishing. I cleaned 'em and coated 'em right, with sperm oil."

Tony asked about the saddle gun and Pop said he'd heard them. As he rummaged through his stores for a used Winchester he said he'd adjusted and reworked right, Chance loaded the bullet loops in her new belt. Tony asked her why she didn't load the gun and when she said she wanted to practice it first, he sighed and said, "If you aim to wear it on the *street*, wear it *right*! Don't *never* sport an empty gun where folks can *see* it!"

She saw Pop's approving nod and sheepishly began to load the cylinder as Tony picked up the Winchester and began to thumb bullets into its tube. Pop told her to hold her arm out straight, and when she'd done so, he nodded again and said, "You don't need the rifle stock cut down. Winchester makes 'em a mite short if you ask me."

Chance nodded and asked if he'd take a check. The gunsmith shook his head and said, "Not hardly. It ain't that I'd expect a friend of Tony here to fob a rubber check off on me, you understand. But I've learned to ask for cash. Feller I sold a gun to for a check one time run into John Wesley Hardin before I could cash it."

As Chance fumbled out a roll of bills, Tony joshed, "I thought your guns was good, Pop."

Pop said, "They are. Where did you think John Wesley Hardin went to get *his* grips adjusted?"

They waited all afternoon and evening, but Brian didn't wire Tony. Tony said it sometimes took a day or so. Brian would have paperwork and some bill collecting chores in Missouri, even if the train had been early.

They ate with the tinkers, but not at their camp under the railroad water tower. It felt good to have a little spending money again, and Chance insisted on treating them all to dinner at a restaurant, which, in Dodge, wasn't saying much. The food was all right, but Annie was scandalized at the prices, and Hughie opined he selected chickens with more care when he stole them.

She wasn't ready to talk to the sheriff yet and she felt uneasy going back to the hotel with Tony, even though he hadn't said or done anything disrespectful after their first moments of awkwardness. She got out of it by pointing out she couldn't go back to the Drover's Rest dressed as a woman. When she said she'd spend the night with the tinkers, Tony just looked wistful and said, "I was looking forward to the expression on that sassy clerk's face. But you're likely right."

The tinkers waited until Tony had walked back to their camp and left Chance alone with them before Annie asked, softly, "Did they trifle with you, darling?"

Hughie snorted and replied before Chance could, saying, "Jasus, you daft auld woman, can't you see the lad's in love with her? It's like a princess he'd be after treating her. Ay, and kill the man who trod on the train of her skirt, I'd vow!"

Chance blushed and said, "Heavens, Tony's just a nice man. He didn't come out here looking for a girl! He and Brian are bounty hunters, not courting swains!"

"Ay, I might have known it was the *pretty* one you'd take a shine to. A gorl would be safer hitching her cart to a lad like Tony than to a high-stepping stud like Brian Pio."

"I'm tired of being just a passenger. I'm taking charge of my own affairs from here on, thank you very much. But what about you two? You said you were looking for work here in Dodge."

The tinker lit his clay pipe and sighed, "Och, these Yanks are all the same, east or west. It's a hard land for a tinker, me darling. For these Americans don't repair anything when they can throw it away and buy another. Do you know, there's a great steam locomotive rusting away just down the siding? Tons and tons of steel they left there, just because it's tubes are leaking a bit and the Baldwin company came out with a more powerful model last year!"

Annie said, "They stamp out tin pots on great machines, too. When these foolish wimmen burn the bottom out, they throw the pot away and buy another! Himself says they make *tin cans* thick enough to use as household wares. It's terrible wasteful they are."

Hughie nodded and said, "The few who do mend their things must have tinker blood in them, too. Back home a farmer is a farmer and that's the end of it. This morning I saw a Yankee farmer and his lad fixing their own windmill! In God's truth I don't know what they might need *me* for in this daft country!"

Chance said, "In the morning I'll want you to help me buy a horse. I can pick my own saddle and harness, but your gypsy eye might catch what mine might miss when it comes to horseflesh." She added, "You'll get a commission on the sale, of course."

"Och, I keep telling you it's a tinker I am and not a burton or a rom, but I do know me way around a horse. As for the silver you keep insulting us with, you gave me back what I loaned you the other night. Ay, and fed us dacent, too."

Annie sniffed and said, "It's not charity cases we are, young miss!"

Chance saw she'd hurt their feelings and asked, "Are you too proud to take a *job* with me, Hughie O'Rourke?"

He frowned through his smoke at her and asked, "What kind of a job would you have for us, Chance McGraw? Sure, you don't even have a *house*, let alone a place of business!"

She stood up and said, "I know. And it's time I looked into that."

Annie asked, "Where are you going? It's past ten or more and you told Tony you wuz staying here this night!"

Chance said, "I'll be back. I'm going up to Madame Moustache's."

Hughie gasped, "Jasus, over me dead body! It's a house of ill repute you're talking about, gorl! What would drive you to such desperate straits when you've a thousand dollars in the Wells Fargo Bank just up the street?"

Chance grimaced and said, "I'm not going there for a job. I need advice from another businesswoman."

A colored maid led Chance to a luxurious red-draped room in the back of the combined bordello and card-house after leaving her to stew alone in the foyer for some time. The place was a rabbit's warren of partitions and sliding doors, so while she'd heard the tinkle of a piano and the laughter of men, she'd seen nothing she could report to anyone, if that had been her purpose in coming there so late at night.

Madame Moustache sat behind a rosewood table, dealing solitaire and smoking a cigar. The madam was a strikingly beautiful brunette of about thirty-five. She wore a low-cut velvet gown of fire-engine red and had her jet black hair pinned up. As she took the cigar from her mouth and stared unwinkingly at her visitor, Chance saw she had a faint growth of downy hair on her cheeks and upper lip. Madame Moustache spoke in a surprisingly cultivated voice, but her words were blunt as she nodded and said, "Turn around and raise your skirts. You're not bad-looking, in a mannish way. If you have a nice ass, you have a job. The house shares even-steven on every trick and, of course, you get room and board as well as Sunday off."

Chance stepped over to the table and placed five twenty-dollar gold pieces near the spread-out cards before she said, "I came to buy, not to sell."

Madame Moustache never blinked an eye. She said, "Well, it's not our regular line, but we aim to please. French Mimi might be willing for a change of pace. But I've only run across women like you a couple of times in this business."

Chance laughed and said, "That's not what I'm buying either. Why don't you let me tell you what I came for before you leap to conclusions?"

Madame Moustache indicated a plush chair with a heart-shaped back and said, "Sit down and tell me your tale, honey. I listen good for a hundred dollars."

Chance took a seat and introduced herself before bringing the madam up to date on her misadventures.

Madame Moustache stared at her with no expression until she got to the rapist with the anchor tattooed on his arm. Then she nodded and cut in, "That one bit Saloon Door Sally, up in the cribs. The professor threw him out. I don't know if he's still in town or not."

Chance nodded and went on. When she'd finished, the madam looked wistfully at the untouched gold between them and said, "I understand how you feel, Miss McGraw. But why have you come to *me* instead of the sheriff?"

Chance said, "I assume you *own* the sheriff and other county officials. You couldn't be running wide open like this without certain understandings with the powers that be."

Madame Moustache hesitated before she nodded and said, "Sure, the boys get a cut. But the last I heard, the sheriff was looking for those rascals anyhow. You don't have to pay the law in Dodge to chase murderers, Miss McGraw. We haven't incorporated the township yet, and I'll admit it's a little wild. But Dodge isn't totally uncivilized."

Chance said, "I know. More's the pity. One of my father's killers has been arrested and taken back to Missouri for a hanging. The posse might catch some of the others and they might not. I meant to kill all seven of them if I could. But I'll settle for any I meet up with."

Madame Moustache glanced at the gun on Chance's hip and smiled thinly. Chance nodded and took a deep breath, then she drew as she rose from the chair, pointing the gun at the window.

Madame Moustache nodded and said, "That's pretty good. Put it away and sit down. I can see you'd beat the average Texas drunk in a showdown, but I still don't see what you need *me* for."

Chance holstered the gun and resumed her seat, saying, "Dodge *is* civilized, as you said. I can't just gun a man without a hunting license. I mean to set up my own detective agency before I use the reward posters and warrants I have on the outlaws."

Madame Moustache nodded in sudden understanding and reached behind her to yank a bellpull. The colored maid materialized in the doorway behind Chance, and as Chance realized she'd been covered all this time, Madame Moustache said, "Lawyer Lockwood's out in the game room, Willie. Tell him I want him."

When the maid left, Madame Moustache said, "You're going about it wrong. You're a woman. The courthouse gang would laugh at you if you approached them with such a plan. I have this property in a husband's name. I'd scratch the bastard's eyes out if he came near me, but he's paid to be my legal spouse. It's a man's world, Chance McGraw. You're going to have to start by getting a man to post the bond and act as the nominal head of your fool agency."

Chance started to protest it wasn't fair. Then she nodded and said, "I have an Irish friend who's looking for a job, and I just thought of another advantage. If *I'm* working for *him*, it might save questions at the coroner's hearings, right?"

"Sure. As a female operative of a man's detective agency, you'd have a freer hand. Is he a good talker?"

"Lord, yes. He could charm the horns off a billy goat."

Madame Moustache began to stack the coins as she

said, "Lawyer Lockwood's a drunk, but he has an in with the right people. He'll be able to post a modest sum in escrow with the county. He'll know all about the papers and such, too. But have you considered that the whole bunch you're after may have ridden out by now?"

Chance nodded and said, "My friends have been looking for them since we arrived. They may have scattered. But Dodge is the sort of town I need as a base of action. I'd never be able to afford what it would cost to set up shop in Leavenworth or any big city."

The maid came back with a bleary-eyed man in a snuff-colored suit. Madame Moustache said, "Lockwood, this friend of mine needs proper papers for a business corporation. She'll be in your office at nine in the morning, so *be* there—*sober*. Any questions?"

Lawyer Lockwood stared owlishly down at Chance and said, "Make it ten and it's a deal. There'll be a fifty-dollar consultation fee up front, of course."

Madame Moustache smiled grimly and said, "No there won't. Miss McGraw is budgeted, and I just said she was a friend of mine. Tell the professor I said your tab out front has been canceled and, for God's sake, stop trying to beat my faro dealer. I *told* you he was crooked the *last* time you ran up a tab, damn it!"

Lockwood grinned and said, "Right. We're all friends, here. You don't know if Saloon Door Sally is still sore at me, do you, Madame?"

"We'll discuss your carnal nature later. Judge Bloomer is a regular customer of mine, too. So make sure you go to him and mention my name when you file this young woman's petition with the court."

"I assume she has a male partner to sign the whatsoevers?"

"She does. If they can't make the bond, tell Judge Bloomer I'll stand good for it. She'll tell you just what she needs in your office. You're too drunk right now to discuss business."

"That's for damn sure," sighed Lockwood, bowing to Chance as he said, "Your servant, Ma'am. But let's make it eleven. I'll have my head in one piece by then, Lord willing."

The lawyer left with the maid. Madame Moustache smiled at Chance and said, "He's no damned good, drunk or sober, but they'll treat you right at the county courthouse now."

As Chance started to thank her, the madam held the stacked coins out to her and said, "Here. You're going to have to pay a file clerk here and a deputy there. Never offer a lawman more than twenty dollars. It's more than they're worth."

Chance looked surprised and said, "I thought *you'd* want something for helping me, Ma'am."

The madam shook her head and said, "You told me they raped you. This may come as a surprise to you, but *we're* women, too! I couldn't take a nickel for the little I can do, honey. Buy some bullets with this cash and shoot 'em once for me!"

Wordlessly, eyes moist, Chance rose and accepted the return of her money. The madam was a little dewy-eyed, too, as she got up to walk Chance out, saying, "You'll let me know if you have any trouble with those courthouse bums, won't you?"

"Of course. You're a great lady, Madame . . . Uh, don't you have a name more seemly that I could call you?"

"Hell, Madame Moustache is my name now, and the name I was born with is unimportant. I follow your drift, honey. But you don't have to worry about my feelings. I don't have any. I'm the best whore west of the Mississippi and I'm proud of it."

In the doorway Chance turned and kissed Madame Moustache on the cheek before she said, "You don't fool me, Madame Moustache."

"Oh, get out of here, you fool kid. I wouldn't hire a girl with such a skinny ass anyway!"

The streets of Dodge were crowded despite the hour and the small size of the town. Chance was aware there were no women on the street as she walked back toward the railroad yards. As she passed two cowhands in a doorway, one of them belched and said, "Well, well, what have we here?" and his drunken companion laughed and said, "Take it easy, Red. Cain't you see she's packing a gun?"

Chance ignored them as she passed, a flush to her cheeks. Even in a riding habit she knew she presented an odd appearance with the holstered .44 riding her hip. There was supposed to be a gun ordinance in Dodge. She'd seen several posters warning of the dire fate awaiting any man found packing a sidearm into town from the loading pens. But the regulation seemed to be ignored by most of the men she passed in the tricky light coming from the windows and saloon doors on either side of the main drag.

She was almost to the end of the street when a short, burly figure stumbled out of a swinging door in front of her. Chance paused to let him get out of the way. Then, as the light from the saloon window hit his face, she gasped and put her hand to her gun. It was Stubby Hawkins, the gang member with the tattooed anchor!

Hawkins saw her at the same time, grinned, and said, " 'Scuse me, honeybunch. I lost a horse out here someplace." Then he swung away and lurched across the walk and down the steps to where a familiar painted pony stood tethered to a hitching rail.

Chance glanced around, saw nobody was near enough to matter, and followed. She caught up with Hawkins as he was fumbling the reins of his mount free. She stepped around the pinto's rump to face him, her back to the dark street. He had his left hand on his saddle horn, preparing to mount up. He saw her there and shook his head as if to clear it. He said, "What do you want, gal? I've been to Big Nose Kate's and I'm tuckered as hell, if you're walking the streets for trade."

Chance said, "I'm not a streetwalker. I'm Chance McGraw. Don't you recognize me, you animal?"

"Aw, that ain't no way to talk, little lady. If we've met up afore, I must have been drunk."

"You were. You couldn't get it up, and you bit me, you son of a bitch!"

The drunken bully's eyes widened and his jaw dropped as he said, "Hell, you *cain't* be that colonel's kid. We *kilt* you!"

Chance took a deep breath, moved her gun hand out to the side and said, "Not quite. *Draw*, you son of a bitch!"

Hawkins laughed and said, "That's loco, honey. You're a *gal*!"

"That didn't stop you the last time we met. Fill your fist, Stubby Hawkins. I mean it."

"Aw, go on, you're funning. Who ever heard of having a gunfight with a *gal*? I'm sorry they shot you, honey. That warn't my idea. I've always been more gentle with my wimmen, as you likely remember with satisfaction."

"I'm warning you. I mean to kill you, Stubby Hawkins. I'm giving you a break you never gave my poor father, but I'm counting to ten and then I'm going to draw."

Hawkins said, "Shit, when you get to ten, take off your shoes and go for twenty. I'd be crazier than you, to have a shoot-out with a woman in the middle of town!"

Chance glanced at his feet as she started counting. If what Tony had said was true, Hawkins wasn't set to go for his gun. Instead he put an unsteady left boot up in his stirrup, grunted, and hauled himself aboard the pinto. As she got to "Six!" he grinned down at her and said, "Nice meeting up with you again, honey. But it's been a long day and I'm off to catch my forty winks."

Chance stopped counting and stepped back as he swung the pony around. She shouted, "All right! This is it! I mean it!"

Hawkins ignored her and spurred his mount to ride away as Chance went for her gun. She drew and trained it on his receding outline as he loped off, not looking back. She cocked the gun and raised the sights to her eye level, cursing herself for not having a horse to follow and for the stupid warning she'd given him. The last thing she'd expected was to be dismissed as a foolish woman!

She saw he was too far and the streets were too

crowded for a clean shot. As she watched him vanish into the gloom, tears of frustrated rage in her eyes, a laconic voice asked, "You pointing that thing at anyone particular, Ma'am?"

Chance turned, and as she spotted the gleam of the town deputee's badge, she sheepishly holstered the gun and said, "Just funning, Marshal."

The lawman shrugged and said, "You ain't supposed to be out here in the roadway, gun or no. Which house do you work for, honey?"

Chance licked her lips and stammered, "Madame Moustache?"

The lawman nodded and said, "I won't run you in this time. But the next time you have trouble collecting from a customer, don't go pointing that fool gun at him on *my* beat, hear?"

Chance nodded and turned away. The deputy said, "Wait a minute, Madame Moustache is up the other way, gal."

She said, "I know. I'm out on a call. That man I just had words with tried to stop me, and, well, you know how the Madame is about service."

The lawman spat and said, "Customer too hightoned to come to a whorehouse like a man, huh? Well, you run along and service him then. What's your name? You ain't bad-looking and I sometimes drop by the Madame's when I gits off duty."

Chance grimaced and said, "Just ask for Skinny Hips. They'll know who you mean."

"I'll do that, Miss Skinny Hips. But I'll get testy as hell if you bring that gun to bed with us, hear?"

The pragmatic businessmen of Dodge were plain dealers who believed in cash-on-the-barrelhead and buyer-beware. So if Dodge wasn't the wild and wooly town Ned Buntline wrote about, it was far from formal. The streets and more important railroad properties were policed informally by men hired by the Santa Fe and local merchants. The military police at nearby Fort Dodge took care of federal violations. Such misunderstandings as the town law couldn't tend to with a pistol-whipping were tried before the county officials. Unlike the town, Ford County was incorporated.

The sheriff was an elected county official who left the running of the railroad town to those more interested unless someone did something serious enough for the county coroner or district attorney to issue a warrant on. It was this divided authority, more than any latent insanity, that accounted for the legendary lawlessness of small Western towns. There were men as rough on the streets of Chicago or New York at the time, but they were far more likely to get arrested. The railroaders and merchants needed the trade of the trailherders who passed through on occasion. So they tended to wink at brawls between nonresidents. But as Lawyer Lockwood explained the next morning when Chance took Hughie to see him, a resident of Dodge had certain rights, and among these rights was the town's vengeance on any wandering Texan who shot out your window glass or anyone important to you.

Lockwood's face was a ghastly shade of greenish gray as he listened once again to her whole story. He was too sick looking not to be sober, and when she'd finished, he said, "I can set up a corporation for you. We'll name Mister O'Rourke here as president. We won't need your name on the corporate papers, and he can hire anyone he wants as a private operative."

Hughie asked, "Will that be legal? Sure, I don't think I'm a citizen of this country."

Lockwood looked pained and said, "I never asked you that, so don't talk about it no more. You speak English, don't you?"

Chance said, "Hughie's confused. I happen to know he's a citizen. After he gets his license, what sort of credentials will *I* need? Do I get a badge or something?"

Lockwood shrugged and said, "You can buy one if you like. Most people don't know this, but a badge has no meaning in law. Anyone can wear a badge if they can back it up."

"That's ridiculous! Are you saying sheriffs and other peace officers have no authority to go with their tin stars?"

Lockwood shook his head and said, "No. They're elected or appointed officials and the law holds they have the same rights as any other citizen to make an arrest."

Hughie blinked and asked, "Jasus! Are you saying any man can step up to an outlaw and tell him he's under arrest?"

"He can if he's tough enough. Common law holds that anyone who sees a crime in progress or spots a wanted man has the legal right to take him before the bar of justice." He belched greenly and added, "That's not saying it's always a good *idea*! Aside from the outlaw getting testy about it, some lawmen frown on citizen's arrest and they haven't all been to law school. The bonded license I'm getting you will save a lot of tedious discussion about it, though. Like Miss Chance here most people think a badge means you're doing something proper instead of just being a busy-body."

He saw the uncertain look in her eye and added, "I'll have some ID cards printed up for you two to fill out as you see fit."

She asked, "What if I have to make an arrest outside the state of Kansas?"

Lockwood shrugged and said, "Bounty hunters have an advantage over regular lawmen that way. That's likely why they're in business. I'll lend you a book about the extradition laws, but you won't use it much. A locally appointed law officer has to answer to his boss or the voters for a mess of rules. A bounty hunter just needs to be tough enough to drag someone kicking and screaming across a state line. Try it on someone who ain't been indicted by a grand jury and you can get arrested. Get him before the judge who issued the warrant and the details don't matter much."

She nodded and said, "A friend of mine took a man who'd jumped bail back to Missouri. Wouldn't anyone in Kansas be interested?"

Lockwood said, "They would if he was a Kansas resident and had friends here. No lawman has much use for a bail jumper. On the other hand if a man was out on bail in Missouri and you tried to carry him back here to Kansas, you'd have his bondsman after you with a writ of habeus corpus and maybe a gun."

"Heavens, I can see it's more complicated than I thought."

"I know. That's why I'm lending you the book. Frankly, I'd try to talk you out of this if I thought you and Madame Moustache would let me."

Hughie asked, "What's this *habeas* stuff, and what's the rule about *killing* people out here?"

Lockwood grimaced and said, "It's in the book, but to put it simple, habeas corpus means 'why hold the body.' Neither a regular lawman nor a private citizen can arrest just *anybody* for the *hell* of it! You're supposed to be able to show cause if his lawyer asks. As for the killing out here, it's the same as killing back there. I've read Ned Buntline, too, but the law is the same all over when it comes to killing folks. You're not supposed to do it."

Chance said, "Come now, they say Wild Bill's killed a dozen men and we passed Boot Hill as we were coming into Dodge."

Lockwood looked disgusted and said, "Wild Bill's score was *four* the last I heard, and he got in trouble over two. Lucky for him he had friends on the coroner's jury. Any citizen has the right to kill in self-defense, and small town coroners don't pick nits if you've been buying drinks for 'em and haven't shot anybody popular. But you do have to answer for a shoot-out before the coroner's jury if you mean to stay in town. Those tales of blowing a man's brains out and just strolling off are for the birds. Even a lawman has to fill out a formal report for the coroner if he's forced to shoot someone in the line of duty."

Chance said, "I'll want some of those forms then.

What about these reward posters that say dead or alive?"

"They mean the wanted man has already been indicted for a capital offense. You take a petty thief dead instead of alive and you'd better have a damned good reason. There's been a lot of discussion about some of the rewards posted by the railroads, banks, and such. Some lawyers hold that Allan Pinkerton could be in a real mess if the survivors of some of his posters wanted to press charges of incitement to murder."

He glanced at the clock on his wall and said, "All of it's in the book I'm lending you, Miss McGraw. If you're not serious enough about this plan of yours to read up on the law, you'd better forget the whole thing."

Chance said, "I wish I could forget, but I can't. While you're drawing up the legal papers, I'd best see about renting an office with quarters. Do you have any suggestions about a permanent address, Mister Lockwood?"

Lockwood nodded and said, "You'll need a mailing address, but prices are dear out here. I know a house down a side street that would do you, but it'll cost you fifteen dollars a month."

Hughie gasped and said, "That's dear indeed! Jasus, we could stay in a hotel for little more!"

But Chance shushed him and said, "It sounds like it will do. How long will it take you to get our license and such?"

Lockwood picked up a pencil and said, "Ought to have 'em by this time tomorrow, Lord willing and I meet the judge in a good mood. I'll write down the address and the name of the landlord you'll want to see about your quarters. Tell him I sent you and he'll treat you right." Then Lockwood paused and added, "Uh, the judge is going to want to see some, well, bond money."

Chance nodded and took out her checkbook. Lockwood shook his head and said, "The judge sort of cottons to cash and carry, Ma'am."

Chance said, "I'll send someone back with cash after I drop by the bank then. What sort of a bond are we talking about?"

Lockwood said, "Shux, you can post the *bond* with a check. The judge gets a couple of hundred for, uh, expediting things. Since you come well-recommended, he'll likely set your performance bond at a thousand."

Chance sighed and said, "A thousand-dollar bond will wipe me out."

But Lockwood said, "Hell, just write the check and forget it, unless you mess up. The county won't *cash* your bond check unless your *license* is revoked."

Chance looked relieved and said, "You had me frightened for a moment."

Hughie shot the lawyer a keen look and asked, "Just what do we have to do to lose our license, sor?"

Lockwood said, "Annoy the courthouse gang, of course. This bunch Miss McGraw is after have no friends in Dodge. Cut the sheriff in for ten percent of such rewards as you collect on the rascals and you can shoot 'em all twice. Just don't get in any fights with people who've come to their own understanding with the local law. Some of the trail bosses and ranchers' sons you might meet here on a Saturday night can be pure obnoxious. They know folks aren't allowed to fight back and it braves 'em up a mite. But, hell, none of 'em are likely to pick on an old man or a woman, so don't fret about it."

Chance said, "I'll take a chance on insufficient funds until we collect a few bounties then."

Lockwood shook his head and said, "No you won't. They'd never accept a bond from a woman. Write out a check to Mister O'Rourke here, and let him post the bond."

Chance started to say it wasn't fair. But she knew she'd be whipping a dead horse in a country that wouldn't let her vote because of her sex. So she agreed. Hughie looked anxious and asked, "Just what happens if something goes wrong and the check is after bouncing?"

"You go to jail," said Lockwood, adding, "Some courts are understanding about overdrawn accounts. Ford County isn't. Too many city slickers have bought cows with worthless paper in the past."

Chance sighed and said, "That's out then. I can't expect Hughie to take such a chance for me."

But the tinker laughed and said, "Och, Jasus, I've always wanted the chance to be a hero for a pretty gorl! If I'm to be a grand business leader of Dodge City, I may as well start learning to be as crooked as the rest of thim. Kiting checks will be a change from poaching, but it has a grand *dignified* ring to it!"

Chance laughed and told Lockwood they'd get the judge's cash bribe to him later that afternoon. He told them he'd have their business set up by noon the following day, Lord willing and the judge needing the money for his bar tab.

As they left to hunt down the address the lawyer had given them, Tony Despres overtook them on the street. He called, "I've been looking all over for you! I was down at the railyards and Miz O'Rourke said the two of you was up at this end of town, but she didn't know just where!"

As Chance began to fill him in on her grotesque "showdown" of the night before, Tony dragged them into a Mexican beanery and insisted they let him buy a round of chili con carne before he opined, "You're still pretty, honey, but you was dumb more ways than I can shake a stick at! What the hell did you think you was doing when you *called* Stubby Hawkins instead of just *gunning* the bastard?"

"I wanted him to know who I was before I killed him."

"And so now he knows they didn't finish the only witness to their crimes, and you didn't kill him worth mention!"

Chance frowned and said, "I was so mad! He just *laughed* at me!"

"Yeah. A showdown with a pretty gal in skirts does take some getting used to. By now he's sobered up enough to reconsider. I'm surprised he was still in town last night. By now he's likely half way to Texas!"

Chance looked sheepish and Tony added, "This agency business is a waste of time, too, even if you was a man. I got a wire from Brian this morning. He had some time on the train to sort things out with Jack Dawson. Dawson's bruised a mite, so he's likely speaking freely. Brian says we was right about the gang laying a clear trail to Dodge, planning to split up here and go their own quiet ways."

"Stubby Hawkins was still here last night, and he said something about a parlor house he'd been to."

"Yeah, Hawkins is likely the dumbest member of the outfit. Brian says he's friends with Big Nose Kate, a businesswoman here in Dodge. I checked her out a couple of hours ago as soon as I got Brian's wire. Old Kate has a new boyfriend. Hard-drinking gambler called Holliday. We don't have no paper on Doc Holliday, so I didn't press it."

"If they said Hawkins wasn't there, they have to be lying!"

"Now just slow down and *think*, dang it. You said Hawkins *bragged* on coming from Big Nose Kate's. It was early, he'd been drinking, and a blowhard like Hawkins ain't about to mess with a man with a rep like Holliday has."

Chance nodded with a frown and said, "I know men brag about the girls they don't get."

"There you go. Old Kate's not bad looking and they say she has a loving nature. He wouldn't have been soaking his head along Saloon Row if he'd had someplace better to spend the night. When I talked to her, she said she ain't seen Hawkins lately, but that she remembers him. She said she had words with him six or eight months ago and warned him not to come back. He likely asked around afore he dropped by to renew their romance, heard about her surly pimp, Holliday, and settled for some drinking and bragging."

Chance said, "You're probably right. But he may still be in Dodge. Even if he isn't, I need to be incorporated *somewhere* before I go looking for him and the others again. Does Brian have any other leads on where the others might be heading?"

"Nails Kinkaid has a brother who owns a saloon in Pueblo, Colorado. He might go there to hide out with free drinks. Sailor Flynn is a lapsed Mormon. Ain't that a bitch?"

"Salt Lake City?"

"Could be. Flynn growed up in Salt Lake. Run off to the California goldfields when he got drummed outten the temple for being less saintly than the Latter Day Saints thought fitting. He signed aboard a clipper, which is how he got the nickname, and he was in Savannah when the war broke out, which is how he wound up a Rebel. He deserted the regular Confederate Army when Grant started winning battles in the Western Campaign and being a Reb got serious. Flynn joined up with Quantrill's guerrillas for a while."

"He must have been one of the border raiders my father fought!"

"Yep. Kinkaid and Hawkins, too. They was with Quantrill when he burnt Lawrence, Kansas. Was your dad riding with the Union when they caught up with Bill Quantrill near the end of the war?"

"Yes. Dad helped identify his body when they found him in the woods after the fight. He didn't talk much about the war, but I gathered the guerrillas rode off and left William Quantrill to bleed to death. Dad said they weren't much when it came to fighting real soldiers."

Tony nodded and said, "That accounts for the grudge they bore him then. Lefty Shaw wasn't with Bill Quantrill in them days. He was too young for the war, but he's made up for it since. Missouri says Shaw was riding with the James-Younger gang a year ago. That accounts for him knowing the older owlhoots. Frank James rode with Quantrill too. Shaw must be sort of ugly, even for a train robber. The James-Younger gang throwed him out on his own after he gunned a little girl in Clay County for no reason anyone can see. The kid was on her way home from school when the gang rode past just ahead of the posse. They say Lefty Shaw just shot her on the fly as they passed. Cole Younger was gonna kill him for it, but Frank James talked him out of it. Shaw has relatives in Clay County, and they might have took it personal."

Chance nodded and said, "Then Lefty is probably back in Missouri."

"That's where Brian figures to look. He wired me to sell the ponies we rode out here and join him back there with our saddles and such."

Chance gasped, "You can't leave now, Tony!"

Tony said, "I just said I was. Brian needs me back there."

"Damn it, I need you *here*! I'll hire you as soon as I get my license from the county, and there's so much I still want you to teach me!"

Tony shook his head and said, "I got a job. You know I'd like to stay and play with you some more, honey. But that's all you're doing here. Playing. As to teaching you more about our business, I thought I just taught you that you was wasting time and money here! You won't even find Stubby Hawkins here in Dodge now that he knows you're alive and here. The local law is looking for him about what they done to them nesters. He's long gone by now."

"You said something about Texas, Tony. Why do you think Hawkins will ride for Texas?"

"He used to ride for a Texas trailherder named Ben Thompson. Thompson's tough and mean, too. If Hawkins can join up with his old Texas sidekicks, no lawman in his right mind would try to take him."

"Is this Ben Thompson an outlaw?"

"No, just crazy. He's an unreconstructed Reb with a bad drinking habit, a lightning draw, and fifty-odd trailhands backing any play he feels like making. He comes up here to Dodge every roundup with a herd of cows to ship. When he and his boys is in town, they board up all the windows and the town law goes on vacation 'til him and his boys has spent their pay and gone home again."

Chance thought and said, "They tell me the fall sales are due. Do you think Hawkins would be dumb enough to ride back north with Thompson's wild bunch if that's where he's gone?"

"Can't say. A month's a long time to a man with Stubby's limited imaginings. But you don't aim to be here a month from now, do you?"

Chance said, "I'm going first to Pueblo. That saloon is the best lead you've given me."

"Honey, that's pure crazy! I told you Kinkaid may be hiding out up there with *kinsmen*!"

"I know. That's why I wanted you to show me some more gunfighting tricks. I'll make it worth your while to stay, Tony."

Despres stared at her from under his bushy brows for a long time before he sighed and said, "Jesus, I'd give an arm and a leg to stay here, even if you don't mean that the way I hope you do. But Brian's counting on me, and I'm not sure I'd be doing you a favor by encouraging your fool notions. You *had* a crack at one of them, honey. You already draw as good as most men, but you froze up when the chips was down."

"That's not true!" she protested. "I had every intention of fighting him! How was I to know he'd just laugh at me and ride away?"

Tony shrugged and said, "The point is that you *let* him. Boot Hill is filled with folks like you, albeit most of 'em was wearing pants when they got kilt. You don't get to be a gunslick by *practicing*, Chance. Anyone can learn to draw good with a little practice. What makes the difference betwixt a gunfighter and suicide ain't in your hands. It's in your *head*!"

"I'm not afraid to kill those . . . those animals!"

"Nobody said you was afraid. It's more than that. It's a thing you didn't *have* last night! Lucky for you Stubby Hawkins didn't have it neither. You both fooled around like young cowboys who'd been reading Wild West magazines."

"Damn it, I was taken by surprise when he refused to fight!"

Tony nodded morosely and said, "Everyone up on Boot HIll was took by one surprise or the other, honey. You see, it's one thing to pack a gun and tell yourself you aim to gun a man. But most folks, when they come face to face with the elephant, hesitate just long enough to think, *My God, this is real.*"

Chance started to protest some more. Then she nodded and said, "All right. Call it buck fever if you like. Next time I'll know better. Why don't you come with us while I rent the house I told you about? Surely you have time to show me a few more tricks before you have to catch your train."

Tony took out his pocket watch and said, "Like to. Can't. I've chores to wrap up and a four o'clock flier to catch. Why don't you come back to Missouri with me instead? We could jaw about it on the train, and Brian might let you tag along when we go after Lefty Shaw."

Chance shook her head stubbornly and said, "I'm tired of just tagging along. If you two won't help me, I'll just have to find someone else."

Tony sighed and said, "Honey, no growed man is about to help a lady get herself shot."

Hughie O'Rourke, who'd been listening quietly, said, "Sure, *I'm* helping herself. Though it's little use I'd be in a gunfight."

Chance shot the tinker a grateful look, but asked

Tony, "Where is the house of this Big Nose Kate, Tony?"

"Not far, but what in tarnation do *you* want with a fancy gal?"

Chance said, "I don't want to talk to her. I want to see if this Doc Holliday is looking for a job."

Chance didn't see Tony off that afternoon. She was busy as well as annoyed. The one-story house they'd rented was just off Bridge Street, which ran north and south from the plaza where it crossed Front Street, which ran east and west just north of the Santa Fe yards. The house was ramshackle and unpainted, but the tinkers pronounced it a grand establishment as they began to unload their cart parked in the side yard. Hughie seemed pleased that the place needed repairs. He said, "I may be after making me fortune in this land as a carpenter. For these people don't build their houses with much skill and that's a fact."

Chance had ordered some furniture and was waiting on the porch for it when a tall man on a big gray gelding rode into the yard and slowly dismounted. As he tethered his mount to the hitching post out front, the sunlight flashed on his badge and she recognized him as the deputy she'd met on Front Street the night before. He walked thoughtfully up to her, ticked the brim of his sombrero, and said, "I figured it might be you, Miss Skinny Hips."

Chance smiled uncertainly. The deputy was young and better looking in the daylight. He wore a drooping moustache in an obvious attempt to look older. His gun was tucked in the waistband of his too short pants, and one might have taken him for a country bumpkin save for the badge and the wide-set gray eyes that were staring right through her.

He said, "I heard about you folks applying for a private law license. That part's up to Mayor Hoover and the county. I'm sort of interested in why you've been asking around for Big Nose Kate."

"Good heavens, you're not Doc Holliday, are you?"

"Nope. The name is Earp. Wyatt Earp. Doc and Kate is friends of mine. I wouldn't want this to get around, but Doc's sort of crazy. When he heard someone was looking for him, he sort of holed up in the Long Branch with his shotgun and started talking ugly. I told him not to gun no she-males 'til I got a handle on what in thunder was going on. I like things peaceable on my beat."

Chance said, "Good Lord, I'm not *after* him! I want to *hire* him!"

Earp looked incredulous. Then he said, "Lawyer Lockwood told me about what them outlaws done when I got your address from him. But you can't hire Doc to shoot them rascals, Ma'am. He ain't even a *dentist* no more."

"I heard he was a killer."

"That's true. You can't hardly beat Doc when it comes to killing folks. But he won't do it for pay. You might say it's his sideline. His main business is drinking, followed by gambling. I could get him a job with the city if he wasn't so moody about regular hours and taking orders. I'd stay away from Big Nose Kate if I was you, too. You see, she likes me 'cause Doc and me have helped each other out in the past. But between you and me she's crazier than he is, and jealous, too."

Annie came out to ask if they wanted tea. Chance nodded and asked Earp to have a seat. The lanky deputy sat on the steps and said he'd admire some tea, but that he had to leave soon.

Chance waited until the tinker's wife placed a tray of tea and biscuits between them on the weathered planks before she explained her needs to Wyatt Earp. The deputy laughed and said, "If that don't beat all. You folks have put up good money to start your own detective agency and you don't have one hired gun between you!"

Chance had been thinking about that. She said, "I've sent for some help. I'm not the frail thing you think either: I can handle a gun if I have to. I just thought Holliday might help me polish up a bit."

Earp laughed again and said, "Doc can't teach you his secret. You wouldn't want his gift if he could give it to you."

"Do you know what makes Doc Holliday so dangerous, Mister Earp?"

"Sure, the poor cuss is already dead. He's got TB. If he don't get killed in a fight, he figures to die slow and dirty with his lungs rotted out. The likker helps, but he never forgets he's dying, so you might say he just don't *give* a hang!"

Chance grimaced and said, "Brrr! That *could* turn a man into a gunfighter!"

Earp sipped some tea and said, "As a matter of fact Doc ain't really all that good. I could beat him to the draw. I know a dozen others who could, too. What makes him dangerous is his total lack of caution. You mess with Doc, and you know you're in for a fight to the finish with a mad dog. *I* can say he's a mad dog 'cause we're friends. He's been known to kill a man for remarking that it might be time for a fresh deck of cards."

He noticed the resigned look in her eyes and said, "Shux, why don't you let us *sensible* lawmen look for them rascals who mistreated you, Ma'am? The DA has a warrant out on the gang and there's some fair lawmen looking for 'em. Aside from the sheriff's posse there's my boss, Marshal Deger, and us five town deputies. If any of them owlhoots is still in Ford County, they figure to join the other eight we got up on Boot Hill afore long."

Chance shook her head and said, "You boys do your job and let me do mine. If I can't get Doc Holliday to give me lessons, who else do you suggest?"

Earp shrugged and said, "I ain't bad, but I *got* a job. There's Luke Short over at the Long Branch. He's likely the fastest draw in Kansas. But he'd just laugh fit to bust if you asked him to give gunfight lessons to a gal."

Chance put down her tea cup and stood up. She stepped away from the porch, whipped out her gun, and fired it three times into the ground.

Wyatt Earp sat there, watching the dust settle as the horse he'd tethered fought to break free. Then he nodded and said, "That was sort of interesting, Ma'am. But make your point."

"Don't you think I'm pretty fast with a gun?" she asked.

He nodded and said, "You're good at shooting *prairie*. But what's all this guff about a quick draw being so important?"

Chance reloaded as she stared at him with a

puzzled frown and asked, "I thought it was the most important part of gunfighting."

"You thought wrong, then," said Earp. He put his own cup down and joined her in the yard. He drew his own gun, quite casually and to her notion not particularly swiftly. He nodded and asked, "Was you expecting me to draw, Ma'am?"

"What do you mean?"

"I'm standing here with my fist full of hardware. That's what I mean. What was you *doing* when I drawed? I'll *tell* you what you was doing. You was just standing there, a gun in your own hand, and you never blinked an eye as I drawed. Had I wanted to, I'd have *kilt* you just now!"

She smiled uncertainly and said, "That's ridiculous! We're not having a gunfight."

He put his gun away with a nod and said, "That's 'cause I didn't *want* one, not 'cause it was *impossible*! I met that fool writer, Ned Buntline, when I was hunting buffalo with Bill Cody. *He* was full of crap about quick draws and fancy gunbelts, too. He kept pestering me to tell him if I was faster on the draw than Jim Hickok, and when I asked how the hell I should know, he looked sort of hurt."

"*Don't* you know, Mister Earp?"

"Not hardly. If me and Hickok had ever put the matter to the test, one of us would be dead right now."

She glanced at the gun in his waistband and holstered her own as she asked, "Could we have a sort of contest—with empty guns, of course?"

He shook his head and said, "Not hardly. I don't want to play ball and jacks with you neither."

"I'll bet you five dollars I could beat you at . . ." she began, and then she found herself staring into Wyatt Earp's unwinking gun muzzle as he said, "You lose. That'll be five dollars, Ma'am."

She said, "Wait a minute, that wasn't fair!"

"Where in the U.S. Constitution does it say a gunfight has to be *fair*, Ma'am? Hell, you could likely whip that pisoliver out faster than me if I was to stand here like a big bird and let somebody say on-your-mark and such. But that ain't the way things happen in real life, Miss McGraw."

She sighed and said, "You've made your point and it was worth five dollars."

Earl laughed and said, "Shux, you already gave me some tea and biscuits, so let's say no more about it. It's been nice talking to you, but I got to take it on down the road."

As he turned away, Chance asked, "Wait, are you a married man, Mister Earp?"

He frowned and said, "Used to be. My Willa died of typhus back in '70, though. Why do you ask?"

"I'd like to know if you'd have supper with us this evening if my furniture ever gets here."

He nodded and said, "I'd be proud to, Ma'am. I sure was disappointed when I asked for you at Madame Moustache's and I larnt you was only funning me."

Chance, or, rather, Hughie O'Rourke, got the detective license Monday morning after Lawyer Lockwood finally found the judge sober enough to sign it.

The weekend had not been entirely wasted. Wyatt Earp had made a mild attempt at seduction in her porch swing after dinner, but he'd accepted her excuse that she needed time to think about his overtures. The next evening he introduced her to Luke Short, the deadly proprietor of the Long Branch Saloon.

The Long Branch was a squalid hole-in-the-wall about the size of a candy store. Luke had named it for Long Branch, New Jersey, his hometown. When Earp took her there at her insistence, Luke Short had led them to the back room for privacy. He said he ran a proper joint and didn't want the boys to think he had women working his barroom.

Like Wyatt Earp, Luke Short thought her ideas were pretty funny. But Chance was learning. She didn't try to get the two experienced gunslicks to *show* her anything. She knew her skills with a sidearm were just a matter of repetition now that she had the basic moves down pat, and her own reflection in the bedroom mirror was the only partner she needed now.

What she wanted from Earp and the sinister saloonkeeper were *stories*, and like most men they loved to talk about their exploits.

Chance was a good listener. Some of the yarns they shared with her were probably bragging, but she listened for the fine points as they swapped tales. When Luke joshed Wyatt about the time he'd almost been killed by Ben Thompson, Chance picked up on the right and wrong moves everyone had made that fateful day in Ellsworth, to the east. She found herself nodding in understanding as she learned how Sheriff Whitney of Ellsworth had died, a surprised look on his face, when Thompson shot him almost as an innocent bystander. Earp said, "I told old Whitney not to git betwixt Ben Thompson and that feller, Sterling, he was gunning for."

Chance said, "I heard about this Ben Thompson. He's supposed to be quick on the draw."

Earp snorted and said, "Hell, Ben and his brother, Bill, was waiting for Sterling in front of Brennan's saloon with *shotguns*! There was no quick draw about it. Everybody told the sheriff Ben was drunk and not to mix in it. But he went in the saloon to make peace with Sterling. Then he come out through the swinging doors, sort of smiling, and Ben Thompson blowed him away without waiting to see who he was."

Luke Short nodded and said, "Never walk through a doorway when there's a man waiting on the other side for whomsoever. Is it true you arrested the Thompson boys for killing Sheriff Whitney, Wyatt? I've always wondered how you got away with that one."

Earp shrugged and said, "Shux, it wasn't that big a boo. I waited 'til the Thompson boys had time to sober some and think about the mistake they'd made. Then I sent word I was coming polite for a peaceable word with them. I had a drink with Ben and told him it'd be better if he went with me to explain it to the judge, and he agreed he was a long way from Texas so what the hell."

Chance gasped, "You mean he went with you, and they let him off?"

"Sure. I told him I'd testify it was a case of mistaken identity. He had about thirty riders in town that day and nobody really wanted to carry it further. Ben paid the fine for disturbing the peace and left town as I advised him. Ned Buntline had no call to write that story about me running the Thompson boys out of Ellsworth. Ben was sort of sensitive about it when I met him later in Wichita. Cost me some sweat and a few drinks afore we made up."

Luke Short laughed and said, "I'll bet if push come to shove, you could take Ben Thompson, Wyatt."

Earp shrugged and said, "Mebbe. I don't aim to find out. I don't reckon Ben does neither."

Chance said, "You mean coyotes hunt rabbits, not each other?"

The sarcasm was lost on both of them. Luke Short nodded jovially and said, "The smartest way to win a fight is not to get *in* one, if you can help it."

"Would you let another man back you down, Mister Short?"

He thought before he nodded and said, "I reckon I'd back down for Doc Holliday or John Wesley Hardin."

Earp agreed, "That Hardin is a mean one all right. Remember the time he was chasing Jim Hickok, spoiling for a fight? I thought I'd laugh fit to bust when old Hickok lit out like a scalded cat!"

Chance gasped, "Wild Bill Hickok ran away from a fight?"

Luke Short said, "Sure he did. Nobody with a lick of sense would face John Wesley Hardin when he was drunk. Old John is crazy cold sober!"

"I thought you men depended on maintaining your reputations."

"Shux, Ma'am. A man can avoid a fight with a maniac without having to apologize. As long as nine out of ten leave you alone, you can hold your head up most places."

Earp said, "I wish them writer fellers wouldn't carry on so about us workingmen out here. I had to pistol-whup a young trailhand who'd been reading crazy stories the other night. Jim Hickok's the one I'm worried about. He sort of *likes* to play up to the stories Ned Buntline wrote about him. Mark my words, one of these days some silly kid's likely to gun old Jim, unexpected, to show us all how good he is."

"It's them unexpected kids you got to worry about," Luke Short agreed morosely. He added, "If you keep your wits about you, you can generally head off trouble if it makes any sense at all. You remember that Iowa hand I had to shoot that night in here, Wyatt? He just come in and started cussing me for no reason. When he got to the part about hearing how quick I was on the draw, I knew what he meant to try next, so I done what I had to."

Earp nodded and said, "Ed Masterson told me about it. He said the kid was still jawing at you when you shot him."

Chance repressed a shudder as that sank in, too. Men like these didn't make the speeches she'd read about. Their secret wasn't fancy gunplay. It was knowing to the split second when gunplay was *called for*!

She felt her own resolve wavering as she realized yet again what she was letting herself in for. But she'd made up her mind, and she encouraged them to keep talking about their deadly skills as she picked up a tactical maneuver here and a bit of deadly strategy there. She was beginning to see that hunting men called for far more thought than other game. There was psychology as well as manual dexterity involved. These laconic, dangerous men had more right to laugh at her than she'd thought. It wasn't just that she was a woman. Nine out of ten trained soldiers would have been well-advised to stay away from them with a gun. She understood now why Brian Pio and Tony Despres had dismissed her as a foolish kid. She *was* a foolish kid. But, damn it, those others had killed her father and defiled her. Maybe, just maybe, if she could remember some of the free advice she was picking up, she might manage to take at least *one* of her father's killers with her.

It was after dark a week later in Pueblo, Colorado. Chance stood near a watering trough near the open doorway of Kinkaid's Saloon. She wasn't sure the Kinkaid who owned the place was the brother of the Kinkaid she was looking for. But it was a place to start.

The sky was ruddy from the ore smelters near the railroad tracks. There was no need for streetlamps in Pueblo. The smelters worked twenty-four hours a day, and the town never slept either.

There were no decent women in this part of town after sundown, but none of the men passing paid Chance much attention as she stood there. She was dressed in jeans and the denim jacket of a cowhand. The sombrero she wore was a man's, too, and her features were shaded by the broad black brim. The railroad conductor had seen her in better light and he'd called her "son" when he'd punched her ticket. She knew she could pass casual examination as a young male rider.

She'd looked in the saloon's open doorway earlier. Nails Kinkaid hadn't been among the customers inside. She hadn't really expected to see him there. Not if he was hiding out.

A man who'd passed her earlier came back down the walk and stopped. He said, "Howdy, son. We, uh, got a gun law here in Pueblo. You're likely new in town."

Chance nodded and said, "I'm reaching for my wallet, Marshal." Then she took the wallet from her hip pocket and opened it to expose the mail order badge and Ford County ID.

The Colorado lawman couldn't read in the dim red light, but he nodded and said, "I figured you was waiting for somebody. Bounty hunters generally check in with us afore they try for anybody here in Pueblo. Saves a lot of misunderstandings, if you follow my drift."

Chance tried for a husky tone as she said, "My boss tells me it's considered fair to deal the local marshal in for ten percent of the reward. The man I'm after is worth five thousand to the Missouri Central Railroad. The State of Kansas is offering five hundred."

"I figured you was a nice young friendly gent. I'd be pleased to help you with the rascal—do you need some backup?"

She started to refuse. Then she said, "I'll put you down as the assisting officer, but I'll take him myself if it's all the same to you."

"By jimmies, you *are* a gent. My handle is Wilson. Jack Wilson. Make sure you spell it right. I can see the flier on whomsoever reads dead or alive, so we'll say no more about it, and I'll just go have me some coffee or something if you don't need me."

She nodded, but said, "I have one question, Mister Wilson. Do you know when that saloon closes?"

"Kinkaid's? It don't. Johnny Kinkaid stays open all night."

"Is that John Kinkaid in there behind the bar?"

"Yep. He lives just over on the next street. Just has to cross his own backyard to get to work. Later in the evening Jeb Forbes tends bar for him until sunup. You ain't after Jeb, are you?"

"No. I never heard of Jeb Forbes."

"We'll say no more about it, then. Jeb's the only one I'm on good terms with. I'll spread the word you're in town and being friendly. None of the boys will bother with this end of town for a spell. I don't remember the name you said you went by, son."

Chance said, "I work for O'Rourke in Dodge."

"Right. It do get tedious with relations looking for you by your right name."

The lawman strolled away and Chance waited until he was out of sight before she moved. She counted the storefronts. There were three twenty-five-foot lots between the saloon and the corner. Chance nodded and walked to the side street. She rounded the block and started counting again. The fourth house from the corner had a porch and lights in the window. She glanced around, saw she was alone, and mounted the steps on the balls of her feet, drawing her gun.

She glanced in the window through the dingy lace curtains. The front parlor was empty. She could see a sliver of light from a rear room as she watched someone moving in the back. She eased to the door and tried the knob. The door was locked.

Chance considered forcing it, but there was a chance she had the wrong Kinkaids. Grimly she retraced her steps to the walk out front. She moved along the block until she came to a weed-grown vacant lot. She made her way between the blank walls on either side and found herself in the yard space in the middle of the block. There were no fences between the cheek-by-jowl houses.

There was little in the way of backyards either. The soil gritted under her boots as Chance made her way to the rear of the Kinkaid house. Across the cindery, bare earth she saw the open back door of the saloon. There was a light in the rear window of the house, too. Chance took a deep breath, drew the gun again, and walked to the window.

Inside Nails Kinkaid sat in his undershirt at a kitchen table. There was a cup on the table in front of him and he was reading a newspaper. He seemed to be alone.

Chance went to the door and tried it. The door wasn't locked. She opened it and stepped inside. Kinkaid looked up at her blankly. He smiled uncertainly and said, "Do I know you, Mister?"

Chance saw his gunbelt was hanging over the back of the chair next to him. She put her own gun in its holster and said, "You know me. The name is McGraw."

Before Kinkaid could answer, a worn-looking woman with ash blond hair came in the side door to ask, "Who are you talking to, Nails?" and that was when Kinkaid made his move.

Chance stiff-armed the woman out of the way as she dropped to one knee and drew. Kinkaid had his own gun in his hand as she fired. Her first round took him under the heart. Her second blew part of his jaw away, and the third missed completely as he went over backward, chair and all.

Chance thumbed the hammer of her pistol to fire again as she trained it on the writhing figure at her feet. Her heart was pounding and her mouth was dry and she felt like she was going to vomit. Until this moment she'd been looking forward to revenge, but even as she told herself the dying man on the blood-slicked linoleum was one of the brutes who'd killed her father and raped her, her emotions seemed all wrong. She'd expected to feel elated, not sorry for the moronic creature!

Kinkaid writhed weakly, stared up at her in wonder, and suddenly went limp. Chance knew he was dead. Nobody had ever looked so dead before. And she knew he'd died still wondering who she was and why she'd killed him.

She told herself it hadn't mattered. It had been him or her, and he'd deserved to die. But the dead thing at her feet refused to look anything like the grinning lout who'd abused and degraded her, and to her numb amazement she didn't feel any different now that she'd killed one of them than she had before. If she felt emotion at all, it was vague regret and a sense of urgency. She'd done what she'd come to do. Now it was time to get as far away as possible. Hopefully without having to hurt anyone else!

The woman who'd come in had fallen to the floor, too, and as she tried to rise she was screaming. Chance said, "Hush up and stay put!" as she moved to douse the light. She stepped over to the window and smashed out the glass as the woman wailed, "I *told* John we had no call letting Nails stay here! Nails never was no good and *now* look what he's done!"

As Chance covered the rear with her remaining two

rounds, a man ran out of the saloon into the yard and Chance called out, "You just stay put, Mister."

The saloonkeeper called out, "Cora? What's happened to Cora?"

"Go to him!" snapped Chance, adding, "If you want to keep him alive, get him out of my gunsights pronto!"

The vapid blonde called out, "Johnny, go back inside! I'm all right, he was only after Nails!"

Chance headed for the front door without waiting to see how they reacted to her ultimatum. She unlocked the front door but reloaded her gun before she stepped out on the far side of the block. She holstered her gun as she tripped down the steps and headed up the block. A man coming out of another house asked what had happened and Chance said, "Don't know. When I hear gunshots, I generally head somewhere else."

The man said, "I'm with you on that, son!" and headed back for his own doorway.

Chance strode up to the next corner and rounded it. She slowed as she found herself back on the main drag. Men were passing her, attracted by the sound of her gunshots. Her ears still rang and her mouth tasted like brass. Now that it had happened, she knew she should feel some satisfaction, but she simply felt drained. She was annoyed with herself for not having considered Kinkaid's kin. Not because she owed his family more consideration than he'd shown hers, but because she just hadn't even *thought* about it in her anxiety to track him down.

She was glad she hadn't had to hurt anyone else. Despite her hatred of the man she'd just killed, she could feel for his bewildered sister-in-law. She and her saloonkeeper husband would be better off without that black sheep younger brother underfoot. Chance hoped in time they'd realize this.

She strode into the town marshal's office and found a gray-haired man sitting at a desk. She took her wallet and the wanted fliers on Kinkaid out and placed them on the green blotter in front of him. He glanced at them, but seemed more interested in the commotion outside. He asked, "What's going on out there? We heard shots."

Chance said, "I know. I just had to shoot Nails Kinkaid. I'm going to need help in retrieving the body peaceable. I'm not looking for a fight with his brother."

The marshal blinked in sudden understanding and said, "You're the bounty hunter Wilson just told me about! You sure work fast, Mister McGraw!"

Chance didn't correct his mistake about her gender. As she'd hoped, the name Dad had picked for her fit either sex. She said, "I'd like to fill out the claims in the name of my agency. Sometimes the survivors can get testy, and I don't want to have it out with anyone I don't have to."

The marshal nodded and said, "Wilson told me you seemed a reasonable young cuss. Johnny Kinkaid's gonna take this personal as hell, but he ain't a bad sort. We'll disremember your name if he asks about you. But you understand you'll have to make a statement to the county coroner and such afore we can let you ride out."

"Wilson told me the form. How do we work your cut?"

The marshal looked pained and said, "I wish you wouldn't put things so *blunt*, son. It's an election year and Johnny Kinkaid is popular in Pueblo."

"Suppose I say your department assisted me in locating the late Nails Kinkaid? The Missouri flier offers the reward for the capture or information leading to the capture."

"That's better. We all know Nails resisted arrest."

The deputy Chance had spoken to earlier came in with another lawman, saying, "It was like I figured. The kid blowed Kinkaid's brother to hash and . . ." Then he saw Chance and added, "I'm glad I found you first. Johnny Kinkaid's just strapped on his guns and he's headed this way."

The marshal rose from his desk with a worried look and muttered, "Oh, hell. This is getting serious. Mebbe I can head him off and cool him down."

Chance said, "That's how Sheriff Whitney got killed in Ellsworth."

The elderly lawman grimaced and said, "I know. Putting you under protective custody won't work neither. If I know Johnny, he'll find enough drinking companions for a vigilance committee, and then where will we be?"

Wilson said, "Hell, let them have it out, Marshal. This kid is *good*!"

Chance said, "I've got a better idea. You fellows will have earned your share of the reward if you'll just send a photograph of the body and the coroner's death certificate to my office in Dodge. Missouri and Kansas don't care if his kin bury him here. They just have to know he's dead. Meanwhile I'd better duck out the back way."

The marshal looked relieved but said, "We need a statement for the coroner from you afore you leave, son."

Chance said, "I'll mail it to you. Where's the back door?"

Wilson asked, "Are you going to let a bartender say he run you out of town, kid?"

But the marshal said, "Oh, shut up, can't you see he's a *pro*? I'll show you out, Mister McGraw. You can use my pony, and I'll get Johnny calmed down after he's proved hisself to ever'body by yellin' up and down the street for your scalp." As they headed for the rear, he added, "I sure appreciate a man who works so neat."

Two days later, seated in the coach of The Denver & Rio Grande Western, Chance stared at the passing bleak scenery of Utah from under the brim of her sombrero, one booted foot braced on the iron frame of the seat ahead as she planned ahead. She was getting used to wearing men's clothing now and more assured of her disguise. She had a tight undershirt binding her breasts under the loose hickory shirt and denim jacket. Everybody walked a little strange in high-heeled Texas boots, and she no longer thought the men who glanced her way had any idea she wasn't just a young cowboy. The wary glances some shot her way from time to time were occasioned by the gun on her hip, she knew. Most men didn't notice and dismissed her as a young saddle bum. Those few who'd made a study of the subject recognized the rig of a gunslick and treated her with desperately casual respect.

Now that the business in Pueblo was over, she'd had time to go over all the mistakes she'd made. She knew she should have gone to the town marshal's first and made her arrangements in advance so that she could have simply vanished after gunning Nails Kinkaid. It had turned out all right in the end, but she now saw how much of it had been beginner's luck. She still shuddered to think what could have happened if there'd been wild teen-agers in the Kinkaid house or if the town law had been less willing to cooperate.

Lawyer Lockwood had wired her back during her layover in Grand Junction. Hughie could sign the statement Lockwood was sending to the coroner in Pueblo. None of them would see any reward money for at least a month, but Lockwood was obviously pleased and willing to wait for his fee. The O'Rourke Detective Agency's credit rating had gone up in Dodge.

The Colorado newspapers had reported the killing in the Mark Twain style favored by small town Western newspaper men. The Pueblo marshal's refusal to name the "private dick" who'd occasioned all the excitement had been blown out of proportion by the rewrite editors, and Chance had been described as the mysterious "Sundown Kid, well-known in Dodge and Texas and reputed to be a reformed border raider." She had no idea how they'd come up with that, but if a hide skinner could be Buffalo Bill, she supposed she could be the Sundown Kid.

The conductor came down the aisle, calling out, "Salt Lake City next stop, folks," and Chance glanced at the shabby carpetbag at her feet as the train passed some loading pens and began to slow down.

She reviewed the little she knew about Sailor

Flynn, the next man on her list. Discreet wires to other lawmen, public and private, had established that the wanted man wasn't hiding out with his hard-working sober Mormon relatives. Informants had spotted Flynn on the streets of Salt Lake City, and it made sense that he'd run for the home territory he was familiar with. But despite the fact there were other bounty hunters and the annoyed Salt Lake police looking for him, Flynn was still at large.

Had he left Salt Lake again? She knew he was familiar with the San Francisco waterfront, too. By now the murder of the family in Kansas had been widely reported, and the California law was covering the Frisco docks and asking questions about seamen looking for a berth on a clipper. Flynn would know this. He had enemies in the East who'd ridden for both sides in the war.

In the past weeks Chance had boned up on every book she could find about law enforcement. She knew most detectives agreed the best place for a wanted man to hide was a big city. Preferably a big city he'd never been to before. That was how a fugitive avoided unwanted chance meetings with old acquaintances who might remember him. On the other hand there were disadvantages to a city you didn't know your way around in. Men who lived in the twilight world of the criminal had to know where the no-questions hotels and boarding houses were. They had to know where a furtive stranger attracted little attention or where a curious police officer would wonder why you were in his neighborhood.

Salt Lake was big enough for a man to lose himself in the crowd, and it had enough transients to justify a few seamy neighborhoods. Sailor Flynn was not a sophisticate. He'd feel safer there than anywhere else.

The train pulled into the depot and Chance rose with her bag. Wyatt Earp had given her an address near the railroad yards, and when she asked for directions, she found it was within walking distance.

As she stepped out into the sunlight and trudged toward the boarding house she was looking for, Chance was glad she was dressed as a man. Wyatt had laughed when she'd told him her plan, but she saw he knew his way around under the wet rocks of the West. The neighborhood was awful. Salt Lake had the biggest opera house west of the Mississippi and was said to be a remarkably proper town, but the clean-living Mormons who lived and worked on the other side of Fourth West Street saw little need for civic improvement down along the tracks. She turned toward the late afternoon sun at First South and followed it across the railroad yards. The street paving ended. The unpainted frame buildings she found herself among smelled of stale cabbage and coal smoke. A fat Mexican girl lounged in a doorway, and as Chance passed, she called out, "Hey, a 'onde va, muchacho? Ju' like three ways for dollar?"

Chance ignored her and the whore called wearily, "Hey, make it two bits and I suck you, too."

Chance repressed a shudder and turned the corner. She passed a grubby little storefront saloon and a pool hall where two youths lounged with bored, hopeless expressions. Chance was tempted to swerve well clear as she had to pass. But she remembered she was supposed to be a man, and she knew any nervousness on her part would alert them as it does a stray cur in an alley. Neither commented as she passed. She was packing a gun and she was taller than either of them.

On the next block she found the boardinghouse

Wyatt Earp had told her about. She went up on the porch and knocked. After a time the door opened and a blowsy woman with gray-streaked brown hair and a rusty black dress opened the door a crack and said, "We don't want any."

Chance said, "I'm a friend of Wyatt Earp. He tells me you rent rooms on occasion."

The woman said, "He does, huh? Well, you go back to the police station and tell 'em it won't work, sonny."

"Wyatt told me about them closing you down as a disorderly house, Mrs. Owens. That's why I'm here. I need a place where I can come and go as need be without a lot of questions."

The woman didn't answer for a time. Then she asked, "Is Wyatt still hanging out with that Big Nose Kate?"

"You know she's Doc Holliday's girl, Mrs. Owens. Are you going to let me in or do we have to stand here all day asking foolish questions?"

The woman opened the door and said, "You understand I don't rent rooms no more. That damned outlaw they shot in my rooms said his name was Smith. How was *I* to know he'd robbed the Union Pacific?"

Chance stepped inside, trying not to wrinkle her nose at the smell of mildew and stale beer as she said, "Wyatt explained. You're not renting me a room. I'm a houseguest. Naturally I have to pay for groceries and such while I'm visiting with you."

"That's true. I figure I need about a dollar a day for groceries these days. Prices has gone up fierce."

Chance nodded and the woman led her up a flight of stairs to a dormer room. As Chance placed her bag on the bed and a silver dollar on the battered dresser, she said, "I won't be taking my meals with you. I, uh, wondered if you had an entrance I could use to come and go as I pleased."

The woman said, "I never lock the back door off the pantry. I don't spend much time back there neither. Go out to the alley and from there to the devil, for all I care. Wyatt likely told you I wasn't a curious lady. But I would like to know one thing and one thing only."

"What's that, Mrs. Owens?"

"Last I heard, Wyatt was working on the safe side of the law. Can I figure you don't mean to rob nobody important while you're hiding out here?"

Chance laughed and said, "I'm working for a private detective agency in Dodge. I'm not here to break any laws. Satisfied?"

The woman looked at least less tense and picked up the silver dollar as she said, "We'll say no more then. Wyatt's all right, but he sure has some funny friends. I was sore as hell the time he sent Doc and Kate to me. I knew Doc had to hide out 'til things cooled down after he knifed Ed Bailey that time. I even lied for them and said they was in Dodge when some of Bailey's friends was looking for Doc and Kate here in Salt Lake. But that damned pair sure made a mess of this house. Doc ruined a dozen sheets by coughing blood all over 'em, and that Big Nose Kate busted my favorite vase, throwing it at Doc one night."

"Wyatt said they're sort of wild."

"Wild? Hell, they're *crazy*! You don't aim to bring no *gals* up here, do you?"

Chance blinked in surprise. Then, remembering the role she'd assumed, she shrugged and said, "Not more than one at a time. I won't let 'em bust up the furniture."

"You men are all alike," the landlady sniffed. Then she shrugged and said, "Well, I'll leave you to whatever. Just leave the, ah, grocery money by the umbrella stand downstairs as you come and go and you'll find I ain't too nosy 'bout what's going on up here."

She left and Chance unpacked. She'd brought her feminine riding outfit from Dodge, and while it badly needed a pressing after riding so far crushed in the carpet bag, she knew most of the wrinkles would repair themselves after the whipcord had hung a while. She smoothed the outfit out and hung it in the one small closet. She put her modest makeup kit on the dresser. Then she tossed the hat on the bed to examine herself in the mirror.

Her face was unblemished now. She was far too tan for a well-brought-up young lady, but even with her hair pinned up, she looked more like a girl without that big battered sombrero. She took out the papers she had on Sailor Flynn and sat on the bed to make sure she hadn't forgotten anything. Then she folded them, put them away, and put her hat back on to leave.

Now that she had a base of operations, her next move was back across the tracks to police headquarters.

Like any town of large size Salt Lake had a regular municipal police force rather than a handful of casual semiskilled deputies. Wyatt Earp had told her how Mrs. Owens had lost her rooming house permit by forgetting the niceties of big town law. Salt Lake City was further west than Dodge or Abilene, but a shoot-out like she'd had in Pueblo wouldn't be handled as casually.

She reached the police station near the Temple grounds just before closing time. She'd planned it that way. She presented her credentials to a desk sergeant, who relayed her to the city marshal's office upstairs. Unlike the marshals in smaller towns the city marshals in a real city were only a branch of the police department rather than the whole show. The Salt Lake marshal's job was that of serving and enforcing writs and judgements. Uniformed policemen policed the streets and kept the peace.

Chance introduced herself again and handed the marshal in charge the warrants for Sailor Flynn's arrest. The Utah lawman wore a bored expression as well as a business suit. He nodded and said, "We know about Flynn. We have some beat cops looking for him, too. The last bounty hunter who came in here offered to split with us."

Chance nodded and said, "My agency mentioned something along the lines of ten percent."

The Salt Lake marshal shot a weary glance at his office clock and said, "Bite your tongue, sonny. You're not talking to a hick in a one-horse town. We're not allowed to accept personal rewards. They expect us to enforce the law on the salary they pay us."

"I know you have a clean department here, sir."

"Then what are you pestering me for? My woman's expecting me, and she puts the meat and potatoes on the table at six o'clock sharp."

Chance said, "I know you and your men are too busy to spend all your time looking for one man wanted in other parts. I've come to concentrate on Sailor Flynn's warrant."

"I know that, damn it. What do you want from me, my blessings?"

"Yessir. I know better than to make a move in your town before I cleared it with you."

The marshal looked pleased, as she'd hoped he

might be. He nodded and said, "Well, I can see you're a polite young gent and a cut above your average bounty hunter. You sure you're bonded and know what you're doing?"

"Yessir, I'll be happy to wait for you to wire inquiries to Dodge before I make any further moves on your beat."

"You know where Sailor Flynn is hiding? Our boys have looked all over for him without much luck."

Chance didn't want any local police around when she met up with one of the men who'd murdered her father. She shook her head and said, "I just got here, sir. It'll probably take me some asking about."

The marshal looked at the clock again and got up, saying, "Hell, I've got to get on home. You come downstairs with me and I'll clear you with the duty officer and give you a copy of the writ we have on Flynn. I doubt like hell you'll find him, for I'm sure he's left town. But you're a nice young gent, and I wouldn't want to see you in trouble if you got lucky."

Salt Lake City was like a houseproud young housewife with a bit more dust than she could cope with. So she swept her unavoidable filth under the rug, or at least down around the railyards where visitors might not notice it.

The Mormon majority didn't drink liquor or even drinks as strong as tea or coffee. Their religion forbade them to smoke. But Salt Lake was an important railroad center and the hub of growing trade. Railroaders and businessmen from other parts either lived there or passed through in large numbers, and the Mormon Elders were reasonable, pragmatic men. So while you found no saloons and few tobacco shops on Main Street and unescorted women seemed unheard of anywhere, they were there. Vice merely kept to the shadows, like roaches, rats, and other unavoidable pests. There were no streetlamps in the trackside slums set aside for "Gentile Trade." The saloons had drapes over their windows, and the piano music wasn't loud enough to spill out on the street. City Hall denied there were any whores in town. Looking for them on the dark quiet streets added a certain piquant adventure for men used to the wide open Barbary Coast or the roaring honky-tonk of Denver's Larimer Street.

Chance moved along the cinder walk in her riding skirts with a new veil covering her woman's hat and half her face. She carried her gun in a velvet muff and was glad she had it more than once, although the men who accosted her with jovial lewd remarks from time to time seemed content to simply curse her when she said no.

She found the house number she was looking for. It looked deserted from outside. Chance went around to the side entrance and knocked the way she'd been told to. A fat blonde wearing nothing but a red silk chemise and high-button shoes opened the door, frowned, and asked, "What do you want, sister? The cribs are full and we ain't taking on no new girls."

Chance said, "I'm here to see Madame Flora. I'm a friend of Madame Moustache in Dodge."

"Shit, I know where Madame Moustache's is. But

Madame Flora won't hire you. Business is awful right now."

Chance said, "You're repeating yourself. Do you want to announce me to Madame Flora or do I just have to announce myself?"

"You talk tough, honey. You must not know who I am. They call me Blue Tooth Mary and I can whip most *men*."

"I see you have a good twenty pounds on me. Don't you think we ought to ask Madame Flora if she wants to see me before we fight?"

The big blonde nodded grudgingly and said, "Come in and let me shut the door. If Madame Flora gives me permission, I might just snatch you bald-headed before I throw you out."

Chance didn't answer. She stood in the gloomy, red-papered hallway while the blonde went to announce her. Another girl in a pink slip came back after a time to say, "Walk this way. Madame Flora says she'll hear your tale, honey."

Chance doubted she could walk that way, but she followed. The smaller whore led her to a cubbyhole office where a motherly looking woman in a purple dress, with hair to match, was seated at a rolltop desk. She waved Chance to a seat on a leather sofa and said, "Be with you in a minute, dearie. These bills are driving me crazy. Look at this one from the water-works. We don't *have* running water on this block and the fucking saints say they've assessed me for water mains."

Chance sat down and said, "Maybe they mean to put water mains in some day."

"Hell, they'll pave the streets and put in lighting *some* day. But *we* won't live to see it! They'll pipe lemonade to every fucking Mormon house in town before they'll see fit to give us a streetlamp on this side of the tracks."

Chance saw her chance to be helpful and said, "I've a hundred dollars here. Will that help?"

Madame Flora looked astonished and said, "You just made a friend for life. We haven't taken in that much all week. You say you've worked for Madame Moustache? Well, you're pretty as hell, but it's only fair to warn you right off that things are slow right now. This damned depression we've been having since the railroad scandals has put most of our regulars out of work. The roundup's starting and the trail herds will be coming in soon, but you may as well know the worse. These goddam Utah cowhands only want to screw. Hardly any of 'em drink, and I ask you, how's a house to make money with sober customers night after night?"

Chance counted out five gold pieces and leaned forward to place them on a corner of the desk. Madame Flora made them disappear and said, "You just saved my life. But what in thunder are you after? It can't be a *job*!"

Chance said, "I'm in a slightly different line, Ma'am. I'm an agent for O'Rourke's in Dodge."

"Fingering for a bounty hunter, are you? Well, *I've* had to do some things my mamma said was wrong in my time. Surely you ain't out to pester one of my whores about some bills she may have run up in the past? I know some girls don't have much sense when it comes to buying pretty things, but if you're thinking of taking it out of their wages, judgement or no . . ."

"We're looking for a man. They call him Sailor Flynn. He's Mormon born, but lives Gentile."

The madam went wooden Indian and asked,

"What makes you think you'll find him here along Parlor-House Row, dearie?"

"The *men* who've been looking for him have checked out the few saloons and pool halls in this part of town."

Madame Flora smiled thinly and said, "I can see why they use you. But I have standards to uphold. You must know it's not professional for a lady in my line to give out information on her possible clientele."

Chance said, "Flynn's wanted a lot of places on a lot of charges, including murder, rape, and infanticide."

"He do sound ugly, but I still got ethics. My mother was a whore before me and she raised me to the code. It ain't considered proper to turn a paying customer over to the law."

Chance said, "We're not the law. We're bounty hunters. Your name need never come into it and there's almost five thousand on Sailor Flynn's head. Ten percent of it's yours if you help us find him."

Madame Flora sighed and said, "Hell, he ain't *that* good a customer. As a matter of fact he only drops by once a week."

"Saturday night?"

"How did you know *that*, dearie?"

"He's on the dodge. The police stop gents on quiet streets at night. Saturday night, with the ranchhands in town, a man walking quiet and minding his own business isn't likely to draw much attention."

Madame Flora chuckled and said, "You do know your trade, dearie. I won't set him up, and you'll have to promise your gunslicks won't do it on this block. Do we have a deal?"

Chance nodded and said, "I'll tell . . . my partner that you and yours are to be left out of it. What time does he generally show up?"

The whore shrugged and said, "Men don't screw by a timetable. The Sailor must be holed up somewhere playing with hisself. He pops in here for a quick lay just after sundown. I reckon he heads for a cardhouse after, like the song says. There's a floating monte game in the saloons along the tracks. I think it's in the Pronghorn this weekend."

"I know the place. I passed it on my way here tonight."

"There you go then. He'll come for a roll in the feathers with Broad Ass Billie early in the evening. She's his favorite. I suspicion he tips her extra up in the crib, but I say live and let live. I'll see she gives him extra French lessons, and he'll leave here barely able to walk. If your gunslicks wait for him down by the Pronghorn, he should be a snap to handle."

Chance started to object. Then she nodded and got to her feet as she said, "We'll forget this conversation in our official report. You'll hear from us after if all goes well. If you warn Sailor Flynn you won't. Remember we offered to cut you in on the bounty."

As she started to leave, Madame Flora said, "Honey, if Broad Ass Billie don't play her part just exactly like I tell her to, she'll leave here sort of bruised."

Chance left the whorehouse and made her way back to the no-questions boardinghouse. She took her time sneaking in. Then she stripped, washed off her heavy makeup, and turned in. It was Thursday night. She had two whole days to kill. Searching for Sailor Flynn in the rabbit's warren all around would not only be futile, it might tip him off if someone she questioned had gone to school with the lapsed local boy.

But there were lots of interesting sights to see in Salt Lake City. She might even go swimming and find out if it was true what they said about not being able to drown in the Great Salt Lake.

It had seemed more like two weeks than two days, but Saturday finally got there. Late that afternoon Chance went downstairs with her carpetbag to settle up with Mrs. Owens. The landlady had been drinking and was looking oddly peeved. As Chance, wearing her male attire, paid her off, the blowsy woman said, "You owe me for the *gal*, sonny. Our deal was for a single room."

Chance stared at her thoughtfully. Mrs. Owens smiled knowingly and said, "That's what I said. You two thought you was pulling something over me, didn't you? I spied her creeping in and out at all hours like a thief in the night. You reckon I was birthed yesterday?"

Chance sighed and counted out the extra silver as the woman looked relieved and in a more mollified tone said, "You should have told me. You knowed I wasn't a busybody. Who was she, another man's gal?"

Chance smiled crookedly and said, "As a matter of fact she *is* spoken for, but she isn't happy with her man."

"I figured she was too sneaky for a whore on call. She looked sort of ladylike, considering. She likely hopes you'll take her with you back to Dodge, too. Women are such fools when they meet young studs like you."

Chance was tempted to enjoy her private joke further by assuring the landlady she had every intention of going back to Dodge with the girl she'd spotted on the backstairs, but her disguise was a serious matter. So she simply shrugged the question off.

Leaving the hideout, Chance trudged back to the main part of town and checked her bag at the depot. She asked the ticket agent for some timetables and went to the beanery next door, where she ate a light supper and studied the railroad schedule. By the time she'd finished it was sundown. Chance walked in the gloaming to nearby Pioneer Park and sat on a bench as the evening grew cooler and the streets got more crowded. She'd never seen the opera by Verdi at the nearby opera house and she had time to catch the first act. But she was dressed sort of rough and she didn't want to cut things too thin.

By nine she was feeling tense and her hands felt numb. She got up and window-shopped along Main Street. If anyone wondered what a young cowhand was looking at in the dress shops, they probably thought he was aiming to buy a notion for his best gal.

At nine thirty she walked back to the depot and found it crowded, as she'd expected. She kept her hat brim low and didn't stare about as she got her bag from the checkroom and strolled out to the platform. The UP Night Flier was loading on time for it's scheduled run to Cheyenne. It would stop in Ogden just up the line before it started up the long grade to

South Pass. Chance climbed aboard, placed her bag on a plush coach seat, and walked to the rear car with her ticket in her hatband. She went out on the rear observation platform and leaned against the bulkhead. Then a million years went by and at last the train was moving.

The Night Flier had cleared the yards north of town by the time the door opened and the conductor stuck his head out. Chance took the ticket from her hatband and said, "I'm not stealing a ride. I just don't feel like sitting yet."

The railroader punched her ticket and said, "Suit yourself, cowboy." As he started to leave, Chance took out her wallet and showed him her badge before she handed him a silver dollar and said, "The Union Pacific is offering a bounty on a man aboard this train. Do you follow my drift?"

"Jesus, you can't have a shoot-out in the coaches!"

"I don't aim to. I figure he'll come back here if he's tense as me. Are you on my side?"

"Not if you mean with a gun. If you're talking about sealing off this end of the car, we might work something out."

Chance nodded and said, "You're in for ten percent. Are you through punching tickets?"

"Sure, what's our play, pard?"

"I'll tell you if I've guessed right after. Take a seat just up front and make sure nobody runs back here if and when you hear the shots. Don't stop anybody from coming back here alone. If you can keep spooning couples from coming back to see the moonlight . . ."

"I follow your meaning, son. I've worked with Pinkertons before. You did say ten percent, right?"

"Yes. It's ten to one the folks I dealt in back there

in Salt Lake City have played me false, so they don't get anything. If I'm wrong, I'll be getting off in Ogden, and it promises to be a tedious wait for another Saturday night with one early train out."

The conductor left and Chance waited, watching the railroad ties recede in the darkness. She was tempted to stand where she had a view up the aisle of the car, but it wasn't dark enough yet and she knew you could see out as well as in through the glass. There were innocent travelers seated the length of the train. Sailor Flynn wouldn't worry as much about that if he went for his gun early.

Chance stiffened as the door grated open again. A man wearing a straw boater stepped out on the platform, smoking a cigar, and for a moment she cursed inwardly, taking him for a damned traveling drummer. Then the stranger sensed her presence and turned warily to say, "Howdy."

Half of his face was to the light from the door. The last time she'd seen those features he'd been raping her by the red glow of her father's burning wagon!

Chance said, "Howdy yourself, Sailor Flynn," and they both went for their guns.

Sailor Flynn was good and on the prod. He fired into the steel deck between them as Chance jackknifed him over his belt buckle with her first round and sent the next two through the space he'd just been standing in. The outlaw fell at her feet, doubled up and moaning as he clutched his guts with one hand and tried to grope for the gun he'd dropped with the other. Chance kicked the gun off the platform as she thumbed her .44 to finish him. Then she lowered the hammer, started to reload, and said, "Just take your time and die slower than my father did, you bastard."

She went to the door and slid it open, gun hand at her side. The people inside were staring pale-faced at her the length of the car. The conductor rose and called out, "It's all right, folks. He's the law."

Nobody else got up as the conductor came down the aisle to join her in the doorway. He whistled softly as he saw what she had done, and she said, "I can take him off at Ogden if I have to. My tale would go down better with Wyoming if we can keep him right where he is until we get to Cheyenne."

"I told you I've been down this road afore, son. I'll wire ahead from Ogden and we'll wrap him in a tarp for now with some ice from the dining car. The UP dicks will pave the way for you up the line if it's true what you say about our company having it in for him. Who is he, a train robber?"

"Among other things. His name is Sailor Flynn. They'll know he used to ride with Cole Younger."

"Oh, you're right. UP will have a brass band waiting for us in Cheyenne. But ain't he still *alive*? I just saw him twitch his boots."

"He's gutshot. It's my hope he won't die in Utah."

"Right. Saves having to tell your tale to any coroner on either side of the state line if the two of us disremember just where it was he breathed his last."

Sailor Flynn moaned and said, "I need a doc, damn it! I'm hurt awful."

The conductor said to Chance, "We won't be across the line until mighty late tonight, son."

She said, "I know. Just lock the door when you leave and I'll make sure he doesn't make a fuss at the next stop. I'll let you know when I need that ice."

The conductor grimaced and said, "Jesus, you sure

play rough. But that's betwixt the two of you, I reckon."

He stepped back inside and locked the door.

Chance hunkered down on her boot heels near the dying outlaw's head and said pleasantly, "We'll be in Ogden soon. Do you think you can be a good boy or do I have to pistol-whip you unconscious?"

"Please don't hurt me no more, kid. You got me dead to rights and I suspicion I'm done for. It's starting to hurt mighty bad."

"I hope so. It'll probably hurt worse when the shock wears off."

"Damn it, you sure are *mean*! What in tarnation makes you gloat so, kid? I know there's paper out on me, but I don't see why you have to act so *personal* about this! I never done you wrong, you damned old bounty hunter."

"Speaking of bounties, I take it Broad Ass Billie told you we were fixing to take you near the Pronghorn, right?"

"Sort of. Old Billie and me had this understanding. You got no call to hurt her, though. Any gal worth knowing would tell her sweetie he was fixing to be took."

"I know. I was *counting* on it. You're dumb, Flynn. I never would have found you if you'd just ducked out the back and crawled back under your wet rock. I figured you'd make a run for it, and this is the first train out before midnight."

Flynn groaned and said, "You must be the Sundown Kid. I heard what you done in Pueblo. How come you're after *us* so serious? There's lots of old boys with more money on their heads."

Chance didn't answer. She'd planned this confrontation for days, but now that it had arrived, she didn't feel like gloating as much as she'd thought she might. Alone the night before she'd fantasized a scene in which she opened her shirt before his dying gaze to let him see he'd been gunned by a woman he'd wronged. But, kneeling over Flynn, she just wanted him to be quiet. She knew he deserved a long, lingering death, but in the end, she knew it would never bring Dad back whether Flynn died in pain or comfort.

The train rolled on through the night, its wheels clicking under them as the badly wounded outlaw licked his lips and muttered, "Jesus, I sure do feel like a drink. You don't have any red-eye on you, do you, kid?"

Chance said, "No," and raised the gun to train it on his temple. He blanched and said, "Hey, I ain't in *that* much pain! Can't we just talk for a spell?"

Chance said, "There's nothing to talk about. Jack Dawson's on his way to a hanging. You and Nails Kinkaid are dead. That leaves four of you for me to track down. I don't suppose you feel like telling me where I could catch up with any of the others, eh?"

"Not hardly. But what in thunder is the *charge* agin' the seven of us, kid? I'll allow me and the boys may have messed up a bit here and there in the past. But the seven of us never pulled no robberies you'd have the same warrants on."

Chance said, "You're wrong. The seven of you rode together the night you murdered Colonel McGraw and raped his daughter."

"Go on, *them* two never pressed no charges agin' anyone. Even if I was to admit being there, which I ain't, I heard there were no witnesses."

"You're wrong again, Sailor. You left a witness. It was me."

The dying man tried to focus on her features as he grimaced and protested, "You're funning me, Kid. Who are you, the colonel's son?"

"No. I'm his daughter. The one you had so much fun with after you shot him down like a dog."

Flynn's eyes widened as he protested, "Go on, you ain't no *gal*! Even if you was, you couldn't be *that* one. Goldy Slade left her dead with a bullet in her brain. You're making this up to trick me into confessing things I don't aim to."

Chance reached for the buttons of her shirt. Then she shrugged and said, "Suit yourself. It's suddenly not very important what you think or don't think, Mr. Flynn."

He was barely paying attention. He groaned and said, "Listen, Kid. I'm really hurt bad. I don't reckon I'm likely to last to the next stop, and it's sort of sissy to die screaming."

"You'll get used to it. I did."

Four days later Chance was back in Dodge. Hughie ınd Annie O'Rourke were overjoyed to see her and ıad begun to worry. Lawyer Lockwood said the noney on Nails Kinkaid was on its way. She still had ›ver half her original working capital even though ›rices in the West were outrageous. The grocery bill lone amounted to nearly ten dollars a week.

Wyatt Earp came calling that evening after work.

He found Chance on the porch in her dress. He seemed to find this amusing.

As Chance sat beside him on the steps, Wyatt said, "The papers are filled with the Sundown Kid and that shoot-out on the UP Flier. I don't reckon you met up with him in your travels, huh?"

"I see you've heard from Mrs. Owens, Wyatt. Does anyone else know?"

"I ain't given to idle gossip, honey. But I'm starting to worry some about this game you're playing. The Sundown Kid is starting to get a *rep*! Me and Luke Short told you how dangerous that can be. You know Ed Masterson?"

"He's another marshal here in Dodge, right?"

"Yep. He's got a baby brother, name of Bat. That's what he tells folks to call him leastways. His real name's sort of sissy. Anyway, young Bat Masterson has been talking big in the saloons and asked his big brother to get him a job on the force here. He keeps hinting he's gunned a few gents, and some folks take him serious. Ed's worried as hell about him getting shot afore he's old enough to shave regular."

"What do Bat Masterson's troubles have to do with me, Wyatt?"

"Just trying to show you how trouble *starts*. Young Bat ain't never shot nobody and likely never will. But any of the wild bunch looking for their own rep might see him as an easy way to look good. The Sundown Kid's made some dead men's kin mighty thoughtful, and there's no telling who might come looking for him. He's knowed to frequent Dodge. A young cowhand was asking for him down to the Alhambra saloon last night."

"Anybody I might be looking for?"

"No. Just a crazy kid. I told him I knowed the Sun

down Kid and that the kid is twice as fast as the papers let on. I might have scared him. I might not have. I'd sure appreciate it if you'd stay in them skirts until he leaves town, honey."

Chance smiled and said, "I don't think I'll need my disguise here in Dodge. Hughie is a born snoop and he looks harmless. He tells me he's been haunting Saloon Row in my absence and that none of the gang seem to be in town."

Earp nodded and said, "I saw Hughie in the Dodge House the other night. I was wondering why he pretended not to know me. But you're right. *I've* asked some too. Hawkins, Slade, and Dodd are long gone. Have you heard anything from them bounty hunters you come to town with?"

She shook her head unhappily and said, "Not a word. I thought at least Tony Despres would wire when he joined Brian in Missouri."

Earp put a casual hand around her waist and said, "Well, I could have told you that you'd never hear from them. They aim to cut you out of any claim to the reward on Black Jack Dawson."

She removed his hand gently but firmly and said, "I've yet to meet Doc Holliday, Wyatt."

Earp said, "I know. I got Kate to take him up to Leadville for his health."

"Is there a sanitarium in Leadville?" She frowned.

Earp shook his head and said, "No. There ain't many *Texans* up there neither. I don't know what it is about Doc and Texans, but they purely rub each other the wrong way. The roundup's almost over and the herds will be coming in to the railyards. I generally like to keep Doc and the Thompson brothers separated. Kate understands. She says she'll keep him there until the frost is on the pumpkins and the town quiets down."

Chance stiffened alertly and asked, "Didn't you say Stubby Hawkins had joined up with Ben and Billy Thompson?"

"Yep, I did. But he won't be riding back to Dodge with 'em so soon. The county coroner has a warrant out on Hawkins for what they done to them nesters just over the horizon."

"He may be feeling brave. We know he's a fool. I've heard everyone in Dodge sort of looks the other way when the Thompson brothers and their ilk ride up from the Panhandle."

Earp looked uncomfortable and said, "That story about me hazing old Ben is part true. The one about me backing down from John Wesley Hardin is a fla lie. Me and the wild bunch has an understanding."

"I know. The point is that you don't enforce th gun regulations when the trailherders ride in an that you don't arrest them unless they molest some body important and popular in Dodge."

"Well, we might look the other way at a little or nery stuff south of the Front Street deadline. Nobod will ride this fur north shooting out the streetlights."

"How many men ride with the Thompson gang Wyatt?"

"No more than fifty, and they ain't a gang. They'r honest trailherders, and Mayor Hoover says they hav a right to let off a little steam when they get paid o for a long hard dusty chore."

"In other words none of you five deputies in tow are likely to be too visible along Front Street whe the herds come to town."

Earp looked defensive and said, "Shux, Luke Sho Kelly at the Alhambra, and other businessmen *li* things that way, honey. They got their own bouncers and know how to collect on busted mirrors. You gotta understand that Dodge *needs* the business we get from the cowhands."

"Heaven forfend that the boys don't feel *welcome*! Do fifty hands have that much to spend?"

"Shux, we ain't keeping Front Street open for just the Thompson brothers. There'll be Shanghai Pierce and the Clements brothers. Clay Allison and King Fisher will be shipping some cows, but, Lord willing, they might not both come personal. It's been said that Clay Allison has bragged he's meaner than King Fisher, which don't seem possible. So far, knock wood, I've never been present when both of them was in the same town on a Saturday night."

"Do you think you could stop them if they decided to settle the argument on your beat, Wyatt?"

Earp laughed and said, "Not hardly. They don't pay the five of us enough to *try*! But don't worry, if they meet up, it'll be down along Front Street, and no matter how it turns out, it'll be a net gain for the ane folks in these parts."

She nodded thoughtfully before she said, "Don't ou see that Stubby Hawkins may feel perfectly safe mong such company? How are you to serve that warant for his arrest if none of you mean to be anyvhere near those riders while they're in town?"

He looked uncomfortable again and said, "You've o call to comment on the sand in my craw like that, oney. You never had to talk to John Wesley Hardin hen he was drunk and on the prod. I did, and we're oth still alive. I faced him in Wichita one time, and was like staring into the open gates of hell. ver'body told me the smart thing to do would be to ave town when Hardin sent word he wanted to see me. But I went. He was sore at me for closing down his favorite saloon and he'd said some awful things about my mother."

"I see. You called his bluff, right?"

"Wrong. John don't bluff worth mention. I asked him could we have a drink and talk some afore we made any horrible mistakes, and like I figured, old John never could turn down a drink. I explained how I'd closed down Rowdy Kate and Rowdy Joe for serving watered drinks and rolling some of their customers in the back room. Hardin said that sounded reasonable, but that he could still beat me to the draw. I told him he was likely right and bought him another drink. By the time I had him too drunk to remember what he'd wanted to speak to me about, I could hardly stand my ownself."

Chance laughed and said, "I'll bet Ned Buntline never printed *that* story! Didn't it occur to you that you had a chance to finish him off once and for all as you drank him under the table?"

Earp nodded and said, "It crossed my mind, but I wasn't *that* drunk. Have you any idea what it would be like to be knowed as the man who shot John Wesley Hardin? Hell, I'd be dead right now instead of telling you about it."

"You've explained the danger of fame. What keeps someone from going after Hardin, himself?"

"Oh, they *do* all the time. That's why John ain't been hanged for murder yet. He keeps shooting folk in self-defense ever'where he goes. One day they'll get him. He knows it, too. That likely accounts for his drinking."

Chance repressed a shudder as she said, "Brrr, let's get back to Stubby Hawkins. Would you say the odds on him riding in with the Thompsons were fifty-fifty?"

"Just about ever'thing's fifty-fifty unless you let Doc Holliday shuffle the deck. But I want you to promise me you won't show your pretty self down near the tracks whilst the herds are in town."

Chance started to argue. Then she nodded and said, "I promise to keep my skirts north of Front Street until they've left, Wyatt."

He wasn't that dumb. He said, "I don't want to see the Sundown Kid south of the deadline neither. If I do, it'll be my duty as a lawman and a friend to lock the young rascal up for his own good."

Later as Chance was having tea with Annie, Hughie came in with Lawyer Lockwood. The men joined them at the table and Lockwood said, "You created some confusion up in Cheyenne, Miss McGraw. There seems to be a mistake about your gender on the coroner's report they sent me."

Chance said, "I didn't make any false statements about my shoot-out with Sailor Flynn. They never asked me if I was male or female, so I never offered an opinion either way."

"I assumed as much. Fortunately we're claiming the bounties on Flynn in the name of the corporation. So I suppose it's all right. I take it you're determined to continue this nonsense about being the Sundown Kid?"

"I more or less have to. The first time I tried to arrest Stubby Hawkins in skirts he just laughed at me."

Lockwood put sugar in his tea and said, "So you told me. You'd attract even more attention if it got out now that two dangerous gunslicks had been shot by a girl. But I don't like it. I think we'd better not put in a claim for either here in Kansas."

"Why not? The Ford County DA posted rewards on them for killing those settlers, didn't they?"

Lockwood looked lofty and said, "Very modest rewards with no comment as to dead or alive. You have to remember none of the gang were ever *convicted* of anything in Kansas. The posters were put out for their capture and conviction."

"Oh. It would be sort of hard to try a dead man, wouldn't it?"

"Exactly. Rewards have been collected on a bandit killed in hot pursuit before a trial. But, frankly, it's a barrel of eels I'd just as soon not open. You'd have to appear before the judge in proper attire for one thing. As your attorney of record, I'd be most uncomfortable trying to explain some of the details and, don't forget, the county would *want* to wiggle out of paying us by digging for improper procedures. It's, uh, *against the law* to wear the attire of the opposite sex in most states and territories."

"Really? I didn't know that!"

"I assumed as much. I gather the laws against transvestism are designed to protect women's privacy in privies, female boarding houses, and such. Most of the arrests I know of have been of men dressed as women."

"Most, Mister Lockwood?"

"Well, they did fine a young lady in Boston for giving a lecture on women's suffrage while wearing pants. I think her name was Miss Bloomer. She has this odd notion that women would be more free wearing these baggy pants she's designed."

He tasted his tea and, having the sweet tooth of most drinking men when they were sober, put in two more teaspoons, oblivious to the horror in Annie's eyes.

Chance said, "Well, let's not bother with trying to collect here in Ford County. The out-of-state rewards on the two I've caught so far have put our books in the black."

Hughie O'Rourke brightened and said, "Begorra, that's the truth. I've been meaning to talk to you about a sideline to our grand firm, Chance. I was waiting 'til we had a lawyer present, for the laws of this land are confusing."

Chance nodded questioningly and the tinker said, "I've made some repairs of this house as you know. The workmanship out here is a mortal sin. Sure, I could slap together a house better than this one for less than five hundred dollars, even doing it right."

"I know it's a balloon-frame shack, Hughie. But we're not paying enough rent to justify building one of our own."

"Och, I wasn't thinking of moving. I was planning to *expand!* This town is bursting at the seams with more people arriving every day. What if I was to put up other housing to rent or sell?"

Chance glanced at Lockwood. The lawyer nodded and said, "A real estate license added to your corporate papers wouldn't cost much, and unimproved land is still cheap at this end of town. Some steady rents coming in would certainly leave you in safer financial shape. You can hardly expect to catch an outlaw every time the bills are due."

Chance nodded and said, "It sounds good. But do you think it's wise to sink much capital into Dodge? These boomtowns have a way of dying on the vine."

Lockwood shook his head and said, "The open range will move west in time, as it did for Abilene and Wichita. But the towns along the railroad tend to survive and grow as the country gets more settled.

I'd be more worried if you were investing in cattle. Beef goes up and down in price. But land just keeps going up. Even with this depression lots in Dodge cost more now than they did two years ago."

Chance smiled at Hughie and said, "I see I'm outvoted."

The tinker said, "Glory be to God. I've been craving something to do with me hands since we've settled down like useless village folk. Sure, I'll show these Yanks how a man builds a house with seasoned lumber and a roof that don't leak!"

Lockwood said, "I know something about a certain tract of land that the owner doesn't. Having friends on the county board gives me advance information on where the future roads will be built. I, uh, assume you all know about, uh, finders' fees?"

"You'll be cut in," said Chance, slightly annoyed. Lockwood had proven himself a lawyer with useful contacts, but his constant need of drinking money reminded her too much of Duncan. Maybe it was just as well that Duncan had been completely useless. Had he had the little ambition of this rustic lawyer, she'd probably still be trying to make a go of it with Duncan. The thought brightened her day and she smiled at Lockwood.

The lawyer finished his sickly sweet tea and rose, saying, "Well, if you folks will excuse me, I have to get back to my office and prepare some more writs. It promises to be a busy weekend."

Chance got up to walk out to the gate with him. She asked idly, "You say you have writs to serve this weekend?" and he said, "Habeas corpus. Saves time to have them signed by the judge in advance. The boys don't like to sit in jail once they sober a mite."

"What boys? What are you talking about?"

"Oh, didn't you know? The herds are coming. You've never been in Dodge when the herds came in. So take some free advice. Lock your doors, board your windows, and stay this side of Front Street until it's safe to walk the streets again."

The first cows came down from the north, summer-fat on the grama and buffalo grass of the Arkansas Divide. The hands who rode in with them were laconic North Plains riders, sitting double-rig saddles and roping tie-down. Most of them wore stovepipe boots and telescoped hats. They hadn't ridden far and many just wanted to sell their stock or be paid off pronto. They opined they weren't looking for trouble from the Texas hands this year. But they refused to check their guns when gently asked, and it wasn't considered prudent to press the matter further.

The herds arriving from the south were bigger and the cows more rangy. It took a tough scrub critter to make it from the dusty Texas Panhandle, and it took tough trailhands to get them through the Kiowa and Comanche unscathed. The southern plains Indians had been nominally tamed by the colored troopers of the Tenth Cav a couple of years back. But many a young brave couldn't read the treaties and a soft-looking white man still tempted roving bands of Indian youths. The Texas hands made it a practice not to look soft. They wore ten-gallon hats and batwing chaps with silver conchos. Their spurs jangled and they cracked their drover's whips more than they really needed to at the tired calico cows as they pushed them up the trail to Dodge. Most Texas hands roped dally-style from a center-fire saddle as they'd learned from the Mexican vaqueros between border brawls. They tended to jeer loudly at lesser men who roped tie-down and drank sissy stuff like beer. Had a psychiatrist been there to give an opinion, he might have said they were suffering from feelings of inferiority. They'd have shot him for suggesting they weren't the cream of the Anglo-Saxon breed, but they did tend to overcompensate for having ridden on the losing side in the recent war, and they had other problems Ned Buntline and the other recorders of the era missed.

Texas had joined first the Union, then the Confederacy, with considerable noise on both occasions. Most Texans were still of the opinion they'd have won the war if lesser breeds like Virginians and such hadn't been such sissies. Added to the bitterness of defeat many Texans with Celtic surnames were all too aware of the newspaper want ads printed in places like Boston that read, "No Irish need apply."

They were uncomfortable in the Union state of Kansas and sure they were being cheated on the price of their cows, overcharged by the local merchants, and dismissed as losers. Hence, like a boy passing a graveyard late at night, Texans of the time tended to be noisy.

This might not have presented as much of a problem had they just been swaggering bullyboys. Unfortunately for those who took unfriendly notice of their manners the Texans were almost as tough as they kept saying they were. Most of them had been raising hell since before they'd known why boys and girls were different, and a Texan who couldn't back his brag with fists, bowie, or shooting iron soon found himself unable to get a job with any outfit west of the Trinidad.

The Clements outfit rode in first, followed by the South Jingle Bob and a thousand head from the Spanish Hat. They were businessmen as well as Texans, so the first order of the day was getting the stock penned, and soon the yards along the railroad were filled with bawling evil-smelling beef on the hoof. A fine film of dried and powdered dung began to settle on the windowsills and furniture of annoyed housewives. Nobody else complained. The smell of cowshit went with money in the bank.

Along the dusty fence lines sharp-eyed cattle buyers mingled with suspicious cattlemen, and an outsider would have expected sudden violence as they cursed each other, red-faced and covered with dust in the hot Kansas sun. But it was generally conceded to be bad business to shoot a man from Swift or Armour just because he called your cow a crippled, scrawny goat, nd the buyers were used to being called "skinflint Yankee sons of bitches" in the line of duty. They knew that they and the whores in town were safe no matter how a Texan yelled at them. Lesser mortals were on their own as the sun sank low and the first aid-off hands moseyed over to Front Street to look or action after long boring weeks on the trail.

Chance waited until well after dark before she rapped on her gun. Hughie O'Rourke met her at e back door, coming in from the outhouse. He oked her over and said, "Jasus, I thought Wyatt arp told you not to dress up like that any more, rl!"

Chance stood there in her male attire and said, "It

would be far more dangerous for me down by the tracks in my skirts. Not only would I have to beat off amorous cowboys, but Stubby Hawkins has had time to think about his close call. He'll be watching for my feminine riding outfit, and he's the kind of man who shoots people in the back."

"Och, do you know for a fact he's back in town then?"

"No. But I know the Thompson brothers are. I tipped our newsboy to keep his eyes peeled, and he was just out front. Ben and Billy rode in just before sundown. They've penned their herd, awaiting later bidding. It seems they don't like the price of beef right now. They must have heard that rumor about the price going up next week."

"Ay, they told me down at Kelly's that the herds are smaller this year because of dry weather. But that's neither here nor there, gorl. You can't go down there among them ruffians on Front Street! Faith, I heard even the *marshal* had pulled in his horns! There's not a lawmen south of the deadline!"

"I know. It makes things simpler if I don't have to worry about that silly transvestite law. Wouldn't you say I could pass for a teen-aged cowboy in this rig?"

"Jasus, you're mad! At least do something about that hat. They'll take you for a Colorado rider with the top flattened down like that."

Chance nodded and took the hat from her pinned up hair as she said, "Thanks, Hughie. That's a point I overlooked."

As she worked the crown of her black sombrero into a Texas crease, O'Rourke said, "I've an even *bet-ter* point for you, me gorl. Why don't you stay here and let me nose about down there before you risk life and limb on a woild goose chase?"

"Do you know Stubby Hawkins on sight, Hughie?"

"Och, you know them rascals rode off before Annie and me found you. But you've described him often enough, and I could ask a few questions and . . ."

"Annie would never forgive me. You'd be in more danger asking foolish questions than I'll be just looking."

"Jasus, I wish you wuz *smaller,* child! The thrubble with adopting children bigger than yourself is that you can't turn them over your knee when they won't listen to you! Will you wait at least until I can get word to Wyatt Earp? He likes you and he might back your play."

Chance put the hat back on, pulled the brim down grimly, and said, "You'll say nothing to Wyatt or any other man I know in town. I'm not *asking,* Hughie. I'm *telling!* Mister Earp thinks less of my idea than you do, and he *is* bigger than me."

The Long Branch would have been crowded with half as many men bellied up to the bar. There were no women present save for Chance as she elbowed her way through from Front Street. Luke Short ran what he considered a respectable joint. He served an honest shot for three cents a glass and neither whores nor obvious cardsharps were welcome. Luke had a baseball bat on the bar, and the mirror had been turned to the wall since she'd last been there. Short and two other men tended the bar for the crowd. A sign above the bar warned against packing a gun or asking for credit. The sweat-stained, dusty hands crowded in the tiny place placed their pennies on the bar before they ordered, but she couldn't spot any who weren't packing at least one gun, and since they were Texans, often two.

Feeling very self-conscious despite her disguise, Chance worked her way to a corner at the end of the bar. She bumped the elbow of a cadaverous man in a black frock coat as she tried to put her money on the bar. She said, "Excuse me," and the man turned owlishly and growled, "Get out of here, kid. This is my corner."

She could see the man was drunk. He looked sick, too. His boney face was chalk white save for oddly red cheeks that made him look like he was wearing rouge. Chance smiled and tried to keep her voice low and friendly as she said, "I'm sorry if I'm crowding you, Mister. But I'll step away as soon as I get my drink."

"That's not *good* enough!" shouted the cadaverous drunk, and as if someone had tripped a switch, the little saloon got very quiet.

Chance saw the men around her were edging away, and one of them murmured to a companion, "Let's get out of here, Jim."

Chance shook her head and said, "Look, Mister. I'm not looking for trouble."

"You already found your trouble, sonny. You just fill your fist when you've a mind to. Fresh kids like you should be stomped before they start to multiply!"

Luke Short came down the far side of the bar and said, "Take it easy, Doc." Then he blinked at Chance and gasped, "For God's sake, what are *you* doing here!"

The man who'd challenged her asked, "Do you know this punk, Luke?"

Short hesitated, confused, then nodded and said, "I do. It's a friend of Wyatt Earp's. They was in here together a while back."

The pale-faced man stared hard at Chance as Luke Short added, "Wyatt won't like this, Doc. The, uh, kid's all right."

"Well, if I can't kill him, I'll let him buy me a drink. I'm Doc Holliday, sonny. Who might *you* be, and what side did you ride for in the war?"

Chance recovered and stammered, "I missed the war by being a shade too young."

"You didn't miss nothing, sonny. I asked for your handle, too."

"Uh, I'm Chance McGraw, Doctor Holliday."

Holliday nodded grudgingly and said, "Well, I can see your manners has improved since you bumped me. We're both having Maryland rye, Luke. The kid is paying."

Luke Short heaved a vast sigh and reached under the bar for two shot glasses and a bottle. He placed them in front of Chance and Holliday and said, "Have a round on the house, uh, gents. Does Wyatt know you're down here, uh, McGraw?"

She picked up the bottle and filled Holliday's glass first as she answered, "No. Did he tell you about my trip to Pueblo, Mister Short?"

"Wyatt don't talk much, but I can read, and I can add two and two. You was in Salt Lake and Cheyenne, too, wasn't you?"

Chance nodded and Doc Holliday suddenly smiled

at her and said, "I'll be damned! You're the Sundown Kid, right?"

Chance glanced at the other men around and saw some had caught the name and were staring at her with wary respect. She shrugged and said, "I'm not trying to advertise it, Doctor Holliday. I wish you'd just call me McGraw."

"Hell, sonny, nobody's about to mess with you with *me* standing next to you." He refilled his glass, drained it, and turned around to loudly shout, "How about it, you Texas sons of bitches? Does any man here want a fight with me and the Sundown Kid?"

Nobody answered. A few men edged out the door. The others found more interesting things to look at as Holliday snorted, "I didn't think so. I don't know where they find trailherders these days. I swear to God I suspicion Texans have to sit down to piss!"

Luke Short couldn't meet Chance's eyes as he said, "Simmer down, Doc. Ben and Billy Thompson is in town and you know how surly they can be about the Lone Star."

Holliday said, "Aw, shit, I'll take on both the Thompsons, Clay Allison, and Hardin, too. I ain't never met a Texan I was afraid of."

He didn't notice when Luke Short reached under the bar and switched bottles. Chance frowned at Short, and he nodded at the new bottle and shook his head warningly. Chance nodded back and poured another drink for Holiday as she soothed, "Here, Doctor, I'm getting ahead of you."

Holliday turned his back on the ugly looks some of the younger hands were now casting his way. He drained the glass, refilled it himself, and drank that, too, before he turned to Chance and said, "I can lick *you*, too, Kid!"

"I'm sure you could, Doctor Holliday. Wyatt told me you were the fastest gun in the West."

"Fuck the West, sonny. I'm the fastest gun in the *world!*"

And then, slowly, like a deflating rubber baloon, Doc Holliday began to sag. As he fell sideways Chance grabbed him. She was strong for a woman and Holliday was amazingly light for his height. Luke Short vaulted over the bar and grabbed Holliday from the other side, saying, "In the back. You know the way."

The two of them half led, half carried Doc Holliday to the back room, where four men were playing cards around a round table. Luke Short said, "Game's over, boys. We're letting our friend here sleep it off on the table."

One of the gamblers protested, "Hell, the game's just starting to get interesting."

Short said, "Take it over to the Alhambra then. This gent who needs the table is Doc Holliday. He sometimes wakes up surly."

The man who'd complained said, "Hell, nobody needs a table *that* bad. Let's go, gents."

As they filed out, Luke Short rolled Holliday atop the table and took his gunbelt off. He said, "We'll leave this on the wall and lock him in to sleep it off. I thank you for your help, Miss McGraw. But for God's sake, don't ever do that again."

"He started it. What did you put in his drink?"

"Chloral hydrate. It ain't as fast as the baseball bat, but Doc's a friend of mine."

"He certainly is wild. Wyatt said he'd sent him to Leadville while the Texans are in town."

"I know. Sometimes Doc don't stay where he's put. But he won't leave *here* tonight. Speaking of staying put, I thought Wyatt told you to stay on the other side of the deadline this weekend."

"I'm looking for a man who may be riding with the Thompson outfit. Have you any idea where I can find them?"

"Good God, no! You think *Doc* here is mean? Ben and Billy Thompson curdle milk just walking past!"

"I'm not after them. I'm after one of their hands, if he rode up from the Panhandle with them."

Luke Short went to the back door and unlocked it as he said, "That don't matter, honey. You take on one rider and you take on his whole outfit. You'd best slip out this way and go on home."

By now she knew better than to argue. She nodded and left the saloonkeeper to lock up after her.

She didn't go home. She started going from saloon to saloon, a trim, medium-size figure in nondescript denim. She tried to look smaller as she moved quietly through the noisy crowds. It was early and most of the paid-off hands were in a jovial mood. She gave a wide berth to those who seemed obvious bullies spoiling for trouble. She knew better than to ask questions. In the Dodge House she watched from a corner with interest when a man asked loudly if Clay Allison had ridden in this year. The sudden drop in temperature as the others moved away from him had been rather frightening. The man had sensed he was asking for trouble, too, and moved out into the shadows, suddenly sober, as a man in woolly chaps had casually reholstered his weapon, spat, and opined, "Just a fool, I reckon."

She never learned if the man in the wool chaps had been the notorious Texas rancher, a friend, or simply annoyed by foolish questions. But it had been an educational experience. Many a man in the crowd rode the thin line between honest cattleman and outlaw. None of them welcomed questions from strangers. She knew if she asked where the Thompson outfit was camped, word of her asking would get there well ahead of her.

On the other hand men who hadn't seen each other recently shouted noisy greetings through the smoke-filled air, and the bars were filled with loud introductions as some hand would yell, "Belly up to the bar, gents. I'm buying a round in honor of the Confederacy and Captain Riggins here!"

At other times she'd hear someone murmur to a friend, "That's Shanghai Pierce there. They say he kilt a man in Abilene."

Feeling more than ever an intruder in a rough male world she'd never known, Chance kept her mouth shut, her ears open, and her face desperately blank as she drifted through the crowd. She was grateful for the treacherous lighting and the wide-brimmed hat she wore as more than once she felt her face flush at the coarse conversations on all sides. She'd known men cussed more when no ladies were in the room. She'd had no idea they made such graphic comments about each other's anatomy. Some of their ideas about *female* anatomy were bizarre as well as vulgar. Chance found herself trying not to laugh as a young hand in the Alhambra boasted of an adventure with a whore named Three Hole Alice that Chance, as a woman, knew to be impossible. When the braggart caught her smiling at him, he frowned and asked what was so funny. Chance said, "I wasn't laughing *at* you, pard. I was laughing *with* you. I've heard about Three Hole Alice."

The boy looked relieved. The slightly older and worldlier hand with him snorted and said, "Hell, I still say it ain't possible for a gal to take on three gents at a time. Where in hell would they all fit?"

The braggart appealed to his new fellow expert and said, "Tell him how Alice does it, pard."

Chance said, "I can't rightly say, since I've never watched her in action. But I've heard the story before."

"You're damned right you have. Ever'body in Dodge knows about Three Hole Alice. Who do you ride for, pard?"

Chance said, "I work for O'Rourke. The name's McGraw."

"Well, I'm Windy Hill, and this here's Pete Verdugo from down Laredo way. We rides for the Thompson spread and you're gonna have a drink with us to Three Hole Alice, hear?"

Chance managed not to gasp aloud. She couldn't believe her luck. She didn't know whether it was good or bad yet. Both the young hands were more than a little drunk and one, at least, was stupid. Her own misfortune in marrying a drunk had taught her about the sudden mood changes of the breed. She decided silence was not only golden, but her best bet.

The one called Windy grabbed Chance by the arm and hauled her toward the bar. His friend Pete moved around on her other side. She hoped it was to get away from Windy's loud voice. Pete was much heavier than her, and as they bellied up to the bar, he was almost leaning against her right side. Her gun hand was blocked from a quick draw. She resisted the impulse to edge away from him. If he was in fact watching out for his noisy friend, a wrong move on her part could confirm any suspicions he had.

Windy started pounding on the bar for service. A weary bartender moved their way and Windy yelled,

"I want three drinks here the day afore yesterday, God damn it!"

Chance reached in her pocket with her left hand, put a silver dollar on the mahogany, and added, "I'm buying. You let me know when that's used up, hear?"

Windy frowned and said, "You had no call to do that, old son. I just got paid. Are you saying I'm a saddle tramp?"

Pete said, "He's being neighborly, you idjet."

Windy thought and then said, "Oh, that's different. I'll drink with any cuss who's *neighborly.*"

Pete muttered, "That's for damn sure." Then he nudged Chance and murmured, "Don't get riled with him, McGraw. He's a good old boy, and he works for the Thompsons."

Chance nodded, but again she avoided comment. Pete was an experienced hand and might clam up if she asked point-blank where their outfit was camped. If she could hold her liquor and avoid a fight with Windy, one of them might spill the one thing she wanted to know.

The bartender put three shot glasses in front of them, held a partly used bottle up to the light, and said, "Two bits more and this is all your'n, gents."

Chance started to reach in her pocket again, but Windy grabbed her elbow and said, "It's my turn, damn it."

Chance nodded and Windy put a quarter on the bar, still holding her by the elbow. Chance forced herself not to resist as the Texan squeezed and said, "You sure are skinny, feller."

"Do you aim to pour or shall I?"

Windy let go and said, "Hell, I'm the host hereabouts. We got us enough here to get drunk as skunks. That is my aim in life tonight."

As he poured, Windy spilled red-eye on the bar, and Pete muttered, "You've got a good start, boy."

Chance just smiled. The more of the stuff he spilled, the less she had to drink. She'd fortified her stomach with Annie's mashed potatoes and two cups of cream before leaving the house. She knew she could hold her liquor better than most women. But there were limits and the night was young.

As the two hands she'd met raised their glasses, Chance did the same. She decided to drink the first one with no tricks. It tasted like shellac smelled. Even Windy gasped for air as he lowered his glass and poured another. Pete said, "You'd best catch your breath between drinks, Windy. I sure don't aim to carry you back to the outfit."

Windy said, "Shit, I'll drink you both into the ground and still get screwd, blewd, and tattooed, hear?"

"He's been on the trail a spell," said Pete morosely.

Chance reached for the bottle and filled Pete's glass as well as her own. She saw Pete was worried about his friend and was holding back. She said, "I'll help you with him if he can't make it home."

Pete picked up his glass and said, "I noticed you helped Luke Short earlier."

"Oh? Were you in the Long Branch when that drunk got sick?"

"I was. We both was. That's why I hauled Windy out. Somebody said that feller you was fussing with was Doc Holliday."

Chance picked up her own glass with a shrug. She'd been right about him wanting to watch her gun hand. She said, "Doc was just funning."

"I've heard about his funning, and Luke Short was

white as a sheet. You must have some rep, McGraw. They say Doc Holliday don't back down much."

"Oh, hell, Pete, I never backed him down. He *fell* down. He was so drunk he didn't know where he was."

"Luke Short said you was a friend of Wyatt Earp."

"I know old Wyatt. He's a deputy marshal here in town."

"I know. What *are* you, McGraw?"

"I told you, I work for O'Rourke. Ain't you heard of the outfit?"

Pete thought before he shook his head and said, "Can't say as I have. Where in Texas is it?"

"It's not a Texas outfit. We're just up at the far end of town."

Pete looked relieved and said, "Oh, that explains how you know Doc and Earp then. I was afraid you might have rode in with a mean rep."

Chance forced a laugh and said, "Hell, you don't have to worry about me and Windy, Pete. I don't pick fights just to prove it's Saturday night."

Windy swung around owlishly to demand, "Fight? Where's the fight? I'm half hoss and half alligator and I can whup any son of a bitch in the house!"

Chance changed the subject by saying, "We were talking about *gals,* Windy."

It worked. The drunken hand grinned and said, "That's a swell notion. Let's kill this bottle and go looking for some *wimmen!* You know where old Three Hole Alice works, old son?"

Chance repressed her distaste as she said, "No. The only house I know is Madame Moustache's. But she charges plenty."

"Hell, we *got* us plenty! Ben Thompson paid us

half our wages with more to come when the cows is sold."

He stepped away from the bar. Then he fell flat on his face. Pete Verdugo said, "Oh, shit."

Chance helped him pick his partner up as Windy marveled, "What's going on?"

Pete said, "You're going to your bedroll, you silly bastard," and Chance said, "I'll help you get him wherever."

Pete nodded and the two of them got on either side of Windy to steer him toward the door. Chance was feeling the drinks, and she knew Pete had a head start on her. They shoved the semiconscious Windy out to the street and off the crowded boardwalk to the dust of the plaza.

Pete said, "This way. Our camp's across the tracks," and Windy protested, "You boys just let me be. I aim to throw up, and then I aim to get laid."

They ignored him and half led, half carried him around a corner. They made it to the tracks before Windy retched and vomited on his boots between them. They waited until he'd done it twice. Then Pete said, "When you taste hair it's time to swallow, 'cause you're throwing up your asshole, you silly son of a bitch."

Chance forced a hearty laugh and said, "We'd best get off these tracks before we get run over."

Pete grunted and they staggered on. Windy was getting heavier and sicker by the minute. Despite being bigger than Chance, Pete let her carry most of the weight. He seemed to be having his own trouble navigating, and she wondered wryly if he knew where he was going.

He did. They got Windy past the south corrals and she saw a string of fires on the open prairie ahead.

Pete said, "Yonder's the outfit. I wonder what they served us back there. My mouth tastes like the bottom of a henhouse."

The camp consisted of four wagons and three fires. Chance could see at least two dozen men hunkered down around the night fires. Others were lounging in or on bedrolls further back from the light. She assumed about a third of the big outfit were across the tracks in town. If Stubby Hawkins *was* with them, she knew it would be suicide to try and take him in this lion's den. But at least she might find out if he was back in Dodge.

A hand packing a Winchester stepped casually in front of them as they approached. Then he recognized her two companions and said, "Drunk again, huh?" and stepped aside.

As they approached the fire, Chance said to Pete, "I see you boys are cautious."

Pete said, "Have to be. Our ramrod, Ben, has enemies."

They steered Windy toward one of the wagons. As Pete indicated an open bedroll on the grass, a feline figure joined them to ask in a disgusted voice about the sagging Windy. Pete took Windy from Chance and literally dropped him on his bedding before he said, "He's only drunk, Ben. This here is Chance McGraw. He's all right. He helped me carry Windy home."

Ben Thompson smiled down at Chance and said, "I'm obliged to you, son. Join us for some coffee and we'll talk about the price of beef."

Warily Chance allowed herself to be led over to the nearest fire. It was a big one. Ben Thompson said, "We got us plenty of firewood this time. Some damn fool strung a fence across the range to the south, so we loaded up a wagonload of free fuel."

As they stepped into the light Ben Thompson said, "Get a cup for my young pard here, Stubby."

Chance felt her heart skip a beat as she stood there, facing Stubby Hawkins across the fire. The pig-faced rapist was squatting on his heels, tending the pot. He glanced up curiously. Chance didn't think he'd recognize her in her male disguise.

But the glow of burning wood was shining up at her face, and he'd seen her features at that angle by firelight before! Stubby gasped, then rose and stepped backward, *going for his gun!*

Chance reacted without time for thought. Stubby fired as she put a bullet in his chest. His hasty round smashed into the fire between them, scattering hot embers in every direction as he fell spread-eagled on his back, drummed the sod a couple of times with his boot heels, and went limp.

It got very quiet.

Chance stood there, frozen with the smoking gun in her hand, as Ben Thompson stomped out a tuft of burning grass and said very softly, "I sure hope you had a good reason for doing that, son."

Pete Verdugo said, "Stubby drew on the kid, Ben."

"I got eyes. But Stubby worked for me. I'm waiting for your answer, stranger."

Chance holstered her gun as she said, "I didn't come here looking for a fight. Pete and Windy never said Stubby Hawkins was riding for you."

"Well, he was, and now you've kilt him. I hope you savvy the spot you've placed me in, kid. There's nothing personal, you understand, but I don't let folks shoot my hands. I'm sorry, but I reckon I'm gonna have to call you on it."

Pete Verdugo said, "Ben, the kid's a friend of Wyatt Earp."

"I don't care if he's friends with the devil incarnate. He kilt one of my hands right in front of me."

Chance faced him in the flickering red glow, aware she was dead. Even if she beat the notorious Ben Thompson to the draw, she was surrounded by his hard-cased crew. They had the drop on her from all sides.

Then another feline figure strode out of the shadows and said, "Just let's ever'body stay put whilst we study on this situation, Ben. We ain't sold our cows yet."

Ben Thompson told his brother, "Stay outten this, Billy. This boy just gunned a friend of ours."

Bill Thompson shook his head and said, "Shit, Stubby never *had* no friends. I *told* you not to hire him. You knowed he was wanted here in Dodge."

"He said it was a mistake, and I figured he'd be safe if he stayed in camp. This young rascal come in here uninvited and shot him all to hell."

Bill Thompson stepped over by Chance and said, "I saw what happened and I heard his excuse. It was a fair fight. I warned Stubby he might get in trouble if he come north with us so soon."

Not waiting for an answer from his brother, the cooler-headed Bill Thompson turned to Chance and added, "Let's hear your tale, son. How come Stubby went for his guns the minute he laid eyes on you?"

Chance took a deep breath, let half of it out so her voice wouldn't crack, and said, "He killed my father. The last time he was in Dodge, I called him on it and he ran away."

Bill Thompson nodded soberly and said, "There you go, Ben. Blood is thicker than employment. The kid had a reason, and he come here innocent, helping one of our other hands."

Pete Verdugo meant to be helpful when he chimed in, "McGraw belongs here in Dodge, Ben. We saw him back down Doc Holliday earlier tonight."

It was the wrong thing to say.

Ben Thompson scowled at Chance and grunted, "*Tough* little townee, are you?"

Chance forced a smile and said, "Not as tough as *you,* Mister Thompson. Wyatt says *nobody* is as tough as you!"

"That's for sure," growled Ben Thompson, albeit somewhat pleased. Then he said, "You got manners as well as a fast gun. What are you, law?"

"I pack a badge. But I really didn't intend to have it out with Hawkins here in your camp."

"You did, though, and now he's dead as a turd in a milk bucket."

His brother said, "Let it go, Ben. It ain't like he kilt an honest hand. We both knowed Stubby was an owlhoot, even if he did rope pretty."

Ben Thompson relaxed slightly and said, "All right, I ain't gonna kill you, boy. But, by God, you're stuck with the cost of a decent funeral for the poor slob even if he *did* kill your dad!"

Chance almost swayed with relief as she said, "That's fair enough. None of you will have to testify for me at the coroner's hearing. He had enough paper out on him to cover a wall and I've got a license."

"What are you, a bounty hunter?"

"Sort of, but his killing my father made it personal. I'd be proud to share the reward on Stubby with you, Mister Thompson."

Ben Thompson swore and said, "Get him out of here, Billy."

Bill Thompson took Chance by the elbow and said, "I'll walk you to the tracks, son. You can pick the body up at the undertaker's after I send him in."

As they left the camp, he added, "That was close, kid. If I was you, I'd stay off the streets 'til Ben and me leaves for home. Stubby will keep a while, and you may have heard my brother's sort of unpredictable."

"I noticed. Do you think he'll change his mind and come gunning for me?"

"Can't say. You was lucky in more ways than one tonight. Ben was sober enough to talk to, and Hawkins gave you no choice. If *I* suspicioned you'd come into our camp looking for him, I'd likely have to gun you myself."

Wyatt Earp was pounding on the door at ten the next morning.

Chance went to the door in her housedress and Wyatt stepped in, roaring, "Girl, have you gone *loco?* I just heard what happened last night. What in the hell are you doing still in town?"

Chance said, "Sit down and I'll pour you some tea."

"I don't want no tea, God damn it! I come to get you *out* of here! You've gone crazy as a bedbug, and now you've got the meanest gun in the world looking for you!"

"Oh, dear, did Ben Thompson change his mind already?"

"Ben Thompson? What are you talking about? Ben Thompson ain't looking for you. It's Doc Holliday! You backed him down last night while he was drunk. It's all over town this morning! Doc says he don't remember having words with the Sundown Kid, but he says if it happened like they say, it won't happen again! He's cold sober and packing a sawed-off shotgun. We got to get you out of town."

"Good heavens, can't you stop him, Wyatt?"

"Stop Doc with a shotgun in his hands? You *have* gone loco! Luke Short and I both tried to talk to him. Luke told him you never *had* a fuss with him, but Doc says he don't care. Folks *say* you backed him down. His honor is at stake. He's so mad, he wouldn't let Luke serve him a free drink."

Chance sighed and said, "Well, it might be a nice morning to take a long ride. I'll change into my riding skirts."

But just then a loud voice called from out front, "I know you're in there, Sundown! Fill your fist and come out, you son of a bitch!"

Wyatt said, "Back door. I'll see if I can stall him."

He went to the window and called out, "Hey, Doc? It's me, Earp."

"I'll take *you* on too, you mealymouthed bastard! I tolt you not to warn the Kid, God damn your eyes!"

"Now, Doc, I come here to arrest him for disturbing the peace. Lower that damn scattergun and we'll talk about it, hear?"

He went to the door and stepped out on the porch.

Then he saw Chance had followed him and muttered, "Oh, Christ!"

Doc Holliday came up the walk, shotgun muzzle lowered and cheeks bright red. He ticked the brim of his hat to Chance and said, "Your servant, Ma'am. I understand the Sundown Kid lives here. I sure hope he ain't important to you."

Chance smiled and said, "He's not here, Doctor Holliday. You can search the house if you like."

"Is she telling the truth, Wyatt?"

"I reckon so. There's nobody here but her and the Irish folks she works for."

"Well, I won't pester folks I ain't looking for. But where's the damned Sundown Kid?"

Chance said, "Last night he was over at the Thompson brothers' camp. He had a shoot-out with a wanted man. This morning he appeared before the coroner to explain his actions and claim the reward."

Wyatt Earp gasped. Doc Holliday frowned and said, "He gunned one of Ben Thompson's hands in Ben's own camp and *lived?*"

Earp recovered and said, "We *told* you the Kid was a *mean* one, Doc."

Holliday shrugged and said, "Well, Ben Thompson has more to look forward to in his old age than me. I don't care how it turns out. I just want to see who's the better man."

Earp grinned and said, "You have my word I think you're the better man, Doc. Luke told you the Kid could have gunned you last night if that had been his intention. He helped Luke lay you out to sleep off a total disaster."

"I know what Luke says. That ain't the point. Word's got about that I ordered the Sundown Kid out of my favorite corner in the Long Branch and that he never crawfished. I dasn't show my face around town 'til it's settled one way or the other."

Chance said, "Can't you say you ran him out of town?"

"Beg pardon, Ma'am?"

"You're still here and the Sundown Kid can't be found. Couldn't that be taken that he's avoiding you?"

"Hell, of *course* he's avoiding me! I've been looking all over town for the sassy rascal."

Earp said, "There you go, Doc. You run the Sundown Kid out of town."

Holliday suddenly grinned boyishly and said, "By God, that's true!" and Chance felt a pang as she realized he'd have been a handsome man if he hadn't been ruined by his illness and hard drink. He touched the brim of his hat to her again and said, "I'm going down to the Long Branch to celebrate. You coming, Wyatt?"

"I'll join you later, Doc."

As Holliday turned away, another man rode up to the gate, swaying in the saddle. He reined in and called out, "Is this O'Rourke's? I'm looking for the Sundown Kid!"

Doc Holliday chortled, "You're too late, Ben. I run him out of town!"

Ben Thompson got down from his mount and hitched his gunbelt up as he walked toward the house, head cocked to one side. Behind him Doc Holliday raised the shotgun muzzle thoughtfully and shot a look at Earp. Earp shook his head and called out, "Howdy, Ben. Heard you had some trouble down to your camp last night."

Ben Thompson stopped, legs apart, and said, "You

heard right. I've been brooding about it now that my cows is sold."

"You get a good price, Ben?"

"Hell, do we ever? What are *you* doing here, Wyatt?"

"Same thing as you, Ben. I come to have a word with the Sundown Kid about his manners. He ain't here."

"I run him out of town," called Holliday.

Ben Thompson stared at Chance and said, "Morning, Missy. Would you be kin to the Sundown Kid? You sort of favor him, but I'll have to say you're prettier."

Chance said, "I don't know if we're related. We're both orphans. This is the O'Rourke detective agency. I'm the office help. Would you like to speak with Mister O'Rourke? He'll be back in a little while. He went to send some telegrams about that outlaw, Hawkins."

"Hawkins worked for me, and, like I said, I've been having second thoughts about that bounty hunter of your'n. I suspicion he knowed Stubby Hawkins was in my camp. He made friends with Pete and Windy just to get at Stubby. I ain't sure I should have let him walk away with my brother like I did. Folks are likely to think I was afraid of the young rascal."

Wyatt Earp said, "Hell, Ben, you know nobody thinks you're afraid of anybody. You couldn't gun a man your own brother backed, could you?"

"Mebbe not. But I mean to have words with that Sundown Kid afore we leave."

"You're wasting your time, Ben. Doc told you he ran the kid out of town."

Holliday said, "That's right. Why don't we all go

down to the Long Branch and belly up whilst we brag on it?"

Ben Thompson said, "You go on ahead, Doc. I'll join you after I've searched ever' saloon in town."

They were still planning the demise of their mutual enemy as Wyatt hauled Chance inside, closed the door, and collapsed weakly at the table. He said, "I don't know whether to laugh or start screaming! Did you really gun Stubby Hawkins like Ben said?"

Chance reached for the tea pot as she said, "You *told* them the Sundown Kid was mean as hell, didn't you?"

"Honey, this ain't only impossible, it's getting *dangerous!*"

"I noticed. How long do you think it'll be before it's safe to show my other self in Dodge?"

"It'll never be *now.*"

"Oh, come now, the Thompsons will be leaving soon, and Doc will be mad at someone else in a day or so."

"Them two is the least of your worries. The Sundown Kid has a *rep!* Do you realize you've kilt three outlaws and faced Doc Holliday and Ben Thompson down all within a month?"

She grimaced as she sat down to pour. She said, "I thought I'd feel better about Dad after I paid them back, but I don't. Four of them are still alive. I know now that even getting *them* won't bring Dad back."

"You're learning, honey. Give it up. You've been too lucky to believe up to now. The trail gets rougher as you follow it. You don't have surprise working for you no more. Them other jaspers know the Sundown Kid is after them, and by now you've been described in every cowtown and hobo jungle. They'll be watching for you. So will a lot of tough-talking punks looking to build a rep."

She stirred her tea and said, "I can't stop now. I'm satisfied now to see Jack Dawson hang, thanks to Brian Pio. But Lefty Shaw, Dodd, and the leader called Slade are still at large."

"Let Pio, Despres, and other bounty hunters look for them. I got a letter the other day from my brother, Virgil. He's out in Arizona Territory and he says things is booming out there. I got to finish my contract with the city here, but I'll likely be moving on. You'd like it in Arizona, Chance. It's pretty country and nobody out there would know us."

She reached across the table to pat his hand and said, "You're very sweet, Wyatt. But you forget I have a job to do."

"Aw, hell, you'd be wiser to quit whilst you was ahead! You ain't halfways down your list and you've already got two experts gunning for you!"

"Wouldn't you do the same if someone killed one of your brothers?"

"That's different. I'm a man."

"My father didn't have a son, Wyatt. I'll just have to do the best I can."

They were interrupted by the return of Hughie O'Rourke. The tinker sank wearily to a seat and gasped, "Jasus, it's a hornet's nest you stirred up, gorl. Where's Herself?"

"Annie went shopping. I'm sure she'll be all right. Nobody's looking for anyone but me."

"Jasus, that's the truth. We got a wire and a money order from your friends, Brian and Tony. It seems young Dodd heard about Kinkaid and Flynn being tracked down by the Sundown Kid. He sent his mother to make a deal with bounty hunters less prone to execution."

"Dodd turned himself in?"

"Ay, in Clay County where they *thought* they'd find him. They split the reward with us. Tony said they owed it to you for scaring Dodd into surrender."

"Tony? Didn't Brian have anything to say?"

The tinker handed her the wire, saying, "It was Despres signed it, as you can see. They must have sent it together, though. Isn't the town of Liberty where they said their headquarters was?"

"Yes, it's the county seat."

Wyatt Earp frowned and said, "Clay County is headquarters for the James-Younger gang, too. Liberty's a rough little town."

Chance got up and said, "You may be right. I'll find out when I get there."

Liberty, Missouri, was older than Dodge and the streets were shaded by elm trees. It lay in the hilly farmlands just east of the muddy Missouri river and served as a market town as well as the county seat. The men she passed walking up from the depot wore bib overalls and straw hats for the most part, though some were dressed as she was in faded denim and felt hats. Only a few wore sidearms, and she was aware of the attention her .44 attracted.

She carried her bag to the small hotel across the

square from the white courthouse. She signed in and washed up before she went downstairs to the dining room to eat before looking for Brian and Tony.

Her order had just been placed before her when a stout man with a tin star pinned to his vest sat down across from her and said, "Howdy." Chance took out her wallet and placed it open on the tablecloth between them. The local lawman studied it and nodded, saying, "Just doing my job, Mister McGraw. We don't see many gents packing guns in these parts. I can see the Missouri Central don't have to worry about you. Who are you after, the James boys?"

She smiled and said, "*They* don't have to worry either. I'm packing Kansas warrants on a pair of rapists and murderers."

The Clay County deputy nodded and said, "Lefty Shaw and Goldy Slade. I read the fliers. Couple of other bounty hunters just brought in their sidekick, Dodd. Kansas can't have Dodd 'til Missouri's through with him, which won't be for twenty years or so."

"He's wanted on a hanging offense in Kansas."

"I know. That's likely why he surrendered himself in Missouri. Do you know Brian Pio or Tony Despres?"

"They're in the same line as me, right?"

"They are, and they might not take kindly to your horning in. There's a lot of paper out on Slade and Shaw. Do you follow my drift?"

"I didn't come here to make trouble. I intend to look up your local dicks before I make any rash moves."

The deputy nodded and rose, saying, "I figured you knew the rules of the game. It's been nice talking to you."

Chance followed him out with her eyes and went

to work on her steak. It was as tough as the rest of the town. Even the apple pie that followed was tougher than it should have been. She wondered where they'd found cardboard the color of pie crust.

She paid, left a dime tip, and stepped out into the gloaming light of the courthouse square. Her stomach felt like she'd eaten a ball of lead and she realized it wasn't the food. It was her nerves. She walked to a bench by a brass cannon on the grass across the street and sat down to study the address she'd written and to get her bearings.

She became aware of a tall figure standing between her and the lamp post by the walk. She looked up from under her hat brim and Brian Pio said, "I'm only saying this once, friend, so listen sharp. I want you to take your warrants and your smart ass off my range. Slade and Shaw are mine for personal reasons. Do you read me, mister?"

Chance laughed and started to rise. Brian moved in like a big cat and grabbed her gun hand and the front of her shirt as he slammed her back down on the bench and warned, "It ain't funny, friend."

"Brian, for God's sake, don't you recognize me?"

He let go of her shirt and tipped her hat brim back with a frown. Then he gasped, "Jesus H. Christ! They told me another bounty hunter was in town!"

As he helped her up, she said, "They told you true. Didn't you read about the Sundown Kid in the papers?"

"Oh, for God's sake! You mean that was *you*, dressed up like this? I thought you'd hired someone in Dodge!"

"I cannot tell a lie. I did it with my little .44. You wired that Slade and Shaw were still at large, Brian."

"They are, but, damn it, that wasn't to get you

here dressed up so crazy! Are you saying you actually beat three grown men in stand-up fights, girl?"

"It's getting tedious repeating it. *You* just took me for a man, didn't you? Let's go over to my place and I'll fill you in on my Dodge City agency."

He nodded and started to take her arm as they crossed the street. She shook him off and asked, "Do you want them to think we're sissies? Just act like I'm one of the boys when we pass through the lobby."

"I'll try, but it won't seem natural. Generally, when I go to a hotel room with a lady, we say our name is Smith."

"That's hardly why you've been invited. I have to use the privy, damn it!"

He laughed and said, "I figured. You even *talk* like one of the boys, wearing them fool pants!"

They went in and up the stairs without occasioning comment. She left Brian in her room as she went down the hall. It wasn't until she met her own eyes in the bathroom mirror as she was washing her hands that she realized how awkward a situation she was in.

In her first surprise at meeting Brian she'd forgotten the grudge she still bore him for the way he'd treated her in Dodge. She still wasn't sure if she was angry with him for having made love to her to distract her or because he hadn't come back for more. She'd just made the tactical error of mentioning intimate matters in the casual tone of old lovers, and no doubt Brian considered himself as such. But this time he wasn't going to get so much as a kiss until he'd explained a lot of things!

She went back to her room and found Brian had hung his gunbelt over the bedpost. She sat primly in a chair near the window and asked, "Aren't we taking a lot for granted, Brian?"

He just looked puzzled. Chance said, "You used me in Dodge. You only made love to me to keep me out of the way while you and Tony stole my prisoner."

Brian laughed easily and replied, "Hell, you know better than that. What happened was . . . Hell, I've never rightly figured out how it happened, and I've studied on it some."

"Is that why you deserted me like a cast-off toy, Brian?"

He shook his head with a frown and said, "No. I knew if I hung around I'd wind up asking you to marry up with me."

"Oh? That's right. I'd forgotten I was damaged goods."

"Chance, you're still talking dumb. You know any man in his right mind would jump at the chance to marry up with a gal like you. I lit out the way I did because *one* of us had to start thinking sensible and, like I said, *you* keep talking *dumb!*"

"My, you certainly have a romantic way of sparking a girl, Brian. I'm so relieved you left me alone in that dingy little hotel to save me for the right man. For a time I was beginning to think you were a love-em-and-leave-em type."

He stood up and came over to her, saying, "Look, back there when . . . when we sort of lost our heads, I said a lot of things and I meant a lot of what I said. But down at the depot in the cold gray light of reality I knew I wasn't right for you."

"Couldn't you have let me be the judge of that, Brian?"

"No. Like I said, one of us had to act grown up."

She didn't answer and he added, "I've kicked myself for it a few times since. The life I lead gets tedious and any man would be happy settled down with someone like you, honey. But you see, it's too late for me to settle down. There's a bullet out there somewhere with my name writ on it, and you're too pretty to wear widow's weeds."

He suddenly laughed boyishly and said, "You look foolish as hell in them pants, too."

She dimpled up at him and said, "I agree. Where's Tony and when do the three of us go after the last two men on my list still at large?"

Brian said, "Tony's out following a lead. We think Goldy Slade and Lefty Shaw are in Clay County. But *you* ain't hunting them with us. I'll take you to a dance if you'll promise to wear a skirt, but I'll be switched if I'll take you hunting outlaws and that's final!"

She stood up, saying, "Tony may have something to say about that, Brian." But Brian said, "No he won't. I'm bigger than both of you. I know he's sweet on you, too, but . . ."

"Too, Brian?" she cut in. He flustered and said, "Aw, hell, you know I'm in love with you, but this traipsing around in pants has to go. It's agin' the *law* to kiss folks wearing pants!"

Chance laughed, a trifle wildly, and said, "My God, you have such a romantic way with words. Kissing folks in pants is almost poetry."

Their eyes met and locked. Brian took her gingerly in his arms and started to say something. Then he was kissing her in mingled passion and confusion. He swept her off her feet and started to carry her over to the bed. Then he stopped and stood there, shaking his head like a stubborn bull with a fly between its horns as he said, "Damn it, let's not go crazy again, girl!"

She murmured, "I didn't start it the last time either, darling."

"Maybe not, but, damn it, I sure wish you wasn't so all fired *willing!*"

She laughed and asked, "Would you feel better if I struggled and said no, dear?"

"Hell, I could *stop* if it wasn't for them smoke signals in your eyes! This ain't going to work, Chance. I'm pure sorry I ever started, but you've got to understand, I can't let you throw yourself away on a man like me."

She shushed him with a finger on his lips as she said, "You're too good for me, too. But don't you think we should pull the shades?"

Wordlessly Brian put her down on the bed, stepped over to the window, and drew the blind. As he turned in the semidarkness, Chance was unbuttoning her male attire. He sighed and said, "I've been trying to figure out how I could get you out of them duds, but . . ."

"Oh, hush and take your own off, you adorable lout. Don't you think I've been thinking about that night in Dodge, too?"

The room was darker when Chance awoke with a start, groped wildly, and saw she was still in Brian's arms. As she snuggled closer, he said, "I've been trying to figure out how I was to get up without waking you, honey."

She said, "You did that in Dodge, you brute. This time you're going to have a harder time getting rid of me. All things considered, I think I'm in love with you. I'll be darned if I understand why."

He chuckled and said, "I told you I was no good." Then he started running his hand down her nude torso as he added, "No good as a husband, that is. I still feel good enough to make love one more time afore I have to go."

"Go? For heavens sake, where are you planning to go at this hour?"

"Have to scout up Tony and see if he's found out anything."

She put her own hand to the back of his as it cupped her breast and said, "In that case I'll just get dressed and come with you, darling."

He stiffened slightly and replied, "Not hardly. Slade and Shaw have friends here in Clay County. One of 'em's called Cole Younger and the others are Frank and Jesse James. I wouldn't let you tag along if your name was Wyatt Earp."

He pressed her breast fondly as he added, "Of course, if you was Wyatt Earp, I wouldn't enjoy this as much. You've got to learn that there's places a man belongs and places a gal belongs, honey. It's tedious to have to keep reminding you."

Suiting actions to his words, Brian rolled over half atop her and Chance protested, "Damn it! I don't want to make love again. I want to help you track those killers down!"

Brian gently but firmly forced her thighs apart with his knee as he soothed, "You can help me best by staying here and waiting where I know you'll be safe."

She was annoyed at his casual assumption that all she needed was "a good lay," but despite her annoyance her body betrayed her by responding, and as she started to protest some more, he kissed her firmly and mounted her again as if he owned her. She murmured, "Damn you, don't *I* have anything to say about this?" and he stopped, his erection inside her pulsing flesh, to ask, "Do you want me to quit?"

She knew he *could,* and the knowledge filled her with mingled rage and respect for his uncanny self-control as she wriggled despite herself and sighed, "Brian Pio, you're impossible!"

He laughed and began to move as he knew she wanted him to, saying, "Nothing's impossible, but I'll allow I'm sort of improbable. You said before you was my woman. Did you mean it?"

"I don't know. I was having an orgasm, and for God's sake, do we have to argue at a time like this?"

He stopped again and insisted, "I want you to promise me something."

"Anything, you idiot!" she husked as another flush of pleasure made her arch her spine. Brian sighed and said, "Me, too. But I swear I'll leave you up in the air if you don't promise to stay here and behave while me and Tony look around. Is it a deal?"

She didn't answer. She couldn't answer as his teasing induced a long drawn out orgasm. Her mortification was eased somewhat as he, too, lost control and pounded her wildly into paradise.

Neither could speak for a time. Then as Chance calmed down enough to breathe again, she murmured, "Hello, darling. For a moment I lost track of you among the stars."

He said, "Howdy. I got sidetracked chasing my own harp music. Do we have a deal or not?"

"A deal?" Chance gasped, going cold in his arms. He said, "Yeah, I told you that you was to be a good little gal and stay right here while . . ."

"Get off me, you . . . you iceberg!"

"Hey, don't get sore, little darling."

"God damn you! I'm not your little darling! I'm taller than half the men I've met, and I've gunned three of the men who killed my father, which is more than either you or Tony can say!"

"Beginner's luck," he laughed easily, and it was the ease in his laughter that infuriated her. Chance shoved hard. Not enough to move his powerful trunk, but hard enough for him to see she meant it. Wordlessly Brian rolled off her, sat up, and began to grope for his boots.

As she watched bitterly, Chance asked, "Are you going to leave a dollar on the dresser before you leave? I can see you're used to just hauling on your boots and walking out with that smug, self-certain smile."

He said, "You're talking foolish."

"Maybe I am. Maybe I'm not used to being treated like a whore."

"Oh, for God's sake, Chance."

"It's my own fault. This is the second time you've done it to me. I swear to God, I don't know why I didn't take Madame Moustache up on her offer of a job! At least a high-class whore is treated with *some* respect!"

Brain turned, the darkness hiding the bewildered hurt in his eyes as he said, "Everything I've said or done since first we met was meant respectful, Chance. If you're too dumb to see that, I can't see how a man is to convince you. I've never been one for fancy speeches."

"Then take me with you. Prove you respect me as a comrade-in-arms and not just as a ball of fluff."

He said, "You ain't a ball of fluff, and you ain't a man I want at my side in a gunfight neither. You're one hell of a woman and I'm scared I'm in love with you. So I'll hear no more about you shooting it out with friends of Jesse James."

She sat up, saying, "Damn it, Brian. I don't want you to just love me as a woman." But he snorted indulgently and said, "I'd look silly as hell falling in love with anything else."

"Brain, you don't understand."

"Sure I understand, damn it. You're a tougher than usual gal who's packing a gun and a grudge and I know just how you feel. But have you ever stopped to think how *I* feel?"

"I know how you feel. You think that old thing between your legs makes you better than me!"

"Not better, honey. Different. Men are men and women are women. If you aim to be my woman, you're going to have to get used to the idea. I don't mean to cook and sew, but I'll help you with the dirty dishes, and if there's any fighting to be tended to in this family, I'll be the one who tends to it."

Chance felt her breath catch as the full meaning of his grotesque proposal sank in. But Brian was on his feet and strapping on his gun as he added, "I'm leaving now. You be here when I come back or all bets are off, hear?"

Before she could answer, he bent to kiss her, gave her a rather proprietory pat, and let himself out. Chance swung her feet to the rug and started to follow. Then she stamped her bare foot and swore.

Who did he think he was to treat her so?

She went to the window and peeked out through the shades. She didn't see Brian, and the night was still young enough for other people to be out on the street. She had no idea where he'd gone and she knew he'd refuse to let her tag along in any case. But there was a hunter's moon, and she'd been making plans of her own before she and Brian had met by chance in the square.

Or had they met by chance? Brain had thought she was the Sundown Kid when he'd approached her. That meant she'd been pointed out. Others in Liberty doubtless had this hotel staked out by now, too, and the men she was after were said to be in with the outlaw gang that practically ran Clay County.

Chance got her carpetbag and took out her feminine riding outfit. Anyone gunning for the Sundown Kid would be expecting her to leave in male attire. Chance was smiling to herself as she dressed after a quick wash. But as she adjusted her veil in the mirror, a small voice asked her, "What do you think you're doing, and what will Brian say if he finds out?"

Brain was a stubborn man who meant what he said, she knew. He'd told her, after as much as proposing, that all bets were off if she defied his orders. She knew he meant the orders for her own good. She knew he'd dismiss her as willful and stupid if he returned to find her hunting on her own. And she knew sickly that Brian would back his words no matter what it cost them both.

Chance picked up her muff and tucked the .44 in it as she cast a wistful eye on the rumpled bed. She had needs and feelings, too, and she knew she'd probably never make love to Brian again now.

"Who wants a man like that anyway?" she sniffed, blowing out the lamp as she let herself out. But as she went down the stairs, her heart already felt the pangs of returning emptiness, and for a moment she was tempted to run back upstairs like the good little girl Brian wanted her to be.

But she wasn't a good little girl. She was a bounty huntress on the trail of killers, and if Brian didn't want her on those terms, so be it.

She ignored the odd look the desk clerk shot her as she crossed the lobby and marched grandly out. Across the street one of the two men lounging in the inky shadows stiffened and said, "The light in the Kid's room is out, and someone just come out the front, Cole."

His companion said, "I see her. It's a gal. The Sundown Kid has human feelings, too, I reckon."

The other took his hand from the Walker .45 at his side as he shrugged and said, "Mebbe. Frank and Jesse say we're not to leave him with any kind of feelings once we get the little bastard in our sights."

Chance, of course, had spotted the gunslicks across the way as she'd left the hotel. She'd hidden her male costume in the bag she carried, so even if they broke in on "The Kid," they'd simply find an empty room and assume he'd gotten out another way. It would have been amusing if the game wasn't being played for such deadly stakes. She was on the streets and safe for the moment, but she'd not only lost Brian. She'd lost her base of operations. Where on earth was she to spend the night?

She knew she could ask directions to Brian's office. He and Tony would be listed in the city directory. If she told Brian she'd only left the hotel because badmen were watching it . . . She'd be exactly the swooning helpless maiden he wanted her to be, and worse yet she knew he'd let her get away with it.

"Damn you, Brian Pio," she told her shadow on the walk ahead of her, "I'm going to find those last two killers and I'm going to bring them to justice, wearing pants or a darned old fig leaf!"

Brian hadn't given her time to explain how she'd caught up with Flynn in Salt Lake. He was so convinced of his own superiority that he hadn't considered the advantages of a female investigator. Maybe if she could show him what a team they'd make . . . and then she sighed and said, "Forget it, girl. You've lost him again, and that's the end of it. You had the choice, you made it, and it's time to concentrate on Goldy Slade and Lefty Shaw. Get those two rascals and you'll have gotten them all!"

Chance paused by a closed shop window to peer at the reflections and make sure she hadn't been followed from the square. She hadn't. The men gunning for her other identity probably thought she was a trollop of the town who'd been up there pleasuring a young man with a growing rep. Chance grinned wryly as she realized this was the second time she'd been mistaken for her own lover.

The poor Sundown Kid would be going out of business just as he was becoming notorious. She wondered what the legend spinners would make of his sudden disappearance. What *was* she going to do with the rest of her life once she'd tracked down the last of the seven? When first she'd started on her quest, the end seemed so far away that she'd never considered it.

She was passing under the last streetlamps now, and she wryly told her lengthening shadow, "You're pretty optimistic for a girl about to face two killers! How do you know you'll *have* the rest of your life to worry about?"

Yet even as she faced that danger soberly, she knew that wasn't what made her feel so drained and empty. Nobody really expects to die, even though reason tells them they must someday. Chance knew her odds on surviving were at least fifty-fifty, but no matter how things went, she'd lost Brian forever. He'd never forgive her for refusing to obey him.

"He's just a stubborn, muley man!" she told herself as she trudged on into the darkness. But she knew that more than Brain's male ego was involved. He sincerely thought she was liable to be killed for one thing, and she knew her quest struck him as something . . . unwomanly?

Chance paused under an elm to look back the way she'd just come. Maybe if she went back and found his office . . . It wasn't as if Slade and Shaw were free and clear after all. Brain, Tony, and dozens of others were looking for them.

Chance shook her head wearily and moved on. Dozens of others hadn't found the last two killers because while other lawmen were good, they were *men.* Brian hadn't let her explain the advantages a female bounty hunter had because he didn't want to hear about them. But she was *good.* She'd tracked those others down by using her feminine advantages as well as a trigger finger just as good as any man's.

"I've still got my agency," she told herself. Even if she managed to bring the last of the seven to justice, there were others just as evil on the frontier. Those poor settlers the seven had murdered might just as well have been murdered by other roving killers. Until all decent people were safe from the likes of Goldy Slade and his ilk, her job was far from finished. Maybe she couldn't have Brian. But she'd still have a job to do!

Yet even as she tried to dismiss Brian, she began to understand him better. Brain, and even Tony, didn't just hunt outlaws down for cash. Despite their cynical talk men like Brian, Tony, and Wyatt felt a sense of mission. They were *needed* in a land still semisavage. Her own bitter feelings of revenge had begun to be replaced by a probably healthier feeling of . . . craftsmanship?

Chance laughed at her own grotesque thought train. But it was true. She did feel a certain pride in the way she'd tracked down killers others had been unable to find. Killing them hadn't been as enjoyable as she'd expected. It had been hard not to feel at least a little pity for a dying creature of any breed. But the *hunting* had felt good and still did. If only Brian had been willing to team up with her. What wanted outlaw would be safe with her and Hughie casting for leads and Brian and Tony moving in for the final showdown?

"Forget it!" she warned herself. This was no time to indulge herself in might-have-beens. She was on her own and on the trail right now. She knew that if she didn't stop mooning over Brian and concentrate on every move in the next few hours, all might-have-beens could be replaced by rest-in-peace!

Madame Sue looked like one of those painted plaster dolls you won in a shooting gallery as she stared at her younger visitor with wary, red-rimmed eyes. Chance had found the house of ill repute where the smirking bellhop at the hotel had told the "Sundown Kid" it would be—a mile outside of town, where visitors to the county seat would neither find it inconvenient to reach nor obviously protected by the local sheriff.

"Let me get this straight," Madame Sue was saying as she counted the money Chance had given her. "You say you don't want to work the cribs, but you want to spend the next few nights in a whorehouse. What happened to the hotel in town, girl?"

Chance said, "I told you I'm on the dodge, Madame. I need a hideout where the men looking for me won't think to look."

The blowsy whore shrugged and said, "I can see you ain't in my line. But you sure are skinny for a bank robber. I've learned not to stick my nose into other folk's business, but I have to know one thing. Are you wanted *serious,* or is it just some bitty mess like poisoning a husband?"

Chance smiled thinly and said, "There are no reward posters out on me, Madame Sue."

"Hell, honey, I'm not the sort who turns folks in for rewards. Some of my best customers have wanted posters out on them. I just want to see if I can help you. Do you have any more money where this came from?"

"I'm not carrying much on me, but I suppose I could get some. Why?"

"Honey, this is Clay County."

"I'm not sure I understand, Madame Sue."

"Sure you do. Everybody knows the James boys, the Younger boys, and Lord knows who else have the law *fixed* here in Clay. You might say fixing the law is our leading industry now that a white man's expected to work his own fields."

Chance met the older woman's eyes in expectant silence and as she'd hoped, Madame Sue explained, "Unless you're wanted on a federal or Missouri charge, whatever it is can be *fixed.*"

Chance made herself look relieved as she nodded and said, "Ah, I understand. Who do I have to see, this Jesse James person?"

Madame Sue laughed and replied, "Of course not, girl. Some of the James-Younger gang drop by from time to time, but, officially, they ain't here in the county of Clay at all. You don't *see* nobody. You, uh, contribute to the sheriff's reelection campaign fund. Do you follow me?"

Chance nodded and to buy time said, "I suppose I could wire for more money. But it might take a few days with the weekend coming up."

Madame Sue tucked the first money Chance had given her in her ample bodice as she smiled and said, "Now you're talking sense, honey. Uh, just so I'll know what sort of contribution they'll be expecting, what sort of mess are you in?"

"I hurt another lady," Chance lied, adding, "We were fighting over a man, who was sort of her husband, and she pressed all these awful charges and . . ."

"For Pete's sake, is that all?" the whore cut in. "I can get you off an assault charge for a hundred dollars. For a minute I thought you'd *killed* someone from the way you was acting."

Chance remained worried-looking. It was important they take her for a petty fugitive, and she'd known in advance that nobody would pay much attention to her made-up charge of small town feuding. But while she seemed to have managed well enough to infiltrate the seamier side of Clay County, the madam's remark about the James-Younger gang had dismayed her. Slade and Shaw were said to be hiding under the protection of their old war comrades here in Missouri. But unless they were actually stupid enough to appear on the premises in the near future, Chance didn't see how this ploy was going to get her closer to them.

Madame Sue rang for a maid and said, "I know this is a dumb question, honey, but you wouldn't want to *work* while you're boarding with me, would you?"

Chance managed not to gag and the worldly Madame Sue shrugged and said, "I said it was a dumb question. Gals who cut up rivals over a man don't have the detachment this trade takes if one's to make real money at it."

A wary-looking colored maid came in and the madam said, "Ruby, this lady will be staying with us over the weekend. Find her a place to bunk and fetch and carry for her, huh?"

The maid nodded wordlessly, and as Chance rose to follow her out, Madame Sue called after them, "We'll talk some more later about them wires you'll want to send, eh?"

Out in the musky, perfumed darkness of the hall Ruby murmured, "You follow me, Ma'am," and took Chance's carpetbag. If the girl noticed it was heavy she failed to remark on it. She led Chance up a narrow flight of steps to a long hallway lined with makeshift doorways of hanging cloth. As they passed one, Chance heard a coarse female voice saying, "Not with your *boots* on, damn it!"

Chance shuddered, and as they passed another crib and she heard a man slobbering drunken endearments to a tittering whore, Chance asked the maid, "How late does that sort of thing go on, Ruby?"

The maid shrugged and said, "The gen'mens usually start leaving about midnight, Ma'am. Tomorrow is a working day."

The maid led Chance into a little cubicle furnished with a narrow brass bedstead and lewd tintypes on the plank walls. The graffiti on the whitewashed planks was dirtier than the photographs. Ruby placed Chance's carpetbag on the bed, but Chance asked, "Isn't there someplace I could stay until, well, things got a bit more quiet around here?"

The colored girl suggested, "Would you like me to show you to the parlor downstairs, Ma'am?"

"I'm not sure. Is it the sort of parlor I'm thinking of?"

"This is a whorehouse, Ma'am," said the maid simply. Then Ruby saw the dismay in Chance's eye and said, "I figured you was quality, Ma'am. They's a side veranda you might sit on 'til it's time to lock the doors."

Chance heaved a sigh and said, "I certainly could use some fresh air. Do you think my things are safe here?"

"No, Ma'am. I'll carry them down to the veranda for you and fetch you some tea."

Chance followed her little benefactor back down the stairs and out to the veranda where Ruby placed her bag by a porch swing. As she turned to go, Chance handed her a silver dollar. The maid looked confused and said, "I ain't paid, Ma'am. I's a slave."

"Keep it anyway," Chance insisted. Then she frowned and added, "What do you mean, you're a slave? The Civil War ended when we were both children!"

Ruby smiled wanly and said, "Please, Ma'am, in Clay County they calls it the War Between The States and it ain't exactly *ended* in these parts."

"Come, dear, you know you're legally free, don't you?"

"Folks don't pay much mind to what the law say in the county of Clay, Ma'am. I heard about the Yankees setting my kind free. But when the sheriff drinks with Jesse James and the county supervisor's kin to Cole Younger, a darky does what she's told, and I was told I belongs to Madame Sue."

Chance knew better than to press the matter further. So she sat on the swing while little Ruby went to get her some refreshments. Chance was beginning to understand just how hopeless Brian thought her idea of catching Slade and Shaw in their own lair was. She didn't only have to track them down. She didn't only have to win. She had to get out of Clay County alive after she'd done it!

Finding herself alone for the moment with time to think, Chance went over the options her distasteful new base of operations left her. Nobody would be looking for the Sundown Kid here. As in Salt Lake she could hope for one or both of the men she was after to frequent just such an establishment. But she didn't dare attempt to bribe the madam or her girls this time. No amount of money on earth would tempt a prostitute with the brains of a gnat to betray a customer under the protection of the outlaw gang that ran the county!

She had a view of the moonlit road out front. But she'd never be able to recognize anyone in this light, even if they appeared. She had no way of knowing if they'd appear at all, and for that matter they could be inside right now!

She was annoyed with herself for not taking the maid up about a seat in the parlor. But did she really want to be inside with Madame Sue's girls? *Could* she sit inside? Chance sat straighter in the swing to see if she could see inside. But the only window in view was dark. As she waited for Ruby to return, she heard a roar of rough laughter above the muffled tinkle of an unseen piano and shuddered. "Face it," she told herself, "you're just not tough enough to pass as one of the girls. Coming out here was a stupid move."

But where in Clay County was it *smart* for her to be right now? She couldn't go back to the hotel. She couldn't go to Brian. She knew sickly that she couldn't stay here for the night. The rough girls working here would never confide in an outsider, and she knew she could never in a million years become an *insider!*

A match flared near the end of the veranda and Chance swung her gaze to see a man standing there, lighting a smoke. Her breath caught as she realized he probably thought she was one of the girls who worked there. Chance didn't know what to say. So she said nothing.

The man stayed where he was, lounging against a post as he shook his match out. Then he said flatly, "You're a whore."

Chance shrugged and replied, "I don't think much of you either," in as brazen a tone as she could manage. The shadowy figure said, "The boys trailed you here, and just now Madame Sue told me the tale you handed her. What's your game, sister? What was all that nonsense about you being a decent gal on the run?"

Chance managed a sarcastic laugh as she replied, "I'll consider telling you my game when you tell me your own, Mister. They call me Skinny Hips. Who are you?"

The stranger answered, "You don't really want to know who I am, Skinny Hips. I know what *you* are because the boys saw you leave a man's hotel room, and the man hadn't registered as man and wife."

"Your boys sound nosy."

"They're paid to be. The man you were with earlier tonight was the Sundown Kid. I'm more interested in what *his* real name might be than I am about your own. What do you call him when the lights is low?"

Chance forced another laugh and asked, "Am I going to be paid for any of this conversation?"

He said, "You're drawing your pay with every breath."

"I don't understand."

"Your still *breathing,* ain't you? Whether you go on breathing or not depends on just how interesting this conversation might turn out. You were about to tell me the Sundown Kid's real name."

Chance made her voice more frightened than it might have been, although in truth it took little acting ability as she heard the sound of boot leather on gravel and realized she was covered by unseen men all around. She said, "He just told me to call him Sundown. I don't write biographies for a living."

"We know what you do for a living. But there's something very odd going on tonight. First the Sundown Kid sends out for a gal, which is reasonable. Then he sends her away, which is also reasonable. Then said gal turns up at a cathouse, pays for lodgings, and says she don't want to work the cribs, which ain't reasonable at all. He gave you the money you gave Madame Sue, right?"

Chance hesitated and then nodded and said, "I got the money from the Sundown Kid's pants. If you must know, he said he wanted me all to himself and paid me extra to be true."

The man laughed cruelly. Before he could say anything else, little Ruby came out on the veranda with a tea tray. She froze in place when she saw Chance was not alone. Chance said, "It's all right, dear. Put the tray here on the swing beside me." But Ruby stood rooted as if turned to stone. The sinister man across the veranda said, "It's all right, girl. Do as she says," and Chance gave him one small point for common courtesy. She realized that to him the colored maid was superior to any whore.

Ruby put the tray down and moved away as if she expected it to explode. As she ducked inside, the shadowy man chuckled and said, "Poor little coon's afraid of me, I reckon. It's a funny thing, I rode for the South, but we'uns never held no niggers."

Then he snapped from whatever reverie the frightened maid had brought to mind and said, "All right, Skinny-Hips. From what I can see of you, I'll buy a lonesome cuss wanting you all to himself for a spell. But what in thunder are you doing *here?* A whorehouse ain't the place to be true and blue to anyone!"

This time Chance's wry laughter was genuine as she thought what Brian, or even Wyatt, would think if they knew where she was right now. But the game she was playing was serious and, thinking fast, she said, "He said something about men watching him at the hotel."

"He was right. Who did he spot, my boys or that damned bounty hunter, Brian Pio?"

"I don't know who your boys are, and the kid never mentioned any bounty hunter. But, wait, he did say something about having words with a lawman of some sort before I arrived."

The sinister stranger took a thoughtful drag on his smoke and said, "That's the first thing you've said I know to be true. A local bounty hunter called Pio approached the Kid in the courthouse square earlier. They went off together somewhere that my boys didn't see. I don't know if Pio's with the kid or agin' him. Old Brian tells me he told the Sundown Kid to leave town. But Brian has been known to fib to his friends, so . . ."

"You're a friend of Brian Pio?" Chance blurted without thinking. And then, to recover, she quickly added, "I remember now. The kid said he and this Brian person had some sort of argument and that was why he couldn't stay at the hotel."

The stranger nodded and said, "I'll buy that. I *like* it, too. He don't know about *us* if he's ducking Pio

But how come he sent you here to this cathouse if he wants you to be his true love? He sure as hell never said he'd meet you *here,* did he?"

Chance felt her mouth go dry as she realized she'd been about to say just that! But of course, if Madame Sue was part of the outlaw establishment in Clay County, any outsider meeting anyone here would be committing suicide, and her questioner would know this!

Choosing her words carefully, Chance managed a light tone as she shrugged and said, "He said I was to come out here to keep this Brian or whatever from finding me. He said he'd meet me later, but not here, of course."

"Now we're getting somewhere! The slippery rascal's fixing to light out and wants some company on the trail! Where were you to meet him, Skinny Hips?"

Stalling for time to gather her thoughts, Chance said, "Listen, I've never set a man up to be ambushed before."

The man reached in his frock coat, took out a small canvas poke, and dropped it at her feet to jingle as he said, "There's always a first time. It can't be far if he said for you to wait out here in this neck of the woods. Has he got friends in the neighborhood?"

"No. He said he needed time to hire a buckboard and leave a message at the telegraph office when the coast was clear. He said he'd pick me up after midnight."

"*Where,* damn it?"

Chance ran her long walk from town through her memory before she replied, "I don't know the name of the place. It's that old deserted place down the road toward town. I don't know what it's called."

The man suddenly grinned wolfishly in the moonlight and said, "It don't matter. I do. The Kid's pretty slick. Nobody ever goes near that old deserted farmstead after midnight. The darkies think it's haunted. What sort of a signal were you to give him when he rode up in that buckboard?"

"Signal? I don't remember anything about a signal. He just said he'd meet me there after midnight if he could."

She made her voice deliberately bitter as she added, "He said he liked my style, but we didn't exactly become engaged."

The man took out a pocket watch and consulted it before he nodded half to himself and said, "We've time to set it up. It's been nice talking to you, Miss Skinny Hips. Naturally you know what'll happen if you try to warn the Kid, right?"

"I don't see how I could. I don't know where he is right now or what you and your friends are planning to do!"

"That's true. That's why I'm leaving you with a poke of silver dollars instead of a bullet in your pretty head."

He dropped his smoke and stubbed it out with his boot in a gesture of smug finality. Chance knew she should drop it while she was ahead, but she said, "I don't know if I can accept money from the man who's going to kill a, well, steady customer?"

The stranger laughed, this time in genuine humor, and said, "Hell, don't let it fret you, Miss Skinny Hips. I never kill anyone unless I have to."

"But you just forced me to set the Sundown Kid up for you and your boys, didn't you?"

"Well, let's say I did and I didn't. The Sundown Kid ain't after me and mine. He's trailing a couple of old boys I owe a favor. They keep talking about how good they are. So tonight I just might let them show me."

"Isn't two against one sort of unfair?"

"Hell, Grant was unfair at Richmond. The Sundown Kid's supposed to be good, too. So let's say we're just giving the boys a few extra chips."

"What happens to *me* if the men the Kid is after don't get him? He'll know I betrayed him, won't he?"

The sardonic figure nodded and said, "Yep. That's the trouble with betraying folks. But I sort of doubt you'll ever meet your loverboy alive again."

As he turned to go, Chance pleaded, "Wait! Aren't you going to put a guard over me, sir?"

"Why should we? You've been paid for the little you could tell us. Like I said, the kid don't figure to last the night. So the only way you could get hurt now would be if you tried to cross us by getting word to him."

"Good heavens. If he knew I'd been talking to you, he'd gun me long before I could warn him of anything!"

"I know. That's why we ain't worried about you. You can stay here and work for Madame Sue. You can take the money I gave you and go someplace else. It's no never mind to us."

And then he turned and melted back into the shadows from which he'd come. Chance's cheeks burned at the contemptuous way in which he'd dismissed her. But her smile was triumphant just the same and she was finding it difficult not to laugh aloud. She'd just been paid hard silver to betray her other self to the very men she hunted!

The little maid came back on the veranda, eyes rolling nervously as she asked, "Are you all right, Ma'am?"

"Of course, dear. But I don't think I feel like tea just now."

"Do you know who that was you was just talking to, Ma'am?"

"I've a pretty good idea, Ruby."

"You was just talking with Jesse James in the flesh, Ma'am!"

Chance picked up the money-filled poke and hefted it before she nodded and said, "I told you I had a pretty good idea. How much would it take for you to get to another county, Ruby?"

"Another county, Ma'am?"

"You know what I'm talking about. There's about fifty dollars here. Two or three would buy you a train ride out of Clay County, or, better yet, clean out of Missouri. You'll need respectable shoes and decent clothes, too. You'd better take it all."

As Chance handed the poke to the only decent girl on the property, Ruby gasped and asked with tear-filled eyes, "Why are you helping me, Ma'am?"

Chance could have told her of a gallant officer and gentleman who'd fought and died, in his own way, so that girls like Ruby could be free. Instead she pasted a brazen smile across her face and asked, "Didn't they ever tell you that all of us whores have hearts of gold, Ruby?"

Chance knew better than to go straight to the abandoned farm after she left the whorehouse. She'd waited until she was well clear in the darkness before she stepped into some roadside brush and stripped off the riding outfit. She'd already put on the boots, jeans, and hickory shirt under it. So she simply had to take the hat, jacket, and gun rig from her carpetbag. She wiped her face with cold cream and a rag before putting on the hat and pulling it low over her eyes. Carrying the bag in her left hand, she stepped out on the moonlit road as the Sundown Kid.

The bag was a bother and she wished she had a horse. But by not renting one at the local livery she'd probably added further to the confusion of the men gunning for her. She was beginning to see how simple moves like paying in advance for extra days and leaving a room without checking out could cover one's trail. She smiled to herself as she thought how many of her spur-of-the-moment moves had added up to the mysterious Sundown Kid. She'd have never come up with the name herself. She'd only dressed as a man at first because they refused to take her seriously as a woman. Her appearances after sundown were just common sense, to avoid recognition in bright sunlight that would betray an obvious lack of stubble on her chin. Now she saw she'd created another mystery as Skinny Hips, the painted whore with a heart of gold and a willing ear for outlaw propositions. They'd never connect her latest disguise with the demure young secretary at O'Rourke's Detective Agency. The science of cosmetics was a wonder. She realized she'd have to invest in wigs and a more complete wardrobe now that she could afford it. But would she need or want to continue with this game if things went well in the next few hours?

Her mental map told her she'd overshot the old farm, and she turned on to a side path. The moon was now behind her and her elongated shadow proceeded her in the dust. The awkward bag was becoming a positive danger now. She opened it as she walked and started discarding things at wide-spaced intervals. She knew passing farm folk would salvage or ignore most of the items. As she passed a cornfield she stopped, grinned, and climbed over the fence to leave the picture hat atop a ragged scarecrow in the field.

Too many people had seen her in the whipcord riding outfit to just abandon it by the side of the road. She waited until it led across a creek and, standing on the wooden bridge, dropped the skirt and jacket in the running water. The bag was empty now. She walked another quarter mile with it before she threw it in the ditch to be found and salvaged by some passerby.

She liked her shadow better now. She moved on, balanced and ready to dart in any direction without hindrance.

It was almost eleven when she made it back to the road the farm was on. She came to the crossroads north of it and melted into a clump of cottonwood. She knew that Brian and Tony had been looking for Slade and Shaw in town. So that meant they hadn't been hiding out in Liberty. They'd approach the ambush from the country outside of town. They'd obviously been hiding out with local farmers sympathetic to the Lost Cause.

She waited tensely as the moon rose higher and the crickets all around got used to her and started singing again. She'd timed it closely, hoping they'd do the same. If the old farm was known to teen-agers in Liberty, they wouldn't want to be there before all good little girls had to be home in bed. If they'd been dumb and gotten there early, she was out of luck. Moving in on the place from any direction would be suicidal. The roofless old cabin had a clear field of fire all around.

She heard hoofbeats and the grit of iron on gravel. She hunkered down. After a long wait a buckboard drawn by a mule rounded a bend to the north. In the tricky light she could just make out two figures on the sprung seat. It was probably farm folk, headed into Liberty . . . this late?

The driver was walking the mule. As they approached, Chance drew her gun, wondering if she should challenge or not. If they were mere innocent travelers, her own ambush would be betrayed.

The buckboard passed at a walk. As she still hesitated, she heard a voice ask, "Why are we dawdling for? Jesse said to git there well before midnight, dang it."

The driver's reply was lost in the crack of his whip and the sudden forward lurch of the buckboard. Chance sprang upright and ran forward in a crouch after the receding buckboard. She holstered her gun, grabbed the tailgate, and swung her boot heels under the bed to brace them against the axle. As she hung there under the wagonbed, the buckboard stopped. A voice said, "Now what?"

Another voice said, "I could swear I heard footsteps on the road ahint."

Chance didn't breathe. The first voice said, "Shit, there's a hunter's moon and I can see clean back to them cottonwoods. Are you spooked already, Lefty? We got to get there and stow this buckboard out of sight, damn it. I swear, I don't see why we brung it in the first place."

"Jesse tolt me to. He says half the town will come running to the sound of shots, and we don't want 'em to find no bodies there."

"Well, damn it, let's *git!* That whore says the Kid expects to meet her there come midnight. We'll be in a hell of a fix if he's *early!*"

The buckboard lurched forward as Chance clung under it, planning her best moves. She could swing up into the bed and have them at point-blank range from behind. But if the mule spooked she might well miss at least one of them in the confusion. She smiled grimly as she saw another advantage to waiting. If the Sundown Kid won right where they'd set up the ambush, his reputation as a deadly fighter would grow to alarming proportions. It wouldn't be enough to kill or capture the last two rapist-murderers. She still had to collect the bounty on them and get out of Clay County alive!

The tailgate's sun-bleached wood was rough on her fingers, and the unsprung wagon bed jolted hard over every bump as she clung there. She knew how far they had to go. She knew she was strong enough, but her hands were starting to go numb. As the wheels rolled on either side of her, Chance let go with her right hand and wiped it on her jeans. Her palms were sweating. She stretched down and dragged her right palm in the dust a moment before wiping it again. Her left hand was killing her, but she wouldn't need it.

They were almost to the abandoned farm when they stopped again. Chance lowered herself to the dirt between the rear wheels. Then she spied the four legs of a horse by the side of the road. Silently she eased up into the tie-rods between the axles and waited. Lefty said, "Howdy, Cole. I thought Jesse said we was on our own tonight."

A voice said, "We just checked with Madame Sue. Skinny Hips ain't in her room. You know how suspicious Jesse is."

"Jesus, you reckon she might have double-crossed us and warned the Kid?"

"Things like that do happen. She said she was sort of sweet on the boy. He's said to be nice-looking."

There was a pregnant pause. Then Cole Younger said, "Me and Ed just had a look at the old farmhouse. It's empty. You boys still want to try?"

Lefty said, "I dunno. That Sundown Kid is mighty mean. Mebbe we should quit whilst we're ahead."

But his companion said, "Look, Lefty, we ain't never likely to get a better shot at him. You want him racking us down one at a time like he done the others?"

"Hell, he ain't about to track us down in Clay County. Our friends own the law here."

Cole Younger said, "You boys are wearing your welcome here a mite thin. The sheriff is broody enough about having to play poker with the Pinkertons and Feds. If you ain't got sand in your craw for esse's setup, I'd advise you to hop a train."

"Damn it, Cole. The Kid may have the depot staked out!"

"No. He don't. *We* do. The Kid ain't at his hotel or skulking about the railroad yards. You can hop the night train or you can try for him yonder at the farmhouse. We're running out of time whilst we jaw about it."

Goldy Slade said, "Let's git on over to the farm, Lefty. I'm tired of looking over my shoulder night after night."

"What if that gal warned him?"

"I don't give a shit. He can't sneak in on us in this moonlight even if he knows. He'll come or he won't. No way he's about to take the two of us forted good behind them logs."

Younger said, "He's right, Lefty. If that gal double-crossed us, the Kid won't be dumb enough to walk into an ambush. He'll wait for another time and place. On the other hand if he *ain't* been warned, you'll never have a better chance agin' him. You do as you've a mind to. I've had my say."

Chance heard him spur his horse and ride away. The buckboard moved forward as she clung to the tie-rods. She felt it lurch around to her left and rattle across a log cattle-guard. She hung down for an inverted view of their surroundings. She saw the dark mass of the old deserted cabin, and when they drove to the far side from the county road and braked to another stop, she twisted like a cat and dropped to her hands and knees between the four wheels.

Lefty got down from the left seat as Slade dropped to the right. Lefty said, "I'll lead the mule to yonder tree and tether him. Check the ruins."

Chance knelt there as the wagon bed rolled off her like a blanket and then she stood up, legs braced, and said, "All right, grab for the moon or grab for your guns!"

Lefty, holding the mule's reins, gasped, "Oh, my God!"

Slade wasted no time in idle conversation, so Chance shot him first as she saw him slapping leather. Slade yelped like a kicked dog and spun around like a top before going down. Lefty let go of the reins and the mule bolted as he dropped to one knee, drawing his gun.

Chance crabbed to one side as he fired. She fired back. Her bullet slammed into Lefty's front teeth, and his head jerked back as if he'd just hit the end of a hangman's rope. He went over backward and lay limp in the moonlight as Chance put a bullet in him for luck and moved in for a closer look.

Lefty was dead and Chance didn't feel as much as she'd expected to either. She knew he was one of the men who'd raped her, but it all seemed so long ago and like it had happened to a stranger. Only the hollow ache they'd left in her heart by killing Dad still remained, and seeing Lefty ashen-faced and dead at her feet didn't do a thing to change it.

Chance turned quickly at the sound of a low groan. Covering Goldy Slade with her weapon she walked over to him and said, "Evening," in a voice that surprised even her with it's casual tone.

The leader and last remaining member of the seven was propped on one elbow, staring fixedly at his own dropped pistol a few feet away in the dust. Chance kicked it within Slade's reach and murmured, "Try again if you like."

Slade stared up at her in the moonlight, his gold tooth gleaming greenly as he half smiled and half grimaced in fear and pain. Slade shook his head and said, "I don't mean to make that mistake again, Kid. That first bullet you put in me smarts enough. I don't reckon I'm gutshot, though. So I'll likely live."

"You're wrong," said Chance, raising the pistol in her own hand. But as she trained the sight on his ugly jackal face, she couldn't pull the trigger! Slade's grin widened as he nodded and said, "The way I see it, you got me for now, but you're going to play pure hell getting me out of Clay County."

Chance lowered her pistol and put it in the holster on her hip before she said, "Come on. It's a better edge than you ever gave my father."

"Do I know your father, Kid?"

"You said you did when you killed him. My father was Colonel McGraw of the Eleventh Kansas, you murderous skunk!"

Slade looked more relieved than upset by the revelation. He coughed, wiped his free hand across his face, and said, "I figured you had personal reasons. But if you're the colonel's son, you was raised as a little gent who'd never gun a wounded man."

"I'm not his son. I'm his daughter. The one you and those others raped and left for dead on the prairie."

Goldy Slade's jaw dropped and he gasped, "You're funning me, boy. I ain't dumb enough to confess things to a man who's about to haul me before a grand jury, but I happen to know that particular gal is dead."

Chance shrugged and said, "I've no intention o proving my identity or sex the way you made me dc it the last time we met. Are you going for that gun o not?"

Slade fell back weakly and said, "I need a doc mor than I need a gun, boy. This jawing's getting tediou

I ain't about to try again against a pro like you and . . ." He went for the gun.

Chance drew and fired without thinking, and this time Slade died, too mercifully, with a bullet in his shattered head. Chance watched as one boot twitched a few times like the tail of a run-over snake and again felt numbly that she deserved to feel more.

Then a rifle spanged behind her and gouted dust and gravel near her right heel!

Chance ran for the cabin and dove headfirst through a gaping window as another rifle ball parted the air just behind her. She landed on her shoulder in the grass and weeds that had replaced the cabin floor. She rolled over and jumped to her feet. She fired blindly through the window to slow down their rush, then moved to the rear doorway as the rifleman put a burst of three bullets through the window she'd just occupied. Chance braced her .44 in both hands and fired in the direction of the flashes. Then she rolled away from the doorway and quickly thumbed the spent cartridges from her gun. She reloaded in the interval she'd bought and moved across the weeds to the road side of the cabin. She saw someone crawling along the fence line on that side and fired. Without waiting to see if she'd hit him she darted back to the far side and fired blindly into the tree line.

A distant voice called out, "Watch it, boys! There's *two* of 'em in there!"

Chance moved back to the front. A voice called out, "Hey, Sundown?" She saw nobody. Moving away from the window so they couldn't aim at her voice, she yelled back, "Who are you and what's your pleasure?"

"We got you surrounded, Kid. You let Lefty and Goldy loose and we might end this friendly."

She thought and yelled back, "They're both dead. We ain't packing paper on anybody else in this county. We'll leave her there if *you* will!"

There was no answer. Chance started circling the interior of the small cabin, risking a peek at all sides as she kept moving. The two bodies lay stark in the moonlight for all to see. The mule had hung up the buckboard in some brush and was grazing nervously in the near distance. She knew she didn't have to worry about a rush from that direction. No gunslick worth his salt would try to creep near a spooked critter. That still left three directions to cover.

She heard pounding hoofbeats. They were coming closer. Chance moved to a window on that side. She saw two riders reining in on the road in the moonlight and yelled, "Get clear! You're in a crossfire!"

A voice she recognized as Brian's called back, "Is that you, uh, Kid?"

"For God's sake, take cover! I'm standing off the James-Younger gang, you fools!"

Brian and Tony rode toward her and Brian said laconically, "No you ain't. We're still alive. They likely rode off when they heard us and half the town coming."

As he dismounted, she heard other hoofbeats in the distance. He came to her as Tony circled the house to cover the back, saddle gun in hand.

Brian met her in the doorway and said, "You little fool! What in thunder are you doing out here alone? What's this about the James-Younger gang?"

"I just had words with them. Slade and Shaw were planning to ambush me here and . . ."

"We heard. That colored gal from Madame Sue

told us when we rode back from a false lead. How in hell did them whores know about it?"

Before Chance could answer, Tony came in the backdoor, saying, "I swear to God, I don't believe it. She even thought to have a buckboard handy! Slade and Shaw are out back, dead as cow pats!"

"They're both mine," said Chance, adding, "I offered to hunt them with you and you laughed at me."

Brian stared down at her in wonder and said, "I ain't laughing now. How in hell did you ever track 'em? They was hiding under the wing of Jesse James!"

"Woman's intuition," she answered dryly.

Tony said, "I'll load 'em on the buckboard and drive 'em to the coroner. You reckon old J.W. Howard is likely to let it go at that, Brian?"

Brian said, "Don't know. Him and me has a sort of live-and-let-live understanding, since he's kin to half the law here. But this lady sort of bent the bargain."

Other riders were out front now, and Brian said, "They won't make no more moves tonight in public. If I know Jesse, he'll wait for a chance to get the Sundown Kid alone."

Tony said, "We'd best stick tight whilst the Kid here appears before the coroner and sends a few wires."

Brian said, "That's what I just suggested."

As she left the coroner's hearing with Brian and Tony on either side, Chance heard a voice in the crowd murmur, "That's him. That's the Sundown Kid. They say he's kilt twenty men or more!"

Brian took her by the arm and bulled through, saying, "Our office is just across the square. We'd best get you under cover afore the crowd thins out."

They led her over to their storefront office and slammed the door in the face of a reporter from Kansas City. The office was dark. Brian took her to the quarters in back and closed that door, too, before he lit the lamp. She asked, "Do you think James and the others will follow us here? You two might be in danger."

Brian said, "Not hardly. This is his home county and they don't look for him at his mother's farm worth mention. But the sheriff would frown on a shoot-out this close to the courthouse. Jesse knows better than to gun a licensed investigator right in town."

Tony asked, "Do you want me to check out the depot, Brian?"

"No. We already know they'll be covering it. Likely with rifles from the rooftops all around." He smiled down thinly at Chance and sighed, "You sure have yourself in the pickle jar, honey. I don't know ho we're to get you out of here, but I'll think of something."

As he went over to the kitchen range to put the coffee on, Chance sat on a bentwood chair by the battered table and said, "It's simple. I'll just turn into a woman again and board the morning train."

Brian said, "No you won't. While you was jawing with the coroner's jury about them boys resisting lawful arrest, I was asking my own questions in the crowd. James is looking for a gal who took his money and played him false. He's got his boys out looking for Skinny Hips Helen, and they say he wants her more than he wants the Sundown Kid!"

Chance lowered her lashes. Brian nodded and said, "I can put two and two together. I'm sort of surprised about you working in a whorehouse, but we live and learn. You must have wanted them two boys mighty bad."

Tony blinked and said, "I don't believe it! Chance wouldn't *do* a thing like that!"

Brian didn't answer.

Chance sighed and said, "I don't suppose you'd believe me if I told you I never worked the cribs?"

"I might, if a young farmer wasn't boasting all over town how good a lay Miss Skinny Hips was."

Chance laughed bitterly and said, "I'm tired of explaining my actions. You just go ahead and think whatever you like."

Tony said, "I believe you, Ma'am. Ever'body knows how young boys brag. I can add one and one, too. You're the toughest lady I ever met. But you ain't *that* kind of tough."

She looked up expectantly at Brian. He shrugged and said, "What's done is done and we'll say no more about it. The point is that you can't get through that gang in skirts, and they'll kill you wearing pants."

"That's not good enough, Brian."

Brian's eyes blazed dangerously. Then he nodded at Chance and said, "I apologize, formal. Now let's coffee up and study on some *sensible* talk. You'll have to hole up here for the next few days at least. We've a spare room for you. Jesse James is a moody cuss, but he can't have his men on the rooftops forever, and he'll think both the Kid and his sweetheart made it out some way if he don't see either of you in town for a time."

She said, "I have to get back to Dodge. Hughie and Annie will be worried about me."

Brian shook his head as he rustled up some cups and saucers. He said, "You'd best let Dodge simmer down some, too. It's my understanding both Ben Thompson and Doc Holliday are looking for the Kid in Dodge." He suddenly laughed boyishly and added, "I swear to God, I don't know how a bitty gal like you can stir up so much trouble!"

Tony sat down, the tension broken, and said, "She *shoots* pretty, too. O'Rourke will know you're still alive and well when he gets the bounty on them two rascals from the Missouri Central and such. *I* don't reckon you should head right back to Dodge, neither. Why don't you take a vacation and let ever'body cool down afore the Sundown Kid puts in another appearance in Dodge?"

Brian said, "I've a better idea. Why does the Sundown Kid *ever* have to surface again?" He nodded down at Chance and continued, "You got ever' member of the gang who wronged you, Chance."

"Dawson and Dodd are still alive, Brian."

"Hell, they're both in jail. Even if one of 'em

should beat the rope, they'll be locked up for years. You've done the deed you set out to do, and I'll have to admit you done it better than most men could have. But it's *over!* There's nothing to stop you from peeling off them fool pants for good and going back to being a pretty young gal forever."

Tony nodded and added, "It's time you settled down."

Chance sighed and said, "I tried that once. It didn't work out. Others are depending on me. We went to a lot of trouble setting up the agency in Dodge."

Brian said, "Well, hell, let Hughie O'Rourke keep the agency and such."

"Brian, Hughie is a harmless old tinker. He can't run the business without my help."

"Let him hire someone then."

"Who's he going to get that's better than me? You've both admitted I'm a better tracker than most men in the game, and I've proven myself in standup gunplay. What are *you* two doing as bounty hunters if it's such an awful job?"

Brian got the perking pot from the stove and began to pour as he said, "It ain't the same. And afore you fly off the handle again, I ain't talking about the pants we got on. We're in this game 'cause it's the only high-paying trade we have. Both of us were off in a war while other kids was getting educated. We don't have business skills, and punching cow pays awful. You're different, Chance. You've got book learning and you know how to talk fancy."

She wrinkled her nose and said, "My, yes, I'm ever so fitted to take my place in a man's world. I might do very well as a schoolteacher or a lady's maid.

Damn it, Brian, you just saw me make over a thousand dollars for a few minutes work!"

Brian muttered, "Jesus, I think she means it."

Chance shook her head as he started to fill her cup. She said, "I'd better not have any coffee, thank you. I'm already keyed up and I'll never get to sleep tonight if I take further stimulants."

Tony said, "I'll drink her cup too, Brian. I purely hope it's strong and stale."

Brian said, "It is. Black as pitch and damn near as thick."

As he sat down, Chance asked, "Do you think you boys should put that awful stuff away this late? It's almost three in the morning and you'll never sleep tonight."

Brian said, "That's the general idea. Your few minutes work is costing us at least twenty-four hours of guard duty. Just let me down this and I'll show you to your room. While you catch up on your beauty rest, me and Tony will be covering the front and back with our rifles."

"Good Lord! You don't think the James-Younger gang will try to hit us in the middle of town, do you?"

Brian didn't answer. Tony sipped his coffee and said, "It ain't likely, but it'll be quiet as hell out there by four or five in the AM. The best way to make sure they don't catch us napping is not to nap at all."

Brian stood up and said, "Come on, I'll show you to the spare room." She rose to follow, nodding to Tony as Brian led her out of the kitchen. He took her to a dark doorway and said, "This is it. Don't light the lamp. The alley windows are barred, but we don't want the glass busted."

"I can undress in the dark. Are you sure you don't

want me to spell either of you on guard? I'm not really sleepy."

"Lay down a spell and see. You've had a lot of excitement in the past few nights. You're likely running overtime on nerves."

She paused, her hand on the buttons of her male shirt, and asked him, "Just how did you mean that, Brian?"

"I mean it like it sounded. Do you always play chess when the name of the game is checkers?"

"Oh? Then you still believe I sold myself as a whore?"

"I don't believe nothing one way or the other these days. I've been lied to all my life. I said I was taking your word about it being just an act. Let's leave her there and forget it."

He started to turn away. Chance put a hand on his sleeve and asked, "Would it make a difference if I could prove I haven't been with a man, present company aside?"

He shrugged and said, "Try to get some shut-eye. Nothing really matters once you study it a hundred years."

"My God, you're bitter! Someone really hurt you once, Brian."

"Everybody's been hurt. Life's sort of tedious that way. I really had no call to mean-mouth you in the kitchen just now. I don't know what got into me."

She sighed and said, "It wasn't the war. My father and other men I've known went through the war. Who put those lines around your mouth, Brian? Was she pretty?"

"Ever'body's pretty when a man is young and foolish. The tale ain't all that interesting even to me. You've got enough other things to worry about come sunup. I'm going out to scout some. So lock the door, brace a chair agin' it, and shoot through the panels at anyone who rattles the nob or knocks. Me and Tony won't awaken you afore you're ready to rise. Anybody else at the door will mean we're both dead."

Chance stared in wonder at the shaft of sunlight lancing through a knothole in the shutters as she realized she'd really been asleep. The angle of the light told her it was at least nine in the morning. She threw off the covers and swung her bare feet to the floor. She went, nude, to the dressing table and poured tepid water from the pitcher in the china bowl they'd placed there with a clean string-rag. She washed the sleep from her face and rinsed her mouth out. She felt a little stiff from her exertions of the night before, but she was wide awake and rested as she dressed.

She strapped the gunbelt on over her jeans and moved the chair away from the door before she listened with her ear against the paneling. She heard no conversation, but it sounded like someone was washing dishes in the distance. She somehow doubted any of the James-Younger gang would be doing that. So she eased the door open and moved toward the kitchen, gun drawn.

She found Tony Despres alone at his cleanup chores. He sensed her even as she put her gun away and turned, a soapy hand on his own gun's stocks. They both laughed.

He said, "Morning. Brian's out exploring. Set yourself down and I'll rustle you up some eggs."

Chance shook her head and said, "I'm not hungry. I'll have some coffee to brush the cobwebs away. I'll fix it myself."

"Yeah, Brian says my coffee makes a tolerable tanning fluid, too."

"That's not why I want to make my own, Tony. I'd like you to run a few errands for me if you're willing."

"Sure, name your pleasure and I'll give her a try."

Chance said, "I'd better write a list. You'll need my dress and hat size. I noticed there's a ladies' shop right down the street. I'll give you the money and . . ."

"Your money's no good here, honey. But what's your play? You can't *go* anywhere, dressed or no, 'til Brian makes sure the coast is clear."

Chance found a pencil stub on the kitchen counter and began to write her needs on a scrap of brown paper she tore from a sack. She said, "They're looking for a young man in blue denim and a painted whore."

"Look, I talked about that to Brian after we'd both had time to steady down last night."

"I know. The point is that the friends of Slade and Shaw aren't out to gun a simple farmgirl. Try to pick out a really country hat to go with the polka-dot dress and pinafore. I can probably get away with the boots, and I'll carry my gun in the traveling basket you'll be buying for me."

Tony frowned and said, "I follow your drift, but you say Jesse James spoke to you face-to-face!"

"It was in the dark, I was wearing heavy makeup,

and I don't think he was looking too close at my face."

Tony shook his head and said, "I can't let you do it, honey. It's just too big a boo."

"All right, I'll just slip out the back and shop for myself."

"Jesus H. Christ! What if somebody's watching the alley?"

"It's possible. That's why I asked *you* to go next door for me."

Tony dried his hands thoughtfully before he decided, "It do make sense to get you out of them *pants.* But if I help you get new duds, you'll have to promise not to try to leave afore Brian comes back. We've got to *study* on this fool plan."

"What time is the next westbound train, Tony?"

"About one thirty. But you ain't getting aboard her. We ain't about to let you sashay down the streets of Liberty in broad daylight, girl!"

"I promise not to board the train for Dodge before Brian says it's all right. Do we have a deal?"

Tony looked relieved and nodded. He said, "I'll go get the new outfit afore the stores get busy with the noonday crowd. You lock the door after me and stay away from the windows."

She agreed and Tony took her list, scanned it, and left by the front door. Chance found a clean pot and brewed herself some decent coffee. Then as the butterflies in her stomach settled down, she decided she had time to fortify her innards for the day. So she scrambled some eggs and made toast.

She'd just finished and cleaned up after herself when Tony rapped on the nearby alley door. Chance let him in and he placed the wrapped packages on the table, saying, "I circled the block twice and they don't seem to be skulking close."

She started unwrapping the packages as she said, "They may have given up. I know Cole Younger and some of the others weren't too keen on backing those two outlaws. I think Jesse's more annoyed at being taken by Skinny Hips than he is at the loss of his old army buddies."

Tony said, "I hope you're right. The trouble with figuring Jesse is that he don't act the way you expect. That's likely why nobody can catch him."

Chance held up the cheap, cotton print dress and said, "Oh, this is perfect, Tony!" Then she took out the perky straw hat with the artificial fruit on it and added, "This is *adorable!* Do you think I should leave the price tag dangling, or would that be too obvious?"

"It cost a dollar and a quarter. The lady in the shop said it was what all the young gals was wearing this season."

He lowered his eyes and said, "You never said nothing about unmentionables, but I throwed in ruffled pantaloons just in case."

"That was thoughtful, dear. I forgot I wasn't wearing anything under these jeans."

"I wish you hadn't said that, Ma'am. I'm trying to be respectful, but you're pushing it to cruelty to animals!"

Chance unwrapped the straw traveling basket and stared down into its emptiness as she murmured, "I'm very fond of you, Tony. I wish I could be a better sport about making it up to you for all you've done for me."

He shrugged and said, "Hell, I ain't no charity

case. I know you don't feel the way about me that you do about Brian."

"Oh, Tony, don't be silly. He's not interested in me. He acts like I was a horsefly buzzing around his saddle sores."

Tony smiled crookedly and said, "Yeah, some boys walk picket fences. Others pull a gal's hair and put frogs down her dress. Brian ain't got much sense about gals."

She started piling the new things in the basket as she asked, "What happened to him, Tony? Some girl really hurt him once, didn't she?"

Tony started balling up the wrapping paper before he said, "Once was enough for a serious cuss like Brian. I don't know the whole tale. But from what I've got out of him a word at a time, she was the girl he left behind him during the war."

"You mean she didn't wait?"

"Worse. Brian wound up in a Yankee prison camp when his outfit had to surrender. By the time he got home, Texas was occupied by Yankee troops. The gal he left behind him didn't like the Reconstruction much. Food was scarce and money was even harder to come by. So she was servicing the Yanks in a parlor house when he come home to marry her."

"Oh, my God!"

"Yep. He throwed the picture locket she'd given him in the Brazos."

"And he's been hating women ever since, the poor thing."

"Well, now, I don't think you could say he *hates* gals. He's a natural man and women sort of cotton to him. He cottons back, in a love-em-and-leave-em way. But meeting you has sort of confused him. You ain't the kind a man can love and leave. Brian ain't the kind of man who can let down his guard. I'd say the two of you have a Mexican standoff."

Chance nodded and said, "You're right. I want to take a bath and get dressed. I notice you've an indoor privy, but I can't seem to find a tub on the premises, Tony."

He bent to haul a galvanized tub from behind the stove as he explained, "We wash up here in the kitchen. I'd sure like to scrub your back, but I'd better go see if I can find Brian. I'll tell him you need a spell of privacy, and we'll be back around noon."

Chance thanked him and put a kettle on to boil as he left again.

But she knew she didn't have time for a hot bath. The clock on the wall told her the eastbound train for Saint Louis was due within the hour. She had just enough time to rinse off and dress if she wanted to board it. Hopefully Brian, Tony, *and* Jesse James would be expecting her to try for the westbound later in the day.

The sun was hot despite the hour as Chance crossed the square clutching her basket primly. She'd braided her hair in pigtails with big pink bows. The perky straw hat sat forward over her new bangs, but she was counting more on her fresh-scrubbed face and farmgirl tan than the little the straw brim might hide of her face.

The depot seemed deserted as she stepped inside and went to the ticket booth. She bought a ticket for Carrollton just up the line and asked if the train was on time. The ticket agent said he didn't know. It usually was. Chance thanked him in her new schoolgirl voice and stepped out to the platform to wait. There were three or four other passengers waiting for the eastbound apparently. Chance went to a bench and put her basket in her lap as she sat down.

A shadow fell across her and she looked up, wide-eyed and innocent. In the bright sunlight she saw Jesse James had granulated eyelids as he stared down at her in silence. Chance lowered her lashes and murmured, "My mother told me not to speak with strangers, sir. No offense, but I listen to Mother."

"You been waiting for the train long, Missy?"

"No, I just got here. If you're worried about catching the eastbound, I suggest you ask inside, sir."

Jesse James removed his hat and said, "I ain't being disrespectable, Missy. I'm sort of with the railroad. I've been asking folks if they've seen a lady we're, uh, suspicious of."

"Oh, dear, you don't mean those awful outlaws are fixing to rob the train again, do you? My Aunt Jennifer's expecting me up the line, but if you don't think it's safe . . ."

Jesse James chuckled and said, "You just go on and visit with your kin, little lady. We ain't looking for train robbers. Are you sure you haven't seen a tall gal in a whipcord riding dress and a picture hat?"

Chance shook her head. Then she murmured, "Wait a minute. I think I *did* see such a person just as I was coming across the square. Would she be sort of, well, wicked-looking and smelling of French toilet water?"

"Keep talking, Missy. Where was she headed?"

"Heavens, *I* don't know! My mother doesn't allow me to talk to people who wear powder and paint!"

Another man sidled up to James and asked, "What have we here, J.W.?"

"This little lady says she might have spied that gal. Over to the square."

The second man said, "She hasn't been here to ask about the westbound. We know she has no ticket. What in thunder do you reckon she's up to, J.W.?"

"Can't say. The point is that she's still in town."

"Hell, we knew that, J.W. The *Kid* ain't rode out neither. We got 'em boxed no matter which way they head."

James frowned and said, "Watch your language. The little lady is blushing." He put his hat back on and smiled down to add, "We won't pester you no more, Missy."

But as they turned to walk down the platform toward the door, Brian Pio tore out of the depot, calling, "Chance! What the hell are you doing here?"

Then he saw James and the other man and froze, his gun hand out to the side.

A million years went by. Then Jesse James said, "Morning, Brian."

Brian said, "Morning, J.W."

"You looking for somebody, Brian?"

Brian had caught on. He nodded, looking past the girl seated on the bench, and said, "Sort of. I can see he ain't here yet. Do you really aim to push it all the way, J.W.?"

As Chance cracked open the basket with her male attire and gunbelt folded inside, Jesse James said, "Well, I'll tell you, Brian. Slade and Shaw wasn't worth much, but the Kid's gal sort of made me look foolish. I'd be willing to let *him* go if he'd hand *her* over. You wouldn't have no way of getting word to him, would you?"

Brian grinned crookedly and said, "I'd be willing to try if I could get *to* the little rascal. You might as well know, my sidekick said he might be over here at the depot. I see now he lied some to *us,* too!"

Jesse James turned, looking past Chance up the tracks as he said, "I hear the train coming. If he don't board her, it'll mean he's trying for the westbound. His gal's still in Liberty, too. Are you listening good, Brian?"

"What's your deal, J.W.?"

"This quarrel I have with the Sundown Kid and his play-pretty ain't none of your business, Brian. He's lied to you and she's lied to us. How do you like that so far?"

"Keep talking, J.W."

"That little gal in the funny hat needs an escort to see she gets to her Aunt Jennifer over to Carrollton. Why don't you be a good-hearted cuss and ride on up the line with her?"

"I don't know her *or* her Aunt Jennifer, J.W.! What on earth would I want to go to Carrollton for?"

"Shux, I'm sure you could find something up the line to occupy your mind for a spell, Brian. With you out of town your partner, Despres, wouldn't make any dumb moves neither."

"In other words you mean to run me out of town?"

"Don't take it so unfriendly, Brian. The little gal is pretty and her aunt might be a good cook. You get on the train with her, and by the time you get back we'll have ridden out. If we don't settle with the Kid and his gal by sundown, we'll figure they slickered us and I'll forget it."

The train was in sight now and slowing for the stop. To buy some time Brian said, "I don't know, J.W. This ain't too friendly."

James said, "Sure it is. Just help the little lady with her baggage and be a sensible gent."

The train hissed to a halt, enveloping them all in steam as Brian said, "Well, I warned the Kid it was his fight on your territory."

He stepped over to Chance and said, "Allow me, Ma'am."

She rose, but said, "I'm quite able to handle my own things, thank you very much!"

But Brian took the basket with a wink at Jesse James and told her, "Sure you are. What have you got in here? It smells like home cooking."

He helped her aboard the train and whispered, "Rear platform, pronto!"

They made their way back to the observation platform by the time the train was rolling again. He peered out through the grimed glass and heaved a sigh before he said, "They bought it! They're standing there like big-ass birds!"

Before he could stop her, Chance opened the sliding door, stepped out on the platform, and waved good-bye. Jesse James removed his hat again and waved it back at her.

She started to laugh hysterically, and now Brian was laughing, too, as the train rounded the bend and picked up speed. And then she was in his arms and he was smiling down at her, tears of relief in his eyes. He said, "Don't ever do that again." Then he kissed her warmly. She clung to him, exploring his lips with hers as their hearts beat in time to the clacking wheels, and she never wanted him to let go of her.

But a voice in the doorway cleared its throat and said, "Uh, tickets, please."

Chance said, "I'm going to Saint Louis, so my local ticket's no good. Could I give you the fare in cash?"

The conductor said, "Sure, if you've got it. How about you, Mister?"

Brian smiled down at Chance and said, "I'm going to Saint Louis, too. Do you have a sleeping car aboard this train?"

"Well, we've got some private compartments up forward. But this train gets to Saint Louis well before bedtime, folks."

Brian looked at Chance again and she nodded radiantly. Brian said, "We want a private compartment anyway."

As Brian took out a roll of bills, the conductor said, "Well, it's none of my business how folks spend their money. We'll be in Saint Louis in about six hours. If you, uh, oversleep, you may miss your stop."

Brian said, "That's all right. We may just decide to ride to the end of the line together."